F
BLA FROST BLOOD #1
BLAKE, ELLY

DATE DUE			
10/28/17			

FROST
BLOOD

FROST BLOOD

ELLY BLAKE

LITTLE, BROWN AND COMPANY
New York • Boston

Little, Brown and Company

Hachette Book Group
1290 Avenue of the Americas, New York, NY 10104
Visit us at lb-teens.com

Little, Brown and Company is a division of Hachette Book Group, Inc. The Little, Brown name and logo are trademarks of Hachette Book Group, Inc.

The publisher is not responsible for websites (or their content) that are not owned by the publisher.

First Edition: January 2017

Library of Congress Cataloging-in-Publication Data
Names: Blake, Elly, author.
Title: Frostblood / Elly Blake.
Description: First Edition. | New York : Little, Brown and Company, 2017. | Series: The Frostblood saga ; 1 | Summary: "Seventeen-year-old Ruby is a Fireblood who must use her powers of heat and flame to help two Frostblood rebels overthrow a maniacal Frostblood king"— Provided by publisher.
Identifiers: LCCN 2016004451| ISBN 9780316273251 (hardback) | ISBN 9780316273268 (ebook) | ISBN 9780316273213 (library edition ebook)
Subjects: | CYAC: Magic—Fiction. | Ability—Fiction. | Fantasy. | BISAC: JUVENILE FICTION / Action & Adventure / Survival Stories. | JUVENILE FICTION / Fantasy & Magic. | JUVENILE FICTION / Love & Romance. | JUVENILE FICTION / Social Issues / Prejudice & Racism. | JUVENILE FICTION / Social Issues / Violence.
Classification: LCC PZ7.1.B586 Fr 2017 | DDC [Fic]—dc23
LC record available at https://lccn.loc.gov/2016004451

10 9 8 7 6 5 4 3

LSC-C

Printed in the United States of America

FOR DARREN, NICKLAS,
ALEKSANDER, AND LUKAS

LOVE YOU FOREVER

PART
ONE

ONE

$\mathcal{J}$ OFFERED MY HAND TO THE FIRE.

Sparks leaped from the hearth and settled onto my fingers, heat drawn to heat, and glittered like molten gems against my skin. With my free hand, I pulled a bucket of melting snow closer and edged forward on my knees, ready to douse myself if the sparks flared into something much larger.

Which is exactly what I intended.

Winter solstice was six weeks away, but my village, high in the mountains, was already blanketed with a thick layer of snow. Grandmother used to say that the true test of a Fireblood's gift was in the cold. But she died before she could show me more than the most rudimentary of lessons, and Mother had made me promise never to practice at all.

It was a promise I couldn't keep. If the king's soldiers discovered me, wasn't it better to know how to wield my heat?

I closed my eyes and focused on my heart, willing the gathering warmth to surge upward and out the way Grandmother had taught me. If I did it right, the bright sparks on my hand would burst into tiny flames.

Come on, little wisp, where are you?

After years of being told to tamp down my fire, keep it hidden, make it invisible, I struggled each time I tried to find it. But there it was, a small, churning tendril. I coaxed it forward, a reluctant thread that grew a little, then a little more.

That's it. I held my breath, afraid to break the spell.

A gust of frigid air whipped my hair across my face. The sparks on my fingers died, and the wisp darted back into my heart.

Mother slammed the door and shoved the quilt back against the crack at the bottom, a deep shiver shaking her fine-boned frame under her cloak. "It's wicked out there. I'm chilled to the bone."

Seeing her tremble, I finally scooted to the side, revealing the hearth. "I thought you were delivering a baby."

"It wasn't time yet." Her eyes widened at the tall flames, then narrowed.

I shrugged, my excitement wilting. "It was so cold."

"Ruby, you were practicing." The tone of disappointment was familiar. "If even one person sees what you're doing, just *one*, they

4

could alert the king's soldiers. With the summer being so wet, and the grains running out, people will do anything to survive, including taking a reward—"

"I know. You don't have to tell me again."

"Then why are you doing this? It's bad enough when you're not *trying* to use your gift." She waved her hand at a pile of half-burned rags. Scorch marks still stained the floor.

My cheeks warmed. "I'm sorry I lost my temper the other day. Again. But tonight I could almost control the flame."

She shook her head in a tense movement that told me there was no use pleading. I wrapped my arms around myself and rocked gently. Finally, her wind-chapped fingers reached out slowly to take a lock of my hair, which she always said was lucky to be black and not red like some Firebloods'. My skin might be a little too sun-kissed for a child of the North, but people didn't look closely in this sleepy village, where no one had powers, frost or fire.

"I understand that your gift is a part of you," she said softly. "But I lie awake at night worrying. How can we keep your secret if you insist on using your fire, even when you know it can spiral out of control?"

It was the same question she'd asked over and over during the past few months, when I'd decided to start practicing my gift. And I replied with the same answer. "How will I learn to control it if I never use it? And if we're not safe here, why don't we go somewhere safe?"

"Not that again. You know we'd never make it to the border, and even if we did, we'd be on the front lines."

"The coast—"

"Is heavily guarded now."

"We should have left years ago," I said bitterly. "We should live in Sudesia with the rest of our people."

She looked away. "Well, we're here now, and there's no sense wishing for what isn't." She let out a sigh as she caught sight of the depleted pile of kindling. "Ruby, did you really need to use half our store of firewood?"

I swallowed past the guilt. "I won't add any more logs to the fire."

"When it burns down, we'll freeze."

"I'll keep you warm. You can sleep right next to me." I patted my mattress, which I'd pulled close to the hearth, just out of range of stray sparks.

Her gaze softened, a smile tugging at her lips. "You're better than any fire. You never burn me, even if I roll too close."

"Exactly. A Fireblood daughter can be very useful."

She gave a bark of laughter and my heart lightened. "I am grateful—believe me." She pulled me into a tight hug, gasping and laughing as she felt the sting of heat coming from me in waves. "It's like holding a cooked chicken. I think you'd better take a walk to cool off. See if you can find some more kindling to replace the lot you used up."

I pressed through drifts, the snow hissing as it melted against my shins above my boots. The wind howled from the southwest, yanking the hood from my head and raking through my hair with pine-scented fingers. The air was bitter, but my skin was still hotter than normal after practicing my gift. Mother had said to gather firewood and bring it home, but she also wanted me to calm down. Surely it was better to expel some of this heat out here, where it was safe?

I had done it before, sneaked out late at night into the desolate, snow-draped woods, my hands thrust into a hastily built fire as I willed myself to control the flames. All I'd managed to do was singe the edges of my cloak.

I gathered a bundle of small sticks, holding them tightly. The forest held its breath, eerily silent but for the rustle of wind in the treetops. Although I knew no one ever came here, I still looked around furtively, my heart beating thickly in my ears. Closing my eyes, I searched for the little wisp of flame I'd found earlier. The sticks grew hot in my hands.

The wind changed direction, barreling in from the north and carrying the dregs of a wet winter storm. I shivered and clutched the sticks tighter, struggling against the cold seeping into my pores and leaching the heat from my body.

Suddenly, the distant sounds of footsteps echoed through the woods.

I dropped the sticks and clambered onto a rock, knocking snow from it in heavy clumps. To the northwest, the path veered down into a gulley, where an overhang protected it from snow.

In a few seconds, I would see whoever approached without being seen myself.

First a hood came into view; then a metal helm flashing between tree trunks washed gray under a steel sky. The blue of the men's tunics shot startling color into the starkly white scene.

Soldiers, breaking the quiet with their heavy, crackling steps and ringing voices.

Blood rushed to my heart, fear blossoming into heat.

I'd been warned a thousand times about the king's soldiers, but I'd always told myself we were too high in the mountains, too insignificant to warrant their search for Firebloods. I hoped they were just passing through on their way from the barren North. But our hut was right along the path they were following. They could easily stop to raid our larder or use our hut for the night. We couldn't risk them getting too near me, feeling the heat of my skin.

I slid off the rock and shot toward home, my shuddering breaths whisper-quiet as I scraped past trees and bushes, using undergrowth and my knowledge of the bend of the land as cover.

When I reached our hut, Mother was sitting by the fire, her long braid hanging over the back of the woven-bark chair.

"Soldiers," I said, rushing to grab her thick cloak, still drying by the fire, and shoving it at her. "In the woods. If they stop here..."

Mother gaped at me for a moment before launching into

action. She grabbed a rag and packed up some dry cheese and bread, then stumbled to the scarred wooden table, where healing plants dried in the warmth of the fire. We'd spent hours gathering the precious herbs, and neither of us could bear to leave them. We packed them as quickly as we could, folding them into scraps of fabric tied with frantic fingers.

The herbs were swept from the table by the wind as the door crashed against the wall. Two men emerged from the snowy darkness, their blue vests each emblazoned with a white arrow.

"Where's the Fireblood?" The soldier's small eyes moved from Mother to me.

"We're healers." Hearing the tremble of fear under Mother's bravado made my legs weak.

With long strides, one of the men cornered me and grabbed my arms. My throat convulsed at the sharp reek of old sweat and foul breath. His cold hand slid to my neck. I wanted to turn my head and bite his wrist, hit him, rake him with my nails, anything to get his hand off me, but the sword at his side held me still.

"Her skin is burning hot," he said with a curl of his lip.

"She has a fever," Mother said, her voice desperate.

I took a deep, shuddering breath. *Hide your heat. Push it down. Calm yourself.*

"You'll catch my fever," I said, trying to keep the tremble out of my voice.

"I can't catch what's wrong with you." He pulled me toward

the door, his hand tight on my arm. I struggled wildly, trying to twist out of his grasp and kicked over a bucket of red berries I had gathered before the recent snow. They spilled across the floor like drops of blood, crushed under his boots as he pulled me out into the moonlight.

Pressure grew in my chest. It was as if the fire in the hearth had crawled into my rib cage and wanted out. Grandmother had described the sensation, but I'd never felt it like this. It stung and burned and pressed against my ribs from the inside. It made me want to rip off my skin just to let it free.

The ache grew until I thought it might kill me. I screamed and a swathe of stinging hot air surrounded me, covering my attacker. He let go and fell to the ground, howling in pain.

I scrambled into the hut where Mother struggled with the other soldier as he pulled her toward the door. I grabbed a log from the woodpile and brought it down hard on the back of his head. He pitched to the side and lay still.

I took Mother's hand, and we stumbled out the door and into the night. The soldier I had burned was still on his hands and knees, pressing snow to his face.

We moved as fast as we could through the thick drifts, away from our hut, away from the place that had always been warmth and safety, a riot of fear and confusion making my mind as numb as my fingers. I had to get Mother away, keep her safe. At a fork in the path, I pulled right, toward the forest, where we could lose ourselves in the pines that grew so thick snow didn't reach the ground.

"Too cold," Mother panted, pulling against my hand. "No shelter there. The village."

We pounded past farms and the shadows of houses until Mother's steps slowed, and I half pulled, half dragged her through the worst of the drifts, which had poured like frozen waves over the path. As we slogged through the shadows next to the blacksmith's shop, I saw orange lights bobbing in the village square.

"Torches," I whispered, pulling back on my mother's hand.

It didn't seem real. I had come to the village at least once a week for as long as I could remember, not just to buy food and supplies, but to get away from the solitude of our tiny hut, to exchange nods and smiles with people, to smell baking bread and the occasional waft of rosewater from the shopkeepers' wives and daughters. Although I couldn't truly call anyone my friend, there were people who always answered when I greeted them, who were glad to take my mother's cordials for a sick father or sister or child.

Now my cozy world had broken like a glass jar dropped onto stone, spilling familiarity and security, never to be gathered back again. The smells were all wrong, the acrid smoke of torches and the reek of too many hard-ridden horses with their unwashed riders.

We wheeled and doubled back, but as we passed a space between buildings, three soldiers wearing the white arrow emerged from the dark like specters, their hands on us before we could move. They pulled us toward the square, where groups of people waited, looking frightened and disheveled, as if they'd been hauled from their beds. I twisted and turned, searching for a way out, but I couldn't leave Mother. She stood quiet and still beside me.

"Is this the Fireblood girl?" The man was tall, with blade-cut cheekbones and a sandy beard, and he spoke with an air of command. His coat shone with polished buttons.

I scanned the familiar faces of the people from my village. Graham, the miller, and his daughter, Flax. The farmers Tibald, Brecken, and Tom, and their wives, Gert, Lilly, and Melody. They had all come to my mother for treatment when they were sick, but surely they didn't know what I was. I'd always been so careful, and we'd been nothing but good neighbors.

A boy my age stepped forward. My heart leaped to see that it was Clay, the butcher's eldest son. At the harvest festival, he had pulled me to the side as the village danced around the fire. His hand had trembled in mine as we shared a kiss in the dark. He'd drawn back after feeling my lips, so hot on his own, but he hadn't pulled his hand away. After that, we'd stolen looks at each other when I went to his father's shop.

"She's the one, Captain," Clay said, his lips trembling. "She killed my brother."

My mother gasped and squeezed my hand. My body had gone numb.

A few weeks ago my mother had been summoned by Clay's father. His infant son wouldn't nurse. The baby's skin was cold.

Mother tried every salve and curative she knew and finally took me with her to see if my natural heat could warm the child's skin. But the baby died anyway. I cried for three days afterward.

"You know that's not true," I whispered. "I tried to save him."

"Fireblood!" said Clay's father. "You brought this on all of us."

I shook my head in disbelief. "Clay? You're the one who brought the soldiers here?"

Clay's face twisted, but he didn't answer. He just turned away.

As if by an unspoken command, the villagers retreated as the soldiers moved closer. In moments, my mother and I were the only ones left, two shivering women ringed by blazing torches.

"There's one way to know for sure," said the captain, holding his torch in front of him with a glimmer of enjoyment in his cold eyes. "Firebloods don't burn."

"Get away, Mother!" I pushed her to the ground.

The torches were almost on us, six or seven coming from all sides, the heat searing my face. The fire from one leaped to the fabric of my dress. Flames ate at my clothes and roared in my ears. My skin was blistering hot, but it didn't burn.

The captain stepped forward, his hand moving to his sword, and Mother threw herself at him. Her nails slashed down the side of his face, drawing a bead of blood. I tried to pull Mother back, but as I came close, the captain's booted foot crashed into my chest. I fell to the ground, gasping, the fire on my dress hissing into steam against the snow.

As I struggled to my knees, he lifted his sword, almost lazily.

Then he slammed the hilt down onto Mother's head with a sickening crack.

She crumpled to the ground like a broken doll, her hair spread over the snow, wispy and delicate, as if drawn with a piece of charcoal. Her long, lovely neck curved like a wilted flower stem.

I crawled to her side and took her shoulders, called out to her. My hands fluttered to her chest, her neck, searching for her heartbeat, strong and steady, like she was. But she lay still.

The world froze.

No. No. No.

The timid little flame in my chest flared to a river of heat, far beyond my control. I didn't care. What was the use in hiding it now? I breathed in a gasp that stole the air from the sky, the trees, the world. The wind seemed to twist around me, the eye of the tornado.

I exhaled.

The flames that covered my body expanded, erupting with a roar and pinwheeling forward. A chaos of writhing, panicked men blurred in my vision as soldiers fell to the ground, pushing their faces and hands into the snow.

My mother's still form lay behind me, her hair and limbs in a tumble. I reached out to gather her to me, but hands seized my shoulders. I lashed out with my fists and searched my mind for that well of flame I'd found in my deepest self.

The heat died as they dropped me into a horse trough, my body breaking through a layer of ice into water that stabbed my skin like needles. Rough wooden walls pressed against my sides. I pushed up, my chest bursting with singeing cold, and was shoved back down. I clutched at the edges of the trough, my nails digging into the wood.

Finally, I was pulled up, gagging out water and sucking in great mouthfuls of icy air.

The captain, his head gilded by a flickering orange light, bent down and grasped a fistful of my streaming hair, shoving his face into mine. His face was red, blisters forming on his cheeks.

"You'll pay for what you did to me and my men. Your whole village will pay."

Fire already blazed behind him, storefronts and houses belching out black smoke. Some of the villagers tried to stop the soldiers, whose torches touched wooden walls and piles of firewood and carts, while they hooted and shouted as if this were an evening's entertainment. Their voices mixed with the wails of those who could only stand by and watch as their livelihoods burned.

Rage mixed with panic, heating my blood and making the water steam.

"A fitting punishment for harboring a Fireblood, don't you think?" said the captain, his eyes glittering.

So everyone would suffer because of me.

"I'll kill you for what you've done this night," I managed to whisper.

The flames cast strange shadows on his leering grin. "Tie her to a horse. We'll take her to Blackcreek Prison."

"But, Captain," said a soldier. "Her fire."

"Then knock her out."

Pain split the back of my head. The last thing I saw before my world faded to black was the white arrow on the captain's chest.

The mark of the Frost King.

TWO

Five Months Later

ℬOOTED FEET APPROACHED IN AN unsteady shuffle, a sign the guards were already deep into their cups. It was just past sunset, the light from the tiny barred window withering into a ruddy glow.

"Wakey, wakey, little wretch."

I lay huddled in my usual position, knees up, arms wrapped around my chest to hold in my body heat, which the stone floor seemed so greedy to leech away. I sat up slowly, my ankle cuff clinking against the chain. Three faces leered at me through the bars.

"What time is it?" Bragger asked, the words tangling together in his mouth. He was thoroughly drunk.

"Time for you to toddle off to your barracks," I replied, voice scratchy from thirst.

He gave a sly smile. "How do you like your new accessory?"

I glanced at the dull gray shackle. "I'm not sure it matches my dress."

He snorted a laugh. "Filthy like the rest of you. And how does it feel?"

"Unnecessary."

"Then I guess you won't be using that heat of yours again anytime soon."

"Depends on whether you decide to show your special attention to any of the other prisoners."

A few weeks before, Bragger and his ale-soaked lackeys had decided they'd had enough of the wracking coughs coming from the older man in the cell next to mine. The man's cries for help cut through the layers of numbness that I had built in my mind. Although the dirty conditions and spoiled food had weakened my health, and my gift, I had managed to reach through the bars to give Bragger a nice jolt of heat on his bare forearm. The beating had stopped, but the prisoner had died that night, and I had inherited his ankle chain as a reward for my interference.

"None of your concern either way, Firefilth," said Bragger. "We might just turn our attentions to you next time. Won't last a day once we're through with you."

Inside, my stomach lurched, but outwardly I was as calm as glass. "You've been promising me that for months, and here I am.

I think you've become rather fond of me. Templeton here has been giving me extra rations."

Templeton, the smallest and quietest of the three, started to protest, but Bragger just grinned. "I won't fall for that again, turning us on each other so we forget about you. I ask you again, you dirty bit of char. What time is it?"

"Time to burn all of you into ashes."

I hadn't realized I'd said the words aloud until he laughed. "Can't have much fire left in you or you would've done that a long time ago. But just in case, Rager, you got the bucket?"

"Right here," said Rager, scraping the metal bucket against the bars.

A key snicked in the lock and the door swung open.

"What time is it?" Bragger asked, low and serious, the tone that told me it would only get worse if I didn't play along.

I gritted my teeth. "Time for my dousing." He smiled into my face, a mask of cruel anticipation.

I concentrated on staying still, not backing away. No matter how I tried, though, I jerked when the frigid water crashed over me, and hissing steam rose from my skin. The guards doubled over with laughter.

"That just never gets old," Bragger said, fouling the air near my face with his breath. "A whistling kettle in the shape of a girl. I wonder what would happen if we poured out all that red tea?"

I lifted my hand slowly to brush back a lock of soaked hair. His eyes followed the movement, alert.

"I'm not scared of you," he said. But he kept his distance as

Rager stepped forward and swung another bucket of water, this one full of chunks of ice that cut my cheeks and tangled in my hair. I gasped, wishing I could control the steam that so entertained them. But then again, without the steam, there would be no fear. I'd seen what they did to the prisoners who didn't scare them.

A third bucket soaked my back. I started to shiver.

"I don't know why the executioner hasn't come for you yet," said Bragger, "but it's only a matter of time."

He gave a swift kick to my shoulder, knocking me off-balance. I curled up in a ball as the cell door closed with a clang, their laughter moving farther away.

I am as cold as the prison walls. I feel nothing.

———

Ice cracked like the breaking of bones.

I woke with a jerk, heart racing. A dark shape, something strange and inhuman, had been hovering over me, touching my cheek in a blistering caress. I blinked away the dream, and the prison came into focus.

Frost swept the prison in a white wave, crusting over stone walls and insinuating itself into every crack and keyhole. It spilled across the floor and hardened into glittering sheets that stopped inches away, leaving me on an island of bare stone.

Booted feet scraped to a halt outside my cell. I stifled a groan. *Not again. No more guards tonight.* But guards didn't smell of oiled leather and soap. My eyes flicked up to a tall, hooded figure hulking outside my cell, a torch held in his right hand. My spine tightened and fine hairs rose on my neck.

Another hooded shape joined the first. This figure was smaller and leaned on a walking stick that he tapped with each step. A short white beard flowed over the collar of his robe.

"So you think this is the one?" He spoke quietly, his refined accent jarringly out of place in this pit of lowborn murderers and thieves.

"Look," said the taller figure, his voice deeper, more vigorous. "See how the ice refuses to touch her?" He sucked in a breath and blew it out with force. The water in the air turned to ice and fell over me in tiny pellets that steamed back into vapor as they met my skin.

I bit off a moan, my eyes wide with terror. So these were Frostbloods, who had a power in complete opposition to my own. I struggled to keep my breathing even, to hide my panic.

"You see?" His voice was low but exultant.

"Sit up, little one," the shorter figure said, tapping the bars with his stick as if knocking at my door. "We wish to speak with you."

I remained still, willing them to move on and leave me in peace. I hadn't felt so frightened since the day the soldiers came to my village. The guards did not have the gift and they still managed to make my life a misery. At least they were afraid of my fire. What could a Frostblood do to me?

"Do as he says," said the man who stood tall and broad and

imposing on the other side of the bars. "Sit up or I'll find a bucket of water, and then we'll see how you shiver."

Defiance heated my skin. I unwound my arms and sat up.

The old man stepped closer. "How old are you?"

I frowned, searching my mind for the answer. Days blurred into months, which could bleed into years in the king's prison.

He seemed to understand my uncertainty. "It has been two weeks since the vernal equinox."

A dull ache spread through my chest. I'd lost nearly half a year. "Seventeen, then."

"You burned the king's soldiers, some of them badly," he said. "Though with the help of skilled healers, they survived."

"A real pity," I replied, my voice as cold as the ice-coated floor.

He chuckled and looked to his companion. "It's curious that her hair is black. The truly gifted often have fiery hair." He reached through the bars toward me. "Show us your wrist."

I brought my hands to my chest. "Why?"

"We only wish to see." His voice was soft, gentle. Without thinking, I lifted my arm, the tattered sleeve falling open to reveal my thin wrist. He took the torch from his companion and held it close to the bars, the light falling on the thick vein that pulsed like a fat red worm under my skin.

"See how it shines so red?" he marveled as I pulled my arm away. He pushed back his own sleeve to show me the vein in his wrist, cold blue instead of crimson. "We wish no harm," he assured me. "We are here to make an offer. If you complete the task we require, you will have your freedom."

My heart fluttered in my throat. The word *freedom* rang in my head like the pure, clear note of a temple bell. The very thought of it was a painful temptation, to feel fresh air in my lungs, the kiss of sunshine on my skin, the play of wind in my hair. I trembled, torn between longing and terror.

There are worse things than dying slowly in a cell.

The two figures loomed still and silent in the flickering light, frost crackling under their feet. Their breath fogged the air with a cold mist.

"What is the task?" I asked.

The old man looked around and shook his head. "It is something you will be only too eager to help us with."

"Why would I help a Frostblood with anything? Except to die."

His weathered hands rose and pulled the hood off to reveal a lined face with skin darker than my own, long and lean with noble bones. His eyes, so light blue they were almost white, burned into me. His lips held the hint of a smile. "Frost and fire were friends once."

"Not in my lifetime."

He looked to his companion and back to me, his expression intent. "Then, perhaps this will interest you. Our target is the throne itself."

I pressed my hands to the cold stone floor to steady myself. It was what I longed for, the *only* thing I'd wanted since the day the soldiers had taken everything from me: to kill the king, who had ordered that raid. If it were not for the king, there would have been no soldiers, no captain, no prison.

My mother would still be alive.

I met the pale gaze, my head spinning. They wanted me to kill the king for them, but at what cost? "You expect me to trust you?"

He spread his hands. "We are here, offering you a way out. If we are discovered, we will be hanged."

"If you're lucky."

He nodded.

"And if I refuse?"

The taller man blew out a breath. "Then you can rot in here until you're nothing but a pile of bones held together by chains."

My lip curled. "One shout and the two of you will rot in here with me."

"A charming offer," said the broad-shouldered figure. "I can't imagine why no one has come for you sooner."

A muffled laugh from the old man. "Enough, Arcus. Do you agree to our terms, girl?"

I considered my options. From what I'd heard from the other prisoners, most of the Firebloods in the kingdom had been killed or driven away. Some were probably rotting in prisons, as I was. But sooner or later, the executioner would come.

I could likely escape from these men with greater ease than I could escape from the king's prison.

I set my jaw and nodded.

The older man bent toward the keyhole and blew into it. Ice spiked around the opening, followed by a loud click. The door swung inward.

"And my chain?" I asked, motioning to my ankle.

He stepped close, leaning on his stick, and sent out another breath. Ice formed in the keyhole of the ankle cuff but melted a second later. He tried again, and again the ice melted.

"Your resistance to cold is too strong. Can you repress your ability, girl?"

I shook my head. Grandmother had died before she could teach me.

A low groan echoed down the corridor from the guardroom.

"The guards are waking," said the one called Arcus. "Stay back."

Before I could blink, he exhaled a blast of freezing air at the chain, pulled a sword from behind his back, and swung it down. I gasped and jerked away as the brittle chain cracked in half. The air echoed with the rending of iron, followed by another distant groan.

"Hurry," urged the old man.

I tried to stand, but a mutiny of pain in my joints pulled me back down. My muscles had grown too weak to support me.

"Carry her, Arcus."

Arcus bent down, his hood stopping inches from me. The scent of soap and horse and leather filled my senses.

"If you try anything," he said, leaning close to my ear, "I'll break your skinny neck."

I glared and held myself still, wishing I could see his eyes instead of shadows. Only his chin and lower lip were clearly visible. Both were strong, well formed, and puckered by a thick, ugly scar. "If you hurt me, I'll burn you so badly even your mistress will run in terror."

He snorted softly, then slid his arms under my back and legs. As he lifted me, the weight of the cuff pulled against my ankle. I grunted in pain and was surprised when he set me down again, pulling a piece of cloth from his robes. He wound it around my ankle under the metal so it wouldn't chafe. Then he scooped me back up.

When my thigh touched the cold skin of his bare arm, he sucked in a loud breath through his nostrils, but he moved quickly and quietly, even with my weight in his arms. As we mounted the crumbling stairs, Bragger stumbled into the hallway, blinking and wide-eyed at the sight of a prisoner being carted away.

Frost fogged the stone corridor and smeared the floor in glittering, interconnected webs. Ice clacked like a thousand chattering teeth as it rushed over Bragger's legs and up his midsection to cover his arms and neck. He opened his mouth, but his words were blocked by the sudden appearance of a mouthful of ice.

I stared at the older man's raised hand, ice crystals shining on his fingers. But I had no time to marvel at the strength of his gift. More guards were grumbling into wakefulness, their voices carrying into the hallway. Arcus strode past the frozen figure to a door propped open by a thin board, the older man following quickly.

As the heavy door clanged shut behind us, I trembled with the reality of escape. My lungs filled with the sweet, clean air of outdoors, my eyes dazzled by the almost forgotten sight of stars, like torches in a darkened room.

Beneath my thigh, Arcus's arm was bitter cold. His breathing had grown shallow.

"My skin burns you, doesn't it?" I asked, noticing his furrowed brow and clenched jaw.

"It is your stench that burns my nostrils, Fireblood, and nothing else. I hope Brother Thistle has enough soap in the abbey to make you bearable."

If he was averse to being near me, that was fine. The feeling was mutual.

"Are you Brother Thistle?" I asked the old man, who was taking labored steps toward a carriage and driver waiting in the shadow of a building across the street.

"That I am, girl. And what is your name?"

"Ruby," I replied. "Ruby Otrera."

"Ruby," he repeated, smiling. "How fitting."

THREE

I HAD FORGOTTEN THE BONE-RATTLING experience of a journey by carriage. Arcus sat next to me, with Brother Thistle in the seat across from us. As we bounced over the rutted tracks that snaked away from the city, I tucked myself into the corner farthest from the younger Frostblood and his icy skin. Even though I was wrapped in blankets, my joints ached with cold, and the waves of frigid air coming from him didn't help.

Arcus gave an exasperated sigh. "I didn't know Firebloods were so susceptible to chills."

I glared at him. My heat had kept me alive when other prisoners had coughed themselves to death or frozen in the night. But over the months, my inner fire had dwindled to the point that I was cold all the time, even if I still felt warm to the touch to Arcus. I doubted he would understand, and with the pain I was in, I didn't care to explain. After a couple of hours, the moans I couldn't stifle irritated him to the point that he agreed to a brief rest.

We rolled to a stop on a deserted stretch of road. The driver stretched his legs while the two hooded Frostbloods trudged off to speak under a large tree, its skeletal branches silhouetted by a bright crescent moon.

"She's a weak little thing," Arcus said, just above a whisper. "I question whether she'll even survive the journey."

"Indeed," said Brother Thistle in an equally hushed tone. "But she survived the prison. She may have hidden strength. And perhaps she has other gifts we have not anticipated."

"Like excellent hearing," I suggested, making the monk startle. We weren't so far that we couldn't turn back to the prison. I couldn't let them see me as weak.

The old monk bowed, his voice edged with chagrin. "My apologies, Miss Otrera."

My cheeks seemed to crack like dry leather, and I realized I was smiling at his discomfiture. It was the first time my face had formed that expression in so long that I had almost forgotten the feeling.

Arcus turned toward me, the moonlight reflecting off the clasp of his cloak. Something about his silhouette and the bright metal sparked a flash of memory of figures moving toward me in flickering torchlight. My smile faded and I huddled deeper into the blankets.

"I will take your rudeness as a sign of improved health," he said.

In a minute we were off again, passing forests and hushed villages. There was just enough moonlight to see the caved-in roofs, doors hanging off hinges, and broken fences. Most of the homes, whether finely built or made of mud and thatch, were abandoned and falling into ruin.

As men and women had marched off to war, the hope of planting and harvesting enough crops in this harsh northern land had gone, too, leaving hunger and starvation behind. The fields stank of decay, even worse than they had months before, when I'd been taken to prison.

An hour or two later, the land changed. Instead of forests and fields, the moonlight silvered low bushes and scrub frosted with snow. We rattled over what felt like a goat path leading up the side of a mountain.

"Are you sure you wouldn't rather just kill me now?" I said through clenched teeth, attempting to keep my innards inside my body with my hands pressed to my stomach. "It would cause less suffering, and the end result would be the same."

"We have a use for you," Arcus replied, "and it doesn't involve watching your bony carcass bounce down the side of a mountain."

He sounded as though he was tempted. Same as I was tempted to push him out of the carriage as we rounded a high cliff. Or maybe set his precious hood on fire.

The land leveled to a high plain hemmed in by craggy slopes

dotted with snow-covered pines. What had appeared to be a pile of rocks from a distance resolved itself into a sprawling building with a tower rising high on one side. The moon sat atop the tower as if someone had jammed a sickle into its flat top.

"The abbey you mentioned?" I asked, noting the heaps of rocks beneath gaping holes in the walls. "The prison is a palace by comparison."

"Feel free to walk back, then," Arcus answered coldly. "I'm sure the guards will welcome you with open arms. And the executioner, too, no doubt."

"The executioner didn't seem bothered with me. No doubt he's preoccupied with the many dissenters rounded up by the king's noble soldiers. He's not likely to remember me until the end of the border wars."

Arcus snorted. "You would be dead by then."

I pressed my lips together. He was probably right.

The carriage pulled up to a stable door, and the driver hopped out while a broad figure shuffled over to help with the horses. Arcus stepped out and reached for me. For a man of such size, he moved lightly. I stiffened as he lifted and tucked me against his cold chest.

"Don't burn me and I won't hurt you," he said, invoking our earlier bargain. Pain distracted me from fear. I bit my cheek and clung to his robe, closing my eyes against the throb of my ankle.

"Tell Brother Gamut our guest has arrived," Brother Thistle said, motioning to a man waiting at the door. "Then take her to the infirmary."

"Guest?" I repeated drily. "Does the abbey welcome many guests with ankle chains?"

"Its standards have fallen abysmally," he replied, stepping over paving stones that had heaved up like jagged fingers. "Which is why this is the perfect place to keep you."

And you, I thought. They had taken me from the king's prison and were therefore just as guilty of crimes against the king as I was.

The large wooden door to the abbey was held open by a man holding a candle, the light reflecting off his shiny bald head, shaved in a white tonsure. He was quite old, with a curved back; large, bent nose; and sunken cheeks.

"The infirmary," said Arcus.

The monk turned to shuffle away into the darkness. We followed the candle as it bobbed along a corridor with arched windows and into a small room with four straw-stuffed mattresses on the floor. One of them was covered in a threadbare white sheet, a thin pillow, and a quilt folded at the foot. It was the first time I had seen anything like a bed in months. I leaned toward it, and Arcus let me down with a thump. I rubbed my hip and glared at him.

He motioned toward me with one hand. "Get her cleaned up."

With that, he turned and left.

"Charming fellow," I said to the monk as he lit a sconce on the wall.

The monk looked at me sharply, but then he nodded. "He can be abrupt, to be sure. But with his history, it is understandable."

"And what is this history that makes his rudeness excusable?"

He turned to me. "Time for questions tomorrow. For now we must tend to your physical state."

I wrapped my arms around myself and eyed him with alarm. The guards had been all too eager to amputate infected limbs. I had threatened their filthy excuse for a healer with blistering burns if he so much as entered my cell.

"Now, now," the monk said, his look softening. "You are in a strange place and you have no doubt suffered much, but this is Forwind Abbey. The brothers and sisters of the Order of Fors have pledged to take in those wrongly persecuted and in need of sanctuary. They may be suspicious of you, but you will not be harmed."

I studied him, the tightness around his eyes, the stiffness of his shoulders. "You're suspicious of me."

He studied me a little too long before replying. "I will judge you by your actions, not your heritage. But I recommend you keep your fire hidden. Not everyone is as accepting as I am, pledge or no."

"You don't need to tell me that."

He nodded and gestured at my ankle. "I am Brother Gamut. It is said I have a talent with herbs. If you will show me your injuries, perhaps I can ease some of your pain."

Reluctantly, I unwrapped the cloth under my cuff. The monk sucked in a breath as he saw the reddened shank that was once an ankle. He seemed to forget his distrust, moving closer to frown at the metal.

"We must remove that at once." He turned and shuffled to the door.

"No swords!" I begged.

He turned back, amusement crinkling the edges of his eyes. "No, child. I have a set of keys that may work. I will return shortly."

I wasn't sure I believed him, but true to his word, he was back in minutes with a set of keys, a bundle of cloth, and a tray that held a cup, a bowl of water, and a mortar and pestle, which he placed on a three-legged stool. His palsied hand trembled as he tried each key, until one of them opened my ankle cuff with a decisive snick. After setting the metal aside, he untied a bunch of herbs from his belt. Carefully separating the stems and selecting certain leaves and flowers, he ground and mixed them with the mortar and pestle, put them in the bowl with water, and placed the linen strips in to soak. I hissed in protest as he cleaned the wound and wrapped the linen strips around my stinging ankle.

He looked at me from under his white brows. "There are signs of infection, but you are fortunate. It is not far advanced. I have herbs that will prevent any poisoning of the blood and ease your pain."

When it numbed, I went light-headed with relief.

"What did you use?" I asked.

"Many plants grow on the mountain. I have been experimenting with what is most effective. This is a mixture of birch leaf, wintergreen, and icetail. My tea will also help."

He reached toward the tray and handed me a steaming cup. A

few minutes earlier, I would have looked suspiciously at the brew, but the monk had proved his abilities with my ankle. I took a sip. The minty taste of wintergreen was laced with an unfamiliar tang that must have been icetail. When the cup was empty, I handed it back.

"May I take a bath?" I asked as he gathered his bowl and herbs. Despite bone-deep fatigue, I longed for the impossible luxury of cleanliness.

"Tomorrow," he answered. "The tincture and the tea are working together to make you drowsy. Relief from pain is a blessing, is it not?"

My eyes were closing, my head lolling onto the pillow. "But Arcus the Angry has decreed I'm to be cleaned up. Do you not fear his wrath?"

He smiled, his hand on the door. "There are things I fear much more."

Light poured through the infirmary window, searing my unaccustomed eyes. I hadn't seen more than dull, indirect light from my small, barred, north-facing window for months. I had become some nocturnal, burrowing animal that cringes back into the velvet darkness of its den.

Currently, my den consisted of a mattress stuffed with straw, a soft quilt, and a thin, down-filled pillow. It seemed a dream: to be free from cold, free from pain, free from being doused with foul water. Thank Tempus it wasn't gruel that sat on the three-legged stool, but a bowl of thick porridge, a slice of cheese, and a glass of water. Squinting against the light, I threw off my covers and crawled over, shivering beneath the wavy glass of the window.

The porridge had a dash of molasses. The cheese was salty and soft. Bliss.

I was back in bed by the time Brother Gamut bustled in with a cup of his healing tea. He bent over, carefully unwinding the linen around my ankle, a task my mother had performed on many a wounded man or woman or child from our village. My chest grew tight, and a strange vulnerability stole over me, as if it were my mother's touch in the monk's gentle hands. I fought against it, desperate for the numbness that had protected me from grief for so many months.

When he was done, I again broached the subject of a bath—a hot one, as I had little energy to heat the water myself. A battered metal tub was carried in by two monks—a tall, thin woman and a stout man—both glancing at me suspiciously.

I ignored their looks, instead watching as bucket after gloriously steaming bucket was brought and poured into the tub.

"Remember to keep your ankle dry," Brother Gamut warned as he and the other two left.

As I sank into the bath, warmth made my blood sing. My power, so long kept limp and weak with poor food, damp cold, and despair, surged outward from my heart. I dangled my injured leg over the edge of the tub and lathered up the soap, my spirit caught between conflicting emotions. The lightness and relief seemed too good to be true.

When I was done, I stepped out of the grime-blackened water and dried off, leaning on the tub for support. Brother Gamut had left a pile of modest clothes. I pulled on the linen underclothes, brown robe, and leather sandals, and was hit by the contrast of my clean self with the stench of the dress I had chucked off. Months in prison had turned my simple blue dress and underclothes into a handful of tattered rags. I picked them up and moved toward a lit brazier near the far wall, then changed my mind and headed for the door.

I had a better method of disposal in mind.

As I turned the knob, I hesitated. Was I allowed to leave? What would they do if I disobeyed their rules? The prison guards might have been afraid to touch me, but Arcus had already threatened me more than once. His frost would protect him from my heat, and he might turn out to be as brutal as the guards.

Although I trembled a little, I pushed the door open. I refused to let fear rule my actions. I was no longer a prisoner, and if they treated me like one, I would escape as soon as I was healed enough to do so.

After trailing down the corridor, avoiding the curious eyes of hooded figures, I leaned a hand against the cold stone wall and cursed the unsteadiness of my legs. I reminded myself that only the day before I'd had trouble standing. This was progress.

A minute later, I found a door that led outside. As I stepped over the threshold, my lungs expanded with a breath of fresh, pine-scented air. I closed my eyes, raising my face to the sky. So many months had passed. I hadn't realized how much I'd missed sunlight and crisp, clean air.

Swallowing the lump in my throat, I left the abbey behind. The snow was mostly melted, with patches left here and there in the shade. A copse of budding fruit trees led to a thin river that gurgled over smooth stones and disappeared into tall grass.

I wanted to be out of sight and not too near dried sticks or bracken. Under a spindly tree, a few flat rocks lined the riverbank, probably to pile clothes on for washing when it was warm enough.

I laid the scraps on the rocks. The morning I had donned them had been the worst day of my life. Although I'd pushed away the memories when I was awake, they invaded my mind every night. I couldn't wipe out the vision of what had happened, but I could destroy this reminder. I held my palms toward the pile and closed my eyes. Heat pooled in concentric rings around my heart. *Let it build. Patience. Steady. Just as Grandmother taught me. Wait until it's ready to spit forth, then harness and control it.*

Controlling it had never been my strength.

I called up every hot urge and feeling that had sat under my skin for months and sensed a crackle just under my breastbone. *Fear. Burning rage.* I poured it all on like lamp oil, ready to ignite.

What I needed was to feel something, something that would make me burn. I pictured Mother's hands curled into claws as she ran at the captain, his sword flashing in the firelight. My name on her lips.

She had needed me and I had found my fire too late.

If only I had known how to control my gift. If only I hadn't used it when she'd told me not to.

It was all my fault. I was responsible for her death and the destruction of my village.

I crumpled to my knees, my palms slapping against the flat stone. The memory was like a flame to dry kindling. The heat grew too quickly, out of my control, spitting from my palms and onto the pile and then to my robe, greedily crawling upward until my clothes were completely alight. Although I knew it would take incredible heat to burn Fireblood skin, it felt as if the flames were eating me alive, searing my eyes, stealing the air from my throat, finding the vulnerable places where I might not be as impervious as I'd thought. It was as if I were back in my village again, the torches closing in from every direction with no escape.

My fists clenched. *Push it away. Control it. Master the fire.* But the fire was its own master and would not be ruled. The burning robes tangled around my feet as I clawed at myself, my mouth open in a silent scream.

FOUR

I WAS DROWNING.

Strong hands held me in the water, like the soldiers on that day. I bucked and clawed. Muffled curses rained down as I was hauled up and rolled onto soft earth, pinned down by hands on my shoulders and the weight of my own sodden robes.

"Let me go," I gasped between coughs.

"Kindly remove your talons from my arms," said a deep voice. His hands lifted, shaking off my curled fingers.

Arcus turned me onto my side and pounded my back as I coughed out water. As he leaned over me, his hood fell open enough to show a well-shaped nose with a strong bridge and a glimpse of scars on his cheeks. Dimly, I noticed that his skin was smooth where it wasn't scarred. He couldn't be more than a few years older than I.

When I could breathe again, I struggled against him.

"If you try anything," he warned, "I'll put you back in the river. A good dunking will cool that fury. Now, what exactly were you doing out here?"

I scooted backward and felt warm rock against my back. "Burning my clothes," I said between coughs.

"You set fire to your own robes while wearing them?" he said doubtfully.

"No," I sputtered angrily. "My old dress. The one I wore in the prison."

"There is a refuse heap just past the stables," Arcus said drily, nodding to the right. "You needn't have started an inferno. Not that I'm against the destruction of those foul rags."

I touched my arms and face, still coughing up bits of river water. My skin was hot, but smooth and unharmed. Relief mixed with embarrassment. I had panicked for no reason, frightened by my own fire.

Arcus waved a hand to the tree behind the rock, which was black along its trunk. "I was out walking when I saw a conflagration rise above the treetops. The fire was clearly out of your control."

I plucked at my robe, cringing away from the cold fabric on my skin. The robes hadn't fared much better than the dress I had come to destroy. It was in blackened tatters, the white linens showing through. Once I might have worried about showing off my underclothes, but Arcus was so stony I doubted he even noticed. I tried not to let my fear of him show.

I took a section of what was left of the robe and began wringing it out. "I suppose you think I should thank you."

"No," he said, his tone stiff. "I don't care for gratitude."

"How very humble."

"Not humble. Gratitude creates a bond that begs further protection or care. I have enough obligations."

"You can rest easy, then. I don't need your protection. I have my gift."

"A gift that led soldiers to your village."

He'd spoken in neutral tones, but his words pierced the vulnerable places in my mind, where guilt was still naked and fresh.

"It was cruelty that led to the destruction of my home. The cruelty of *your* people with their border wars and raids on villages."

"Perhaps if the Firebloods had negotiated instead of resorting to assassinations—"

"Frostblood history," I said with disdain. "Forgive me for distrusting your version."

"What is your version, then?"

My version came from my grandmother, who'd told me that fire and frost had fought for dominance for as long as anyone could remember. Frostbloods eventually took Tempesia in the North, and Firebloods settled in the Fire Islands of Sudesia. But when the islands had no more land to offer, Firebloods sailed to southern Tempesia and worked for generations to till and improve the soil of the Aris Plains. As their skills grew, they were accepted as valued farmers—until Frostbloods decided they wanted the land for themselves.

But history could be twisted and warped to suit the person telling it. I wouldn't convince Arcus of anything, and he likely had no trouble painting his own people as rightful rulers and victims of rebel attacks.

"My gift can heal," I finally said, taking a different approach. "Heat has the power to save lives."

"It can also ruin them," he replied. "It can maim and kill. You burned those soldiers savagely."

I sat forward. "Frost can be just as dangerous! Who are you, so perfect and beyond reproach? You haven't even told me what you expect me to do."

He paused. "Brother Thistle thought it best to wait before telling you."

"Why? He thinks I'm weak like you do?"

He shook his head. "I knew it the moment I saw that"—he gestured to the tree—"cloud of fire. Your power is wild. Dangerous. Before we can trust you to know more, you need proper training."

"And who, pray tell, is going to do that? I'm sure the king has killed all the Fireblood masters by now."

I had never met a Fireblood master, of course, but when I was little, Grandmother had told me there was a small handful left in Tempesia. Masters train for years until they have complete

43

control over their gift, and only a Fireblood or Frostblood council of masters can decide if that person has truly done so.

Arcus stood and brushed off his robes. "You're right. There are no Fireblood masters left. But there are Frostblood masters. One of them lives in this very abbey and is willing to teach you."

"Not you."

"No. Brother Thistle. Surely you've noticed the magnitude of his gift?"

I had. In the prison, frost had grown wherever he stepped. Even the carriage had crackled with it. And he'd wielded his power with great precision when he'd unlocked my cell.

I wanted to learn that kind of control.

"Supposing I agree," I said, "how would he teach me?"

"You've already agreed or you wouldn't be here. And I'm no teacher. You'll have to ask Brother Thistle about his methods."

"I will."

Fatigue pulled at my bones. I pushed myself up and started back to the abbey.

Arcus caught up with two long strides. "Perhaps with some control, you'll be an asset to our plans instead of a danger to yourself."

"I'm no danger to anyone but the people who hurt me."

"And not much danger to them right now."

"I suppose you're an expert in rigid self-control," I said. "It must be easy when you're frozen inside."

"Those who can't control themselves will find themselves under the control of others. It's a lesson you'd do well to learn."

"If you try to control me, it's you who will be taught a lesson."

My foot hit a clod of earth and I stumbled, the ground coming up to meet me. Arcus grabbed the back of my robe and hauled me upright, his derisive snort bringing more heat to my cheeks.

"If you wish to threaten me, best wait until you're steadier on your pins." Before I could protest, he swung me into his arms with ease. "I'm growing accustomed to carrying this bundle of crackling firewood."

Crackling firewood, indeed. No doubt that meant I was skinny and unpleasantly warm. Well, he was intolerably cold. I shuddered against the chill from his chest, resisting the urge to push my way free. That would only reinforce his opinion of my wildness.

He took me to the infirmary. I told him to put me on the floor, as I didn't want to soak my pallet with my dripping clothes. He set me down quickly, my hip again meeting the floor with a thump.

I glared. "Perhaps Brother Gamut could teach you how to be gentle while Brother Thistle teaches me control."

"Listen carefully." He towered over me, his steely tone making me wonder if I had pushed him too far. "There are rules to your stay here. You may move about freely in the abbey with the exception of the dormers, where the monks sleep."

I snorted. "Not somewhere I'm likely to frequent, is it?"

"In fact," he continued, "it would be better if you stayed away from the monks altogether, with the exception of Brother Thistle and Brother Gamut. The rest would just as soon turn you in to the soldiers rather than risk bringing them to the abbey. Or risk being burned in their beds."

"Only if they give me good reason," I replied with sweet poison.

"Pay attention because I'll only say this once. The river is your boundary to the north, the stables to the east, the road to the south, and the edge of the woods to the west. If you pass these boundaries, you'll receive a sound thrashing from me, and you will lose all freedoms and privileges."

"You lay one finger on me and I'll—"

"Burn me so badly my mistress will run in terror. I'm afraid that threat holds little weight with me, Lady Firebrand. Get yourself dried off before you take ill. You're weak enough as it is."

He walked out and closed the door with a quiet thud, leaving me steaming in my wet robes.

FIVE

$\mathcal{I}$ SPENT THE NEXT THREE DAYS IN the infirmary, seeing no one but Brother Gamut and drinking cup after cup of his tea. When resting bored me to distraction, I started a routine of limping around the room at intervals, with breaks in between. It was surprising how quickly I gained strength with the help of Brother Gamut's herbs. For the first time in months, I started to feel safe.

Until I woke on the third night with the taste of ashes on my tongue.

My fingers dug into the quilt as I tried to shake off images of buildings wreathed in flames. *It was just a dream.* But the acrid smell wouldn't leave my nose. I sat up, rigid with fear.

Fire.

I threw on my robe, slammed the door open, and ran as fast as my ankle allowed down the corridor and out through the cloister. Following the haze of smoke, I rounded the northwest corner of the abbey. Brothers and sisters ran from the river to the church, tossing buckets of water at the flames spitting from the north door, their wide-eyed faces and clenched hands appearing white in the firelight. One of the sisters cried out as heat washed over her, the water from her bucket hitting the door with a hiss. Then she wheeled around and ran back toward the river.

"Where is Brother Thistle?" I shouted as I drew close. His frost was worth a thousand pails of river water.

One of the monks pointed at a figure stretched out on the ground. I ran over and fell to my knees. Brother Thistle's chest rose and fell too quickly.

Brother Gamut shuffled over to us, a bent silhouette against the orange glow. "He fell asleep at his desk in the chapter house. Brother Peele found him and carried him out."

"We must wake him," I said. "He can put out the fire."

"We have tried. He won't wake."

My heat would hardly help in this situation. I knelt by the monk and gently shook his shoulder. If only I had some strong-smelling herbs to put under his nose to rouse him.

Pounding hoofbeats shook the earth. I turned to see a massive white stallion draw to a halt and Arcus swing from the saddle.

"What did you do?" he demanded as he rushed forward and fell to his knees on the other side of Brother Thistle. Shadows hid his expression, but the accusation was clearly directed at me.

"I did nothing," I said coldly, "except try to wake him."

Brother Gamut cut in to explain what had happened to Brother Thistle. As he spoke, a shout came from one of the sisters who had been accounting for everyone. "Sister Pastel isn't here!"

Brother Gamut's hands knotted as he looked at Arcus. "She must be in the library."

Arcus pushed up and ran for the north door. He blasted the iron door handle with frost and yanked the wooden door open. Smoke billowed out and hungry tongues of flame licked at the edges of the frame. Arcus's whole body was tensed, but he didn't move. Something about his posture reminded me of a small animal facing a predator, its safety dependent on perfect stillness.

I left Brother Thistle and ran to Arcus's side. "What is it?"

He shook his head.

"Use your frost to fight the fire as you go," I said, perplexed. "Is there something wrong? Is your frost...not strong enough?"

"Of course it is!" he barked. "This is nothing."

He put his hands in front of him. The air crackled with frost, but it melted instantly against the raging heat. My eyes widened as I saw how his arms trembled.

"You're afraid of fire?" I asked, thunderstruck.

He rounded on me with a furious glare, but his breath came in short bursts, his chest rising and falling like he had just run for miles.

I waited to feel triumph at his weakness, but my thoughts were clouded with worry. "Where's the library?"

"Just past the church," he answered. "Third door."

I nodded. "I need a pathway out. Try your best to clear the hallway. And have Brother Gamut ready to help when I bring Sister..."

"Pastel," he supplied. "But you can't go in. The roof could collapse."

"Then I'll have to get out before it does." I turned and bolted through the doorway and into the church, ignoring Arcus's shouts behind me. A wall of fire blocked the opening to the corridor. I closed my eyes and threw myself through the flames, tumbling onto the stone floor to quench my robes.

I opened the third door and found a room lined all around with books. Brushes and pots of ink sat in neat rows on tables in the smoke-filled room. Between two arched windows, there was a tapestry of Tempus, father of the four winds, whipping up a storm to punish disobedient sailors.

"Sister Pastel?" I called, my voice shrill.

A tall, robed figure was sprawled on the floor beneath the tapestry. I recognized her as the sister who had eyed me suspiciously as she'd helped bring in my bath the day after I'd come to the abbey. I slid my hands under her arms, grunting with effort as I lifted her. The temperature of her skin was cooler than mine, but nothing like the frigid sting of Arcus's skin. She clearly had no gift of frost to protect her from the flames that filled the corridor.

The windows were the only possible exit. I gently set Sister Pastel back down and picked up a wooden chair, smashing it against one of the windows, which shuddered but didn't break. I tried to smash the glass with my shoulder but bounced off, my arm screaming with pain. I fell back a few paces and was about to try again when a low voice called, "Stand away!"

I covered Sister Pastel with my robes as best I could and shielded my head with my arms. There was a deafening crash as the beautiful colored glass exploded inward, spraying vivid shards onto the floor. A rush of fresh air cleared my head as Arcus scrambled over the frame and into the room.

I ripped the tapestry from the wall and threw it over the jagged glass. Together, we lifted Sister Pastel over the windowsill and climbed out. As Arcus laid her on a hillock a short distance away, I put my hands on my knees and took great gulps of air, then spun around, heading back to the library.

Although my mother had taught me basic letters, it was my grandmother who had taught me to read and love books, bringing several volumes whenever she visited. And my mother's compendium of herbs had been invaluable. The thought of all those precious books in the library dissolving into ash was unbearable.

"What are you doing?" Arcus shouted.

"Saving the books!"

I heard pounding footsteps before he grabbed my shoulders and turned me to face him, a dim outline in the faint glow. "Leave them! The fire won't spread that far."

He ran along the abbey wall, and I followed. On the north side, the monks kept their vigil with buckets of river water. Arcus told them where he'd left Sister Pastel, then ran to Brother Thistle's side.

"How is he?" Arcus asked Brother Gamut.

"Still alive," the monk answered, looking fretfully toward the roaring fire.

Arcus nodded and rushed back to the abbey's large wooden door, the place where he had looked so lost and frozen only minutes before. The flames belched out brilliant embers that burned to black in the orange light. His brow furrowed as he spread his arms wide and clapped his hands together. Frost crusted over the stone and melted. Another clap and more melting frost.

Arcus fell to his knees in the dirt, his palms slapping the heated ground as his back rose and fell with labored breaths.

"Just need a minute," he said. "Harder than I expected."

"You're overheated, most likely," I said. "When I'm wet or excessively cold, my gift is weakened. The same must be true for you when your skin is hot. You've been near the fire for too long."

He made a noncommittal sound. I figured it was as close to agreement as I would get. I waved to a monk who was running forward with a pail of water.

"Wait," I called, grabbing the bucket as he slid to a halt. "Bring more water, please. Here, to me."

And I turned and dumped the bucket's contents over Arcus. He gasped and shook the water from his hands. "What are you doing?" he said, outraged.

"Cooling you off. Ah, another bucket. Good." I sloshed the pail of river water over his head.

"While I appreciate your help, you don't have to drown me."

"Fine, then you do it." I handed him a third bucket from one of the sisters.

Glaring at me, he dumped it over his own head, then moved back in front of the burning doors, clapping his hands and sending out frost. It seemed for a minute that the raging flames would devour the church and the whole abbey with it. But, gradually, the frost stayed for longer and longer on the heated stone. He threw clouds of it whistling down the corridor, and the flames receded, gasping out fat puffs of smoke.

In a few minutes, it was done. The fire was out. A chorus of coughing echoed in the silence. One of the monks fetched a torch from somewhere in the abbey and came to stand near Brother Thistle, along with several others who looked down at him with concern. I stood on the outside of the group, wishing there was more I could do.

A man turned to face me, his bushy brows drawn together and his round face twisted in a scowl. I recognized him as the other monk who had brought my bath the first day, along with Sister Pastel. "You went right through the fire. You're a Fireblood!"

My whole body filled with the need to run, get away, all my memories swirling up and closing my throat.

"She is a refugee, Brother Lack," said Arcus, moving from Brother Thistle to where I struggled to stand my ground. "We have offered her a home because hers was destroyed. Her blood is irrelevant."

I looked sharply at Arcus. He was defending me?

Brother Lack whirled on him. "She is a danger to the abbey and everyone in it." Each word was delivered with the force of a nail being driven into wood. "She is a Fireblood and furthermore a criminal. She had an ankle chain when you first brought her. I saw it myself!"

"She is no more a criminal than any of the other hundreds of unfortunate Tempesians who have tried to defend themselves against attacks."

"And what of the king's wrath when our transgression is discovered?" Brother Lack demanded.

A weak voice laced with indignation came from behind him. "Have you forgotten the aim of our order? To heal the sick and offer refuge to the persecuted?"

We moved to gather around the lean form of Brother Thistle as he raised himself onto one elbow before succumbing to a fit of coughing.

Arcus crouched down and took his shoulder gently. "Easy, my friend. You breathed in a good deal of smoke."

Brother Lack continued to stare at me as if I were a viper about to strike. "Perhaps she is persecuted for good reason. Perhaps the gods punish her for her sins. I remind you that I come from the South. I have had experiences with Firebloods. They are a dangerous, shifty, untrustworthy lot, with no adherence to any of the values we hold dear."

"You forget yourself," warned Brother Thistle, breathing heavily, his deceptively soft tone making the hair on my arms stand up. "Her only sin is being a Fireblood, and that is no sin at all." He coughed a few times more and continued. "If compassion is so abhorrent to you, perhaps I should question your dedication to the tenets of our order."

"*My* dedication? I have devoted my life to the order. I only suggest we maintain the purity of this holy place. The fact that you have brought a *Fireblood*—"

"And remember," Brother Thistle cut in softly, "I decide who belongs here. The order bestowed that authority on me and no one else."

There was a pregnant pause, full of the sounds of Brother Lack's quickened breathing, a battle of wills waged in stern faces. Finally, his nostrils flared but he bent his head stiffly.

"Forgive me. I misspoke."

"All is forgiven," said Brother Thistle, a new series of coughs taking hold of him.

Brother Lack raised his head. "The fact remains, she started a fire that could have killed you."

"It wasn't me," I said, agitated. "What reason would I have to do this?"

Arcus considered me silently and I realized I had plenty of reasons. To distract them so I could run away. To take revenge on Frostbloods. And he'd seen me lose control down by the river when I'd burned my clothes.

Some of the other monks muttered to one another, distrust and concern shadowing their faces. Fear and anger pulsed in hot waves from my chest to my fingertips.

"We can debate this for the rest of the night," said Arcus, speaking loudly over their unrest. "Meanwhile your brother's and sister's injuries go without tending. You have my solemn vow that I will watch the girl closely. We will discuss this tomorrow."

He spoke with the uncompromising tone of command. Most of the monks nodded and started to disperse. Brother Lack held his ground, standing with crossed arms and glaring as if I might rush forward and engulf the abbey in flames at any second.

"Follow us," Arcus said to me, his tone blunt but not hostile. "Brother Lack, I will depend on you to see Miss Otrera into the abbey."

He and another monk lifted Brother Thistle. It didn't escape me how carefully Arcus handled him, as if he carried the sleeping form of his own father. There was clear respect, even affection, between the two, and the thought made my chest ache with a kind of jealousy. It had been a long time since anyone had treated me with tenderness.

They moved along the outside of the abbey toward the infirmary. I followed slowly, my ankle stiff from exertion and the cold night air.

Brother Lack moved to my side, leaning over to mutter in my ear. "You may have Brother Thistle fooled, but I see you for what you are: a vindictive Fireblood intent on destroying a place that worships the god of the north wind. I don't know how you wormed your way in here, but I promise you this: I won't rest until you are back in prison, where you belong. Even if I have to take you there myself."

The bright intensity of his small black eyes showed that he was dangerously sincere. What would it take? One simple message alerting the soldiers to my presence. Or perhaps one night

I'd find myself hauled from my bed and shoved into a carriage bound for the nearest garrison. I had made a mistake of letting relief convince me I was safe here. I would never be safe with followers of Fors; I had to remember that.

Arcus appeared in the doorway to the abbey. "Inside," he commanded.

There was no more time to hesitate or wait for my body to heal. Any fate was better than finding myself back in prison.

I would leave tonight.

S I X

THE INFIRMARY WAS QUIET—A THICK, cloying silence that makes you fancy you can hear impossible things like a spider's progress over the windowsill or the swish of a mouse's tail dragging on the floor in the dark.

I lay on my usual cot pretending to be asleep while Brother Thistle and Sister Pastel slumbered in adjacent cots. Arcus had chosen the mattress closest to the door, a shadow guarding the abbey from my dangerous presence.

At first I'd feared that Arcus planned to keep awake all night to watch me, but after giving me a stony look and ordering me to sleep, he settled down on his bed. He gave no indication whether he was grateful for my help saving Sister Pastel, or whether he believed I had started the fire in the first place. Perhaps at that moment he didn't care. He'd moved slowly and seemed very tired, as if the effort of putting out the fire had taken every scrap of strength from his body.

When everyone's breathing was slow and even, with only a rattling cough occasionally breaking the silence, I picked up a pair of leather boots that sat discarded by Brother Thistle's feet, which were not that much bigger than my own. I took a thick cloak that hung on a peg on the wall and crept barefoot to the door.

As I turned the knob, it creaked slightly. I froze and glanced sharply at Arcus's solid bulk. He slept on his side, his hood still firmly covering half of his face. Was that a slight hitch in his breathing? I waited, silent and breathless. Finally, when he didn't move, I turned the knob and opened the door.

I felt my way in the silken dark to the arched eastern door of the abbey before putting on the boots, then crunched over the frozen ground to the kitchen, where I found a leather satchel and filled it with apples, hard cheese, a bit of dried meat, a few nuts and seeds, a sharp wood-handled knife, and a waterskin.

I knew from Brother Gamut that a small room adjacent to the kitchen served as an apothecary, where he dried and ground his herbs. Glass bottles lined the shelves. Inspecting each label, I chose the ones I thought most valuable. If the abbey had any silver or gold adornments—candlesticks and such—I would have taken those instead. But I hadn't seen anything worth stealing.

I found a second leather bag and filled it to bursting with glass bottles, careful to wrap each in linen bandages.

When I reached the stables, the horses grew agitated, perhaps still unsettled by the smoke that lingered in the air from the church fire. One of them was Arcus's massive, fiercely elegant white stallion. He snorted and stamped and rolled his glinting eyes at me. Instead, I approached a yellow-coated mare that greeted me with a blink of her soft brown eyes. I stroked the space between them and was relieved when she didn't shy from my heat. In minutes I had her saddled.

We left the stables and rode west. As the mare proved steady and I found my seat, I lengthened the reins, the muscles of her back rippling. A sensation of freedom shot through me, heady and wonderful, and I squeezed my legs tighter, eliciting a burst of speed from the mare's flanks. Every breath exploded in my ears as I waited for a shout from behind me or the jolt of hooves clattering across the forest floor.

But then I crossed the western boundary Arcus had set, and the quiet woods folded around me like the arms of an old friend.

The mare found a path through tall, fragrant pines and leafless oak and sycamore trees, and I let her follow it.

I would find a port city where I would sneak onto a ship. Tevros was northwest of Tempesia, but I wasn't sure how far or where it was from here. As I considered which direction to go, my stomach rumbled out a reminder of a more immediate problem.

I leaned over to check on the leather satchel that held the food—and cursed. It wasn't there! It must have become dislodged when I'd let the mare gallop and would be too hard to find in the dark. I struggled not to panic.

If I had better control of my gift, I could use it to hunt, to roast a squirrel or winter hare where it stood. But that kind of deliberate use was well beyond me. I'd have more luck making a trap, but I had no knife to cut twigs or branches, as it was in the same satchel as the food. I could only hope the path led to a village.

Rather than riding into a gorge, we stopped for the night under a canopy of pines. The next morning, I watched the sunrise paint the mare in streaks of gold, like butter melting on a soft piece of freshly baked bread.

"I'm going to call you Butter," I told the horse with a pat. She snorted softly in reply.

While Butter ate withered grasses, which I hoped wouldn't make her ill, I gathered some edible roots for a meager meal. My throat was parched with thirst, but there was no sign of water until the afternoon of the second day, when a distant rushing noise brought Butter's ears up. A lively river churned over rocks. After drinking our fill, we followed the river's course until it veered over a cliff. From there, we turned south and found path after winding path as the sun set again.

It was eerily quiet. An acrid, burning smell tainted the clean forest air. It wasn't the smell of freshly burning wood, but the stale echo of things burned and left to decay.

We came upon a maze of wooden buildings, houses, and shops that were broken and charred and caving in on themselves.

Soldiers had been here.

I barely breathed. If there was even a chance that they waited anywhere nearby, we would turn and leave as swiftly as we could. But I couldn't afford to pass up the possibility of food if any was left in some abandoned larder. I was already weak with hunger. And it was clear the village was abandoned.

One of the houses was less damaged than the rest. Inside, I found turnips, a few potatoes, a half-melted round of cheese— worth its weight in gold to my ravenous eyes—and a metal flask. I gathered it all quickly and remounted Butter, riding for another hour before resting.

The next day, we found a thin stream covered in ice. I broke the surface and filled my flask. I ate the cheese, but the turnips and potatoes were too hard and would need cooking to be edible. There was little shelter on the next stretch of rocky land, so we kept on without resting until night fell.

I was a jumble of aches and bruises, barely upright on the horse's back, by the time lights flickered on in the distance, appearing and disappearing between the trees like playful spirits.

The trees gave way to a clearing, where a dozen wagons were arranged in circles around campfires. I halted and slid off the horse's back in the cover of the pine boughs, well out of the firelight.

People were sitting in clusters, turning spits made of tree branches. My mouth watered as the juices from a skinned hare dripped into the fire with a hiss. They divided the rich-smelling meat into portions, but to my frustration, they didn't take out sleeping rolls or retire for the night in their wagons after eating. Instead, they gathered at the center of the clearing, jostling for the best seat on one of the fallen logs that had been pulled into a semicircle around a fire. A woman with chestnut hair, her face carved in strong, striking lines, came forward and invited a girl of about nine or ten years old to choose a tale.

I sat on the ground on a bed of pine needles, my back against a tree trunk. Butter stood a few yards behind me, content to rest.

The girl chose the origin story, how the Frostbloods and Firebloods came to be. With her hands in her lap, the old woman seemed to grow taller and statelier in the dancing orange light. All faces leaned toward her, their excitement palpable as they listened.

"In the early days," said the storyteller in her low, melodious voice, "people had no frost or fire. They lived with the animals, wearing the skins of those they hunted, and were barely more than animals themselves. The gods of the four winds lived in the sky, each keeping to their own kingdoms, isolated but equal.

"Only Fors, the god of the north wind, was lonely. He wanted there to be someone like him, someone who reveled in blistering cold and biting ice." Her hands moved like white birds among the flickering shadows. "So he swept his hand to the glacier at the top of the world and gathered the coldest pieces. Then he shrank himself into human form and watched the human tribes as they warred with one another, endlessly killing and being killed."

"How were they killed, Magra?" asked a girl in a fascinated whisper.

"Kaitryn!" said her mother. "Don't ask such morbid questions."

Magra smiled and leaned close, as if she was familiar with the girl's thirst for gory details. "Any way you can think of. By their own hands, by stones and swords and axes."

"I bet it was terrible," the girl said with delight.

The storyteller nodded. "Fors said to the woman who ruled the tribes of the North, 'Here, take my ice and use it to freeze your enemies. Then no one will be able to defeat you.' He put the shard of ice into her wrist, and the vein turned blue. The woman's body became cold and her eyes turned pale. She raised her hand and smote the enemy tribesmen with deadly showers of frost and snow until everyone who was left ran from her in terror."

The girl clapped her hands, and some boys inched forward on the ground, their eyes bright in the firelight. Even the adults were still and silent, their gazes rapt.

"But Sud," said Magra with a stern look, "the goddess of the south wind, had loved a warrior of the defeated tribe, and it pierced her heart to watch him die. She saw how formidable the icy warrior woman had become and was afraid that she would kill all the other tribes."

Magra put out her fist as if she were holding something. "So Sud swept her hand into the great volcano, pulling out drops of bubbling lava. Then she shrank herself into human form and watched the people as they struggled to find food and to keep themselves safe from the ice tribe."

She opened her hand and spread her fingers as if she were bestowing a gift. " 'Here,' the goddess said to a chieftain who ruled a tribe in the desert. 'Take this lava and use it to melt the ice of your enemies. Whoever defies you shall be burned. Then you will need to fight no more.' She put the drop of lava into the wrist of the chieftain, and the vein bubbled hot. The man's body warmed and his hair turned red. He raised his hand and cast fire at all his enemies, and no one dared defy him."

Magra made a sweeping gesture, her long sleeve billowing out, and the children shrank back, as if fire might spring from her fingers.

"Over time, the other tribes made alliances with frost or fire, the Fireblood and Frostblood leaders having reached a truce. Each claimed their lands on the earth. Maps were drawn, and the people found peace."

She paused as if that were the end of the story, and the listeners seemed to hold their breath.

"But Eurus, god of the east wind, was filled with envy. He went to Neb, the mother of the winds, to complain. He wanted to create his own creature. Neb was tired of her children fighting, so she declared there must be balance in all things. Whatever Eurus made, his sister Cirrus, goddess of the west wind, would have to make the opposite."

She held her hands palms up as if they formed two sides of a scale.

"Eurus, excited and filled with purpose, swept his hand into the depths of the ocean, down, down to the darkest shadows in the deepest caves. He pulled out a handful of absolute darkness, then, sure that he had found the best gift of all, shrank himself into human form and watched the tribes as they struggled under the rule of frost and fire. 'Here,' he said to a powerful shaman. 'Take this darkness and use it to erase all of your suffering—you will never feel pain again.' He put the darkness into the man's wrist and the vein turned black. But instead of finding relief, the man fell to the ground, writhing in pain and begging for mercy. In minutes, he was dead."

The eyes of the younger boys grew round. Kaitryn leaned forward.

"Eurus tried over and over again, but no one could survive his sweet oblivion. So the god of the east wind divided and sprinkled his darkness over the world, and wherever it fell, a shadow came to life."

She lowered her voice until it was eerie and soft. Fine hairs rose on the back of my neck. "But the shadows were hungry. They devoured the animals and people and were never satisfied. And if a shadow, called a Minax, took a special liking to you, it would seep beneath your skin, turning your eyes and your blood black. You'd become vicious and wild, cunning and bloodthirsty, eager to do its bidding and lose yourself in its blissful darkness."

I rubbed the back of my neck with my hand, trying to erase the chill that danced down my spine. From the day I'd been taken to Blackcreek Prison, I'd had nightmares about a living shadow, the most frightening part of the old stories preying on my fear and isolation. In the dreams, a dark shape would touch my cheek in a painful, blistering caress. I'd wake up shaken and terrified.

"It was a dark time," said the storyteller. "But the creatures weren't allowed to roam free for long. Cirrus, the goddess of the west wind, who loved peace above all things, made a hole in the earth. She forced the living shadows into the darkness below and created a Gate of Light at the entrance, which the Minax could not pass through."

Magra opened her hand to the sky. "Then Cirrus swept her hand into the vivid sunset and snatched a ray of light, which she trapped in a crystal. She shone the light onto two mountains, changing them into sentinels and putting them to sleep until called on to guard the Gate if it ever fell under attack. Finally, she called the fiery chieftain and the icy warrior woman and commanded them to mix their frost and fire to help her seal the Gate."

"I bet they fought," said one of the boys.

"No, they didn't," Magra said. "They worked together because that was what the goddess wanted. Exhausted from her labors, she fell to earth. A wisewoman called Sage took Cirrus to her mountain cave and fed her broth and meat and nursed her back to health. In gratitude, Cirrus put the last bit of sunset from the crystal into Sage's wrist, turning her blood and hair to gold. After that, she could heal the sick and see danger before it happened. She is the third sentinel guarding the Gate of Light, and she won't die until the last Minax is destroyed."

"But the shadows are all trapped underground," Kaitryn said.

"Ah. Some say Eurus kept two of his favorite creations on the earth by hiding them where no one would find them. So Sage must keep watch until they are destroyed as well." Magra put her hands in her lap and sat back. "But the world has grown weary of stories now," she said, slowing her voice to signal the end of the story. "And only children listen."

Memory shuddered through me. My grandmother had always ended her origin story with the same phrase.

"I'll always listen to the stories," said Kaitryn. "And then I'll tell them to others on my adventures across the sea, to the Fire Islands of Sudesia and to the west, where there are monsters, and then I'm going to get a sword and—"

"Mam says you're too sick to travel," said one of the boys. My eyes flicked to Kaitryn. She didn't look ill, though her cheeks were a little flushed.

"I'm going to get better!" she said angrily. "I'm going to find somewhere with no soldiers and no bad people and a king who isn't mad."

Her mother's eyes widened. The circle of listeners went silent. "Hush, child," said a man in a low voice.

"I don't care," said Kaitryn, but more quietly. "His soldiers burned our homes."

"They burned my village, too," I said in a whisper so soft even I could barely hear it.

"It's time for bed, you little ones," said Kaitryn's mother, taking the hand of each child. "We travel again tomorrow. In two days, we'll reach the coast. You need your rest."

So the coast was only two days away. Perhaps I could follow in their wake, stealing food at night and using their path to find my way safely down the mountain.

One by one, the fires were extinguished, and everyone shuffled off to the wagons. Unfortunately for my hopes of pilfering food, a tall, bearded man remained as sentry, leaning his back against a wagon as he took a swig from a flask.

After a while, another man joined the first. He wore a patch of dark fabric over one eye.

"Anything?" he asked, pulling his rumpled cloak more tightly around himself.

"Unlikely," the bearded man answered. "The soldiers moved on. The Fireblood is halfway across the sea, if she has any sense. If not, they'll run her to ground between here and the coast."

I sucked in a breath as my heart took up an irregular beat. I wasn't sure how many other Firebloods were out there, but I had to assume they were talking about me.

The man with the eye patch hacked and spit on the ground. "That's what I think of that stinking Fireblood. She escapes from prison and we all suffer for it."

I clamped my hand over my mouth.

"They say Firebloods are the dangerous ones. But I don't see none of them burning down my house."

"We'll go back in the summer," said the bearded man. "Though I wonder what's the point of rebuilding when they can take it all away again. Only the injured and ill left to defend our homes."

The other man scoffed. "No doubt they'll soon decide we're fit enough. Never mind this"—he pointed to his eye patch—"or your tree branch of a leg. Fat lot of good we were when they raided us."

The bearded man sighed. "I still don't sleep nights, thinking about a Fireblood wandering free with fire in her fingertips."

I'm not a threat! I wanted to scream it so loudly that they would somehow believe that it was true. The Frostblood soldiers were the threat. That captain who killed my mother, cutting her down like she was nothing.

"The reward, though. Five thousand coin. Think of it." The bearded man gestured with his flask, pointing to the right. "I could hire a ship bound east, buy some land on some empty island, build a house. Find a cure for Kaitryn."

The man with the eye patch put a hand on the other man's shoulder. "The healer in Tevros will fix her up right enough. You'll see."

The bearded man handed over his flask. "Take the watch," he said, limping stiffly to one of the wagons.

Five thousand... I moved deeper into the trees, struggling to muffle my gasping breaths. I would never be safe. The soldiers were so close, raiding the countryside in search of—it could only be me. If I followed the villagers to the coast and we hit a stretch of open ground, I'd be easily spotted. Then again, with the twisting, tree-lined mountain paths, there was usually somewhere to hide.

A chorus of coughing pierced my fog of indecision. It was a child's cough and it came from the clearing. I moved closer until I could see. The bearded man with the limp carried a small form while a woman followed closely behind.

"Magra!" said the man, pounding on the side of one of the wagons. "Please, help us. Kaitryn is having another spell."

The storyteller came out, shivering in the cool air. "I don't know what else we can do. All the herbs perished in the fire. And even if I had my cures, I've tried everything."

"But it's so much worse now." The woman who must be Kaitryn's mother twisted her hands together. "She breathed in the smoke...and it was already bad enough. It's been such a wet winter." She took a shuddering breath. "You must be able to do something."

"The only thing we can do is keep her as warm as possible," Magra replied gently.

The girl was coughing so hard she could barely draw breath. Her mother started crying in stifled sobs, trying to block them with a fist.

I tried to think of what Mother would do. It was a wet cough, not a dry one. That ruled out steam infused with the essence of needleflower or nightbrace. I'd have to feel her skin to know if she had a fever, and I couldn't do that without revealing myself. But I could judge by the sound. I ran through all of Mother's patients in my mind until I remembered one whose cough had sounded similar. It had been a boy a few years older than I, with wracking coughs so severe he had started bringing up blood. She had used some kind of tincture on his chest. I closed my eyes and tried to remember. Eggswort. No, that was red and the tincture had been yellow. I could almost picture her hands as she crushed the herbs. Suddenly, it came to me.

"Essence of wintergreen and spiny meadowvale," I whispered.

I crept back to the saddlebag, patting Butter as she gave a soft whicker, and rummaged through until I found the bottles I'd snatched from Brother Gamut's apothecary. It took several minutes of unstopping each and sniffing carefully, but I found the two I needed. Clutching them tightly, I hovered near the edge of the trees.

Someone had fed and stoked the campfire. The man with the limp sat with Kaitryn close to his chest, a blanket wrapped around her small frame. He patted her back gently while the girl's mother stroked her toffee-blond hair.

It made my chest ache. My mother would have done the same thing, hovered over me, done anything she could for me.... She *had* done that. Her whole life had been about protecting me. And to see this spirited little girl who had vowed to sail the oceans struggling even to draw breath—I knew I wouldn't be able to leave things be. I had to help.

After a few minutes, the girl's coughing eased.

"Best stay close to the fire," said the mother. "Too cold in the wagon."

The man nodded and they huddled together, adjusting position a few times before their breathing changed and it was clear they had fallen asleep. It would be near impossible to get close without waking them.

I went back to Butter and riffled through the saddlebag again, this time searching the bottles by size. It was the smallest I wanted, the one that was carefully labeled as producing a deep sleep from one drop of its fumes. I wondered if Brother Thistle had used this concoction to subdue the guards in the prison.

Once I found the tiny bottle, I moved behind the wagon where the man with the eye patch stood watching Kaitryn and her parents with a somber expression. I put a drop of potion on the edge of my cloak and crept with painstaking care toward the sentry, on his right side, where he wore the eye patch.

Just as I was poised to leap forward, he pushed away from the wagon and walked off. I cursed softly, drawing back into the shadows. But if he was checking the borders of the clearing,

I would have at least a couple of minutes before he returned. I would have to be fast.

Leaving myself no time to second-guess my decision, I moved to the family huddled by the fire, quickly putting the soaked edge of my cloak to their faces, first the father, then the mother. They were already asleep. This would just make their sleep a little deeper.

I stared at the little girl, so soft and vulnerable, yet so tough in her own way, her body fighting that incessant, tiring cough. I couldn't risk using the sleeping potion on her with her breathing already troubled. Instead, I shook her gently.

"Kaitryn," I said softly. "Wake up."

It took a few more shakes and repetitions, but she finally opened her eyes. "So tired," she said blearily. "Go away."

I smiled. "I have medicine to help you breathe better."

She stared at me with a furrowed brow. "I don't know you."

"I'm a friend, I promise. You can't go on any journeys if you can't breathe right. Isn't that so, little sea captain?"

After a few seconds, she nodded warily.

"Good girl. I'm going to put a few drops on your chest."

She let me put the drops on the clammy skin over her sternum—one, two—and then I tucked the blanket back.

"Breathe now," I said, conscious that my time was running out. The sentry could be back any second. "Any better?"

She took a few breaths and coughed. I scrunched up my brows, thinking hard. When Mother had treated the boy with

74

the cough, she had me come put my hands on his chest to warm him.

"I forgot, little sea captain. We need heat." I put my hands on her blanket over her chest. "Is it growing warm yet?"

"A little," she said.

I needed to send out more heat. But how much was too much? The baby I had tried to warm, Clay's brother, came into my head. Maybe it *had* been my fault that he died. Arcus had said I was wild, uncontrolled. Could I trust myself to do this?

Kaitryn let out another cough. I didn't let myself think. I sent out a pulse of heat, then concentrated on keeping it steady and unwavering. This was a much softer process than making fire, just raising my own temperature. I could do this.

After a minute, Kaitryn's cold little hand covered mine, then quickly pulled away. "Your hand is so hot."

I held my breath, waiting for her to yell for help. Instead, she blinked and smiled. "I don't feel like coughing anymore."

"That's good." I fought the urge to laugh with relief. Carefully, I handed over the bottles and explained how her parents needed to administer the same medicine, always with heat.

She nodded. "I'll remember."

I smiled in approval. "Clever girl. Now here's the important part. You need to buy more herbs when you get somewhere proper, like a village with an apothecary or a healer. Essence of wintergreen and spiny meadowvale." I made her repeat the words three times. "A good healer will know the herbs by the smell," I told her, "but in case you don't find one, at least you'll know—"

"Who in blazes are you?" said a low, threatening voice.

My head snapped up. Standing a few feet away was the man who wore the eye patch, obviously shocked to return from his rounds to find a stranger chatting calmly with one of the village children.

I stood up quickly, showing my palms. "Just a refugee like you. On my way to the coast."

"And where's the rest of you?" He scanned the woods. "The rest of your party?"

"Gone. Killed when the soldiers came."

He shook his head. "They may burn our homes in a drunken rage, but soldiers don't kill people, least not so many. Unless you're caught hiding a Fireblood."

I forced my expression to smooth and lifted my chin. "Well, I didn't stick around to find out."

"What were you doing?" He gestured to Kaitryn.

"Healing her. With herbs. Kaitryn, hold up the bottles."

"Micha," said the man, nudging Kaitryn's father with his boot. "Dierle. Wake up."

When they didn't wake, his jaw hardened. "What did you do to them?"

"I was afraid they wouldn't let me near Kaitryn, so I made them sleep more deeply."

"You poisoned these good people with your foul concoctions? For all I know they're dead!"

I shook my head. "They're fine! They should wake within the hour. Check them yourself. They're both breathing."

He moved toward them, bending down to put his ear to their chests. As he half crouched, I saw the moment his muscles coiled just before he launched himself at me.

SEVEN

HE LEAPED WITH STARTLING SPEED. I grabbed the potion-soaked corner of my cloak and brought it to his nose. His arms wrapped me in a tight grip, but he took a breath, and that was his downfall. His eyes fluttered and I shoved him away hard with both hands.

I spun away and ran toward the trees as he shouted for help. In my panic, I went too far left and had to retrace my steps to find Butter. For a moment, I thought I'd lost her. Then her coat made a yellow smear in the dim light, and I wanted to cry out with relief. Thank Sud I'd left her saddled.

"Just me," I said, low and reassuring, running a hand along her neck before hopping onto her back. "No time for sleep, girl. We need to move."

The trees, though not chokingly thick, were too close for a gallop. We could only walk, putting slow and steady distance between us and the torches spreading into the trees as they searched for the intruder.

If I was lucky, Kaitryn didn't have time to tell anyone about the temperature of my skin. And there had been layers of clothing and thick cloaks between me and the man who had grabbed me. They might give up the chase quickly, glad to have driven me away.

As long as they didn't know I was a Fireblood.

Butter kept a good pace, especially when we came across a thin, frozen stream and were able to follow its banks unobstructed by trees. Eventually, the torches fell so far behind they were no longer in sight. I forced my tight muscles to relax. We had escaped.

As we stopped for the night under a bit of hollowed-out cliff, I chewed on that word like a dog gnaws on a piece of dried leather.

Escape.

That was all I seemed to do anymore. Run away. I had escaped the prison, the abbey, and now a camp of refugees. Was that what my life was now? An endless series of close shaves until my luck ran out?

I would never be safe in Tempesia. There was nowhere I could hide that someone wouldn't turn me in to the nearest garrison for that reward. I had hoped to get to the coast and stow away on a ship, but if that was what the soldiers expected me to do, they would be watching every road, checking every berth.

The real problem was my conscience. It wouldn't stay quiet anymore. As long as the king lived, there would always be another captain, another raid, until my people were extinguished, and maybe not even then. When Arcus and Brother Thistle had come to the prison, they had offered me a chance to strike at the king. I hadn't known whether to believe them, but had agreed because it was better than dying a slow death.

But what if Arcus and Brother Thistle had a real plan to overthrow or kill the king...and I was part of it? I had been too scared and weak to feel that I could be of any help. But after seeing the suffering that followed in the wake of my escape—the burned villages, the misplaced people, the little girl gasping for every breath, her medicine burned along with her home—wasn't I obligated to try?

I wasn't being noble. There was nothing noble about a thirst for revenge. It was about getting what I wanted, a chance to kill the king. And no one else would have to suffer because of me.

I looked at the stars for guidance, then turned Butter back toward the abbey.

After some wrong turns and backtracking over the next few days, we entered the massive stretch of forest only a day's ride from the abbey, weaving through trees with weathered gray bark that matched the sky. At midday, clouds began dropping fat flakes that wheeled in the breeze like tiny doilies crocheted from silk thread. In the afternoon, the wind changed, beating sideways from the north. The snow became heavy, wet, and laced with sleet. It hissed when it first touched my face. Soon, my skin cooled and I could no longer feel my cheeks.

Everything was violent white. The wind hit my eyes like invisible needles, making them water. I could barely see a few feet in front of Butter's ears. We could walk right off the edge of the mountain and I wouldn't know it until we were halfway down.

There had been a depression in the cliff face forming a sort of cave somewhere behind us, back when the breeze was light and playful. I should have stopped. I should have known better than to underestimate a winter storm in the mountains.

Cursing myself, I pulled back on the reins. I was fairly sure I could survive the night. My heat should keep my insides from freezing. But not Butter. She had no defense against the cold. The temperature had dropped sharply. For her sake more than mine, we needed to go back and find that bit of shelter.

Then again, we could be hours from the abbey. I didn't know how long we'd been in the woods or how far we'd come.

"We'll keep going," I told her. "The snow is too thick to go back. You'll find your home, won't you, girl?"

I urged her forward and she trudged on. Whether she knew her way or not, the mare's pace slowed steadily over the next hour or two until she finally stopped.

"Just a little farther," I told her, rubbing her ice-crusted neck. But the truth was, there was no way to get my bearings in this endless wash of white. I slid off Butter's back into a thick drift and put my hands on her side.

"A bit of heat for you," I said, pushing some out carefully the way I had with Kaitryn. It seemed to revive her, though it left me shaky and weak. We hobbled side by side for another eternity through the rising snow.

I could no longer feel my feet. The wind had calmed, but the snow kept falling. It looked like a flurry of feathers to me now. I wanted to reach up and grab some and rub them against my face. I felt strange. And so tired. It would be nice to sit and rest, just for a little while.

No sooner had the thought crossed my mind than I sank down, my back against the trunk of a tree.

"Just for a moment," I said, realizing that I could barely feel my lips. Perhaps I had been wrong. Perhaps a Fireblood could die in the snow, if she were cold and tired enough and without food for fuel. The thought was distant, though, and was more curious than alarming. I closed my eyes.

Dimly, I heard Butter nicker and felt her nudge my cheek with her cold, cold nose.

A golden-haired woman was staring at me with an urgent expression, a crease marring the gold-dusted skin between her brows, amber eyes sparking.

"Wake," she said. "Your time hasn't come yet." She looked behind her fearfully. A shadow fell over her face. "You must save yourself."

"Fors tried to kill me," I whispered. "He sent a storm to freeze me."

"Get up, child. He needs you."

"Fors?" I asked, my brain muddled by a strange lethargy. "Why would the Frostblood god need me?"

My muscles twitched as if trying to pull me up in spite of myself. I moaned as I became aware of the wicked cold biting at me like gnawing teeth.

A sinuous black shape took the golden woman's place, hovering over me. I had a sense of malevolent eyes fixed on me, though the shape was faceless. My skin seemed to grow painfully tight. A dark tendril reached out, and I knew in some deep part of my soul that if it touched me, I would never be the same again.

I woke with a jolt. It was still daylight. I still sat against the tree. The drifts were higher now, halfway up my chest.

With a fierce effort, I broke free of the snow and pushed up, groaning as feeling returned to my limbs like tiny, stabbing knives. Searching the trees, I saw no sign of Butter. I was torn between anger at her desertion and relief that she might still be alive.

Cursing, muscles burning, I pushed through the heavy drifts, step after aching step. I still didn't know if I was going in the right direction.

"Butter!" I called over and over, my voice ragged. As if she even knew a name I had just given her and was biddable enough to obey me, a stranger who had stolen her in the night. Still, she was my only hope of finding my way out of the woods. I looked for tracks, but they must have been covered under snow. "Butter, if you don't come back here right now, I'll make sure you eat stale oats for the rest of your life!"

Suddenly, there was an answer: a distinctly horsey snort from a distance to my left.

"Butter, here!" I cried, hope surging into my chest.

But it wasn't Butter who emerged from the whitewashed trees. It was a stallion made of snow, with sapphires for eyes, and a rider cloaked in black.

The captain had found me.

I turned and ran, but the drifts caught at my feet. I tried to find fire inside myself, but I was too cold. I could barely warm myself.

A hand came to the back of my cloak, lifting me bodily onto the horse, the front of the saddle pressing into my stomach. I lashed out with my elbows. The stallion danced in agitation.

"Stop it!" a voice said.

I looked up. He wore a hood pulled low and underneath that a mask that covered the top half of his face. But I knew those well-formed lips, twisted with anger.

"Arcus."

"So pleased you remember me. Now, stop struggling before I dump you in the nearest snowbank. I've been on horseback for five days trying to find you, and I'm not at all sure you're worth the trouble."

His anger came off him in waves colder than the north wind. I threw a benumbed leg over the stallion's side and gripped the pommel.

"How did you find me?"

He unclenched his jaw to answer. "When Wheatgerm returned to the stables, I followed her tracks until they disappeared. And then I heard someone bellowing nonsense, and I knew it must be you."

"Who the blazes is Wheatgerm?"

"The horse you stole from the abbey," he said as if talking to a simpleton.

"You mean Butter. And I didn't steal her. I borrowed her. I take it she's safe?"

"Cold and tired, but safe in the stables eating like she's half starved. Which she probably is, thanks to you. And her name isn't Butter."

"It is now."

"She's not yours to name."

"She's mine in spirit now that we've had an adventure together. And her name suits her. She's soft and yellow, like butter."

He made a disgusted sound. "If we all had names to suit us, you'd be called Thorn in My Backside. Or Plague of the Gods."

I prickled at his scathing tone. "And you'd be Miserable Blockhead."

"Is that the best you can do?"

"Give me time. I'm half frozen."

Now that I was out of the snowdrifts, feeling returned to my legs, warmth flowing back into my chest. The only part of me that wouldn't warm was my back, pressed against Arcus. With each movement of the horse, I became more aware of the unfamiliar sensation of being so close to a male body for this long, his upright posture unyielding as I swayed, braced on either side by the rigid confines of his arms.

"You're freezing me," I complained to cover my discomfiture. "Perhaps your name should be Icy Tyrant. No, wait. Frigid Despot."

He made no effort to mimic my teasing tone. "I don't much care what you call me. If it weren't for Brother Thistle's urging, I would have left you to die."

After that I was silent all the way back to the abbey.

EIGHT

THE NEXT DAY, BROTHER GAMUT chastised me for running away, especially in winter with no provisions. I had bathed and dressed in dry clothes and sat on my pallet in the infirmary while he forced me to drink cup after cup of hot tea.

I took another sip. "I thought you'd all be glad to have me gone."

He regarded me with his gray eyes, his bushy brows lifting. "Things were refreshingly peaceful for the past few days. Truthfully, there were those who hoped you wouldn't come back. However, the brothers and sisters trust Brother Thistle and are loyal to him. He gave many of them homes and purpose when they fled from provinces where the fighting has spread. If he says we must hide you here, they will comply with his wishes. And you won a few hearts when you saved Sister Pastel from the fire."

A few days ago, I would have made a stinging remark. I wouldn't have let myself care, or admit I cared, what followers of Fors thought of me. But I found myself strangely glad to have won a bit of their trust.

"How is your ankle?" Brother Gamut asked.

I shrugged. "Your tea is helping."

"Good. Now, drink up. You're to meet Arcus in the library for a chat."

I groaned. "A lashing, you mean."

"A tongue-lashing, perhaps. He will be calmer once he has an opportunity to vent." He paused. "I believe he was worried about you."

I scoffed. "Arcus is a block of ice. If he has any feelings, they certainly aren't wasted on me."

"It is not easy for a Frostblood to admit his feelings, or even allow that he has them. Logic and self-control are prized among the followers of Fors. But we must go now. You mustn't keep him waiting."

I heaved a sigh and followed him from the infirmary.

⌒〜

As we entered the library, a tall monk with a blade-thin nose sat at one of the tables, her long-fingered hand holding a brush. She wielded it with careful confidence, every movement small and precise. I noticed that the tapestry of Tempus, cleaned of smoke and soot, had been hung over the broken window.

A figure brooded behind her in the darkest corner of the room. Arcus. His presence pulsed in the air with an almost audible hum. He sat in the wooden armchair I had used to try to break the window only days before, his fingers drumming a rhythm on the armrest. "Sister Pastel, would you be so kind as to give us the room?" he asked.

Sister Pastel looked up and noticed me. She inclined her head solemnly, and I nodded back, relieved to see that she was recovered after the fire.

As she left, I examined the table. It appeared she'd been working on a parchment with colorful illuminations depicting the goddess Cirrus, dressed in pristine white robes and casting her benevolent gaze upon a field full of fat sheep. The goddess of the west wind was also the goddess of rain and farmers. Sailors, too. In fact, she was the goddess of many things that were favorable. Not like Fors, his icy sword vowing revenge on anyone who defied him.

From the corner of my eye, I caught Arcus gesturing for me to sit. I shook my head.

He stood and took a step closer. My whole body clenched.

"You left," he finally said.

Heat crept up my neck. "If you plan to thrash me for violating your precious boundary, you could have picked a better spot. You wouldn't want to stain any of the books."

He said nothing, but he fairly vibrated with tension. His looming size, coupled with the waves of cold fury that came from his skin, were enough to set my heart into a rough canter.

I knew what he was doing. The guards had been experts at it. They had been too scared to come near me but had still found ways to torture me with discomfort and fear: a bucket of icy water, a heavy object thrown at me as I cowered in the farthest corner of my cell, a crash of steel sword against metal bars just as I was falling asleep. Stillness was a kind of violence in the hands of people who played at handing out pain.

Disappointment sheared through me. For some reason, I hadn't thought Arcus was one of those people. I didn't doubt he would punish me. I just hadn't thought he'd make a game of it.

"Having fun?" I taunted, my lip curling.

"I told you the rules," he said in a low voice.

"And I broke them." When he still didn't move, my voice rose. "Let me make it easier for you. I wish I *had* lit that fire in the church. I wish the whole abbey had burned to the ground!"

"I never wanted you here in the first place."

It surprised me to find that his statement hurt. He had implied it before and said worse, that he would have let me die in the woods if it weren't for Brother Thistle. But it had been said in anger then, and now he was calm and cold. I reminded myself that I didn't care how he felt.

"Unfortunately, you're a necessity," he added grimly. "You're the key to getting everything I need. And because of that, you can't just wander away whenever you feel like it. Too much depends on you."

"Funny how you still haven't told me why you need me. It would be wiser to run."

"I'd drag you back."

"So your plans don't involve my willing participation? I can just be forced into it?"

He was silent. A telling flare of his nostrils was an admission.

I crossed my arms. "You need me willing. And that means I need information."

"And if you're captured, you'll tell the soldiers everything. I can't take that chance."

The silence lengthened and pulled thin until I could no longer bear it. I shook my head and turned away. "Next time I leave, I won't come back."

"I took you from the prison!" he said, his voice raised. "I saved your life."

I spun back, my skin heating. "So what—I'm your slave now?"

Another voice came from behind me, a cultured voice raised in shock. "What is the meaning of this shouting?"

I half turned to see Brother Thistle in the doorway, his brows drawn into a scowl. He might have looked like any old man, such as I'd see tending chickens in my village or gathering herbs on the mountain, if it weren't for the frost-misted air he exhaled and a thin layer of ice crystals that coated the stone floors of the hallway behind him.

"It's not like you to lose your temper," he chastised Arcus.

"She would try the patience of a god," Arcus muttered, throwing himself back into the chair.

Brother Thistle motioned to another chair, which sat in front of the table with the book on it. "Please sit, Miss Otrera."

I sat. He pulled a wooden stool close and looked at me long and hard. "Why did you leave?"

"Why do you think? I have no urge to go back to prison."

"You won't go back."

"Brother Lack said he will not rest until the soldiers know where I am."

Arcus sat forward in his chair, gripping the arms as he glared at Brother Thistle. "I warned you. I told you he couldn't be trusted. You insist on seeing the best in people."

"We can discuss that later. Right now we need to ask Miss Otrera why she didn't come to us for help and instead rode off into the woods."

"I was scared," I said honestly. "You haven't told me why you brought me here, what part I'm supposed to play in this plan to overthrow the king. And you seemed to believe I started that fire."

"Did you?" asked Arcus.

"I don't believe you started the fire," Brother Thistle said quickly. "And I understand your fear. But you must promise never to leave again. It is very dangerous in the surrounding villages."

"The soldiers are searching for me, I know. I passed a ruined village and came upon an encampment of refugees."

"You didn't allow them to see you." When I remained silent, Arcus added, more urgently, "Did you?"

"Well, not intentionally."

Arcus swore and my voice rose. "I had to help a sick little girl! And I don't believe they knew I was a Fireblood." I had no urge to tell him how she had touched my hand and remarked on the heat of my skin. "They're moving on to the coast. I don't think they'll search for me, even if there is a reward of five thousand coin on my head."

More swearing from Arcus. Brother Thistle raised his hand. "We knew there was a reward, though I didn't realize it was so significant." He closed his eyes and massaged his brow. "My concern is if these refugees tell the soldiers of your presence. There is a lesser reward for information of your whereabouts."

"Oh," I said. "I didn't know that."

Arcus threw up his hands. "Would it have made any difference?"

"Probably not."

"Promise you won't leave again," said Brother Thistle softly. "And then we can discuss what you want to know."

I shrugged. "Tell me everything you're planning and then I'll decide."

Ice crackled over the floor from Arcus's chair.

"Is that his version of a tantrum?" I asked Brother Thistle.

"The patience of a god," Arcus muttered.

"Enough," said Brother Thistle. "If you can't promise, I can tell you nothing. The lives of too many people depend on us."

"And you would accept my promise?"

He looked intently into my eyes for so long that I thought he wouldn't answer. "Yes," he said with gentle conviction.

I let out a long breath. "I came back, didn't I? I decided I wanted to help. I promise not to run away again."

"Then it is time to discuss our purpose in bringing you here." He leaned forward, his hand on his walking stick. "We heard rumor of a prisoner of the king who was a powerful practitioner of the art of heat."

The art of heat. Grandmother had told me that was how it had once been known. Respected. Revered. Frost and fire working together to achieve their goals and make better lives. That was a long time ago.

"Before going to the prison," he continued, "we troubled ourselves to find out more about you. For instance, none of the people in your village had the gift, including your mother."

My hands curled into fists inside the sleeves of my robe. "My mother," I said softly, "had a gift more essential than the ability to heat water without benefit of fire. She was a brilliant healer."

He inclined his head. "So we have been told. Another reason you interest us."

"And why exactly do I interest you?"

"For one thing, there are very few of your kind left in Tempesia. Few with powers of your magnitude, at any rate. It is quite possible you are the most powerful Fireblood left in the kingdom."

A wave of disorientation had my hands grasping the arms of

94

my chair. In my village, I had felt alone, misunderstood. But at least I cherished the thought that, one day, another Fireblood would help me understand what raged inside my heart and how to live with it, how to harness and use it without fear of hurting everyone around me. Now it appeared I was alone.

"So they were all killed in raids," I said, needing to be able to imagine their deaths, to show my respect by doing that small thing.

"Some in raids, yes," he said. "Others died in prison. But the strongest are often taken to the king's arena."

I sat up straighter, surprised. "I've heard a champion who wins in the arena can receive his freedom, sometimes even gain a place in the king's court. But I thought it was only Frostbloods."

"That was once true. The entire practice ended under the previous king, Rasmus's older brother, who didn't care for needless bloodshed. King Rasmus has resurrected it. He takes the most powerful Fireblood prisoners and matches them against his Frostblood champions."

"Can a Fireblood win their freedom?" I asked.

He hesitated. "We have never heard of a Fireblood coming out alive."

So even the most powerful of my kind had been cut down for the king's entertainment. "How did it come to this?" I whispered. "Grandmother always told me that frost and fire used to live in peace."

Brother Thistle spoke. "When Firebloods came across the sea searching for new and fertile lands, even our myths and traditions set us up as rivals. Peace was established, but eventually Firebloods pushed the boundaries of their territories, fighting with landowners, demanding more farmland."

"That's not fair," I retorted. "That was all settled. It was King Akur who pushed to change the boundaries that had existed for hundreds of years. Firebloods had made the land what it was, and he tried to take it back."

Brother Thistle inclined his head. "The Firebloods were far outnumbered, so they resorted to assassinations of high-level Frostbloods. When that didn't force King Akur's troops back, they killed some of the most valued members of his court."

"And his wife," said Arcus, his voice grating compared with Brother Thistle's softer tones.

"Regardless, King Rasmus is only taking up where his murderous father left off," I said.

"He is far worse than his father ever was," said Arcus. "King Akur was at least generous with alms for the poor and improvements for cities. Rasmus uses the treasury to make more weapons, train more soldiers. He tortures anyone suspected of treason, kills the barons who oppose him, and crushes any hint of rebellion by sending all the able-bodied men and women off to the borders, where they can do nothing."

"And everyone left behind starves," I added. "Thank Tempus the abbeys and their monks appear to be safe, though. And... whatever you are." I waved a hand toward Arcus.

He was no monk; that was for certain. There was just nothing *monkish* about him at all. He carried himself like a warrior and spoke like a nobleman. His cloak and boots were fine, yet he hid himself in an abbey.

"King Rasmus still honors the god of the north wind," Brother Thistle replied. "He wouldn't risk angering Fors by harming his devotees."

I shifted in my seat so I faced Arcus. "And how do you suppose I'll manage to kill the most powerful king in our history?"

"He is not the most powerful king in our history," Arcus retorted. "Ruthlessness is not power. Tyranny is not strength."

I was startled to hear him echoing my own convictions. In fact, much of what he'd said I agreed with. "So even you, a Frostblood..." I said. "You hate the king, too."

"We are against the way King Rasmus carries out his rule," said Brother Thistle, glancing at Arcus. "We are against his lack of compassion."

"Lack of compassion?" Sudden anger brought me to my feet. "Is that your pallid description of a king who would send his soldiers to raze an entire village because of *rumors* of a single Fireblood?" My chest heaved. "The home I loved, my mother, everything is gone—all because I was born with a gift I cannot help, cannot control, and can never, ever be rid of!"

A flame burst from my palm and danced across the floor, sliding up a table leg. Arcus leaped to his feet, slicing the air with his hand. Frost doused the fire before it could spread to the parchment laid out on the table. A smudge blackened the polished wood.

"Calm yourself," he said, breathing hard.

I curled my hands together. I hated the loss of control that came with strong emotions. Slowly, I returned to my seat and wrapped my arms around myself, glaring at the floor. "I say we show the king a similar *lack of compassion*. String him up and set the frost wolves on him. It would be a kinder death than he has granted to many."

"Miss Otrera, we do not disagree with you," said the monk, his eyes on my fisted hands. "To heal the kingdom, we must end King Rasmus's reign."

Relief surged through me, though I still simmered.

"Perhaps we can continue this discussion another day," he said. "It is easy to forget that you have been through a great ordeal and are still healing."

I tucked my shaking legs further beneath my robes. It would do no good to lose my temper with these men. If all I did was spit and claw like a feral cat, they would never trust me.

"Thank you for the herbs and food," I said sincerely, trying to sound calm. "Brother Gamut has taken good care of me."

"The first order of business is for you to heal," said Brother Thistle. "Any other matters can be discussed when that has been accomplished."

"Any other matters," Arcus said, his commanding voice resonating in the small room, "will be handled when I say it is time to handle them. We sit by and wait while the throne—"

Brother Thistle held up a hand. Surprisingly, Arcus went silent.

"Trust me, my friend," said the monk. "We have waited all this time, searching for the girl. Time is our enemy, but sometimes patience is necessary."

Arcus stood abruptly and brushed past my chair on his way out of the room. A rush of frigid air stung my cheek as he passed.

NINE

OVER THE NEXT COUPLE OF DAYS, MY temper cooled as my health improved. I asked Brother Thistle for more information about my task, but he told me to focus on healing and more would be revealed when he felt I was ready. After three days, Brother Gamut declared me recovered enough to train. He brought clothes and left me to dress in a woolen cloak, faded white shirt, and red tunic over dark leggings. Leather boots were laced tightly to my feet, and my hair was tied back with a piece of string. I was instructed to meet Brother Thistle at a spot between the abbey and the woods, where a copse of trees would shield us from any curious eyes.

On the way to the westward door, I passed by three monks, a man and two women. The man wore his hair in a tonsure, but the two women just wore their hair cropped very short, barely long enough to brush their temples. They all moved to the side as I passed, doing nothing to hide their aversion. Clearly, my rescue during the fire hadn't won over everyone. Perhaps they still thought the fire was my fault.

Preoccupied with my thoughts as I exited through the westward door, it took me a moment to notice that Arcus was waiting.

He wore a blue tunic and black leggings that fit snugly over the thick muscles of his thighs. His shoulders were made broader by shoulder guards that shone silver in the weak sun. He wore a sort of hood with no cloak and the same mask from when he found me in the snow. It extended partway over his face, covering his nose and cheeks.

When his eyes met mine, I froze as if I were wrapped in frost.

They were light blue, little chips of ice that glinted like frozen jewels. They were eerie, stunning, beautiful eyes. *If ice can ever be beautiful.*

I nodded in greeting and walked forward. He fell into step beside me, his strides shortened to match mine.

"Couldn't resist an opportunity to watch Brother Thistle knock me down?" I asked.

"A great deal depends on you." His tone was cordial but detached. "I need to be sure your training goes well."

"Why? Your role in all this remains rather murky."

His jaw tightened, but his tone remained light as he changed the subject. "I should have told you before; I thought it was brave of you to go after Sister Pastel." He paused. "Thank you."

I stopped in shock and turned to him.

"For rescuing her when I hesitated," he finished, meeting my eyes.

"Not so brave for a Fireblood." I fiddled with the edge of my tunic as we continued walking. "And I wouldn't have been able to get her out without you." I grimaced. "Anyway, if history is any lesson, I'm more in danger of setting myself on fire than anything else."

"Well, don't," he said sharply. "I don't fancy carrying you all the way to the river."

"You could just throw frost over the flames," I pointed out.

"And you would welcome the sensation of ice on your skin?"

I glanced at him. "Is that why you tossed me in the stream instead? You were being considerate?"

"I was being practical," he answered, still looking forward. "Water douses flames. Your heat repels frost. It was easier to push you in."

His reasoning was sound, but his remark about carrying me *all the way* to the river still rankled. "You speak as if I'm as heavy as an ox," I said. "Last week I was a bundle of sticks."

"You're still too thin."

"Perhaps if I gain some weight, you won't call me a stick anymore."

"You may hope to one day be a branch."

I glanced at him sharply, unable to repress a little flutter of delight that he was bothering to joke with me.

"A log, even," I suggested.

"Doubtful," he said wryly. His eyes settled on my leg. "You're limping less noticeably. Your ankle is healing."

"Yes." It still ached, but perhaps Brother Thistle would go easy on me, as it was our first lesson.

We arrived at the scrubby bare patch, our booted feet crunching bits of dead grass wet with recently melted snow. The air smelled of woodsmoke and pine. Birds piped from distant trees. Tendrils of mist snaked along the ground, slowly lifting as the sun rose.

"Good morning, Miss Otrera," said Brother Thistle, dressed in his usual robes and leaning on his walking stick. "I trust you are ready for our training?"

I nodded. Arcus stood off to one side, close enough to hear but not close enough to be in the way.

"Sit," the monk commanded. We both sat, and I hoped I wouldn't stiffen so much that I couldn't get up.

"Close your eyes," he said.

I closed one but kept the other open, not relishing the sense of being completely vulnerable. I wasn't ready for a surprise attack.

"Both of them."

I sighed and closed both eyes.

"First we must clear your mind."

My eyes popped open. "My mind? What has that got to do with anything? The heat comes from my heart."

"Which is controlled by the mind. Which you would know if you had learned to master your gift."

I followed the monk's instructions. He gave me a strange

word, either ancient or gibberish, and I repeated it over and over. The idea was to get to a place where my mind was completely clear. I thought I was doing quite well until a loud sigh issued from the monk.

"Miss Otrera, a hummingbird is capable of more stillness than you. Perhaps if you didn't fidget quite so much, your mind would be quiet."

I looked up at him, stung by his tone. I hadn't realized I was fidgeting.

"Trying to make my mind quiet makes me fidget," I replied. "And if you're trying to teach me patience, perhaps you should have some yourself."

He blinked in surprise, his cheeks darkening slightly.

"You may be right," he said, standing and leaning on his cane. "But what you do not realize is how little time we have. It is spring now, when your power waxes and mine wanes. At summer solstice, you need to be ready for your task."

A mixture of excitement and fear surged through me, making my fingertips tingle.

"That is just over two months away," he continued, "which may seem like a long time to you. But it takes years of practice to effectively learn this. So in the time we have, we must do what we can. And I suppose I must be satisfied with the outcome."

My skin heated at his resigned tone. There was implied censure in his words, as if he expected to be disappointed.

"Your body temperature is rising," said Brother Thistle. "Good."

"You can tell from so far away?"

"Of course. And so can you, with others. You only need to pay attention. Attune yourself to things outside you instead of constantly being preoccupied with your own thoughts."

There was the censure again. My blood heated further.

"Good, Miss Otrera. Now, let us do a test to see how much control you already have. Channel your anger and burn that small shrub over there, as you did the table leg in the library."

"But I didn't mean to. That happened without me thinking about it. I'm only good at heating things, not making fire out of nothing."

"Do not think about fire. Only think of making the essence of the thing hot, and it will burn."

Although his words echoed what Grandmother had taught me, it was hard to trust the advice of a Frostblood.

"Forgive me, Brother Thistle, but what do you know of the art of heat?"

He inclined his head. "Where I grew up, there was a great Fireblood master nearby. I used to watch the students in his school as they trained."

"A school?" I asked with a rush of curiosity.

"High on a hill next to a temple of Sud. I suspect the master knew I was watching. He was a fair-minded man. Even-tempered for a Fireblood."

"Did you ever train with them?"

He shook his head. "That was not allowed. I trained on my own and came to realize that many of their same techniques could be used with frost. When I came here from Sudesia, I was far ahead of many of the other Frostblood warriors."

"You came from Sudesia?" I said, unable to keep the surprise from my voice. "And became a Frostblood warrior?"

He straightened and leveled me with a piercing look. "Indeed."

I imagined a younger Brother Thistle, his face unlined, his hair dark, his chest covered in leather or armor. He wasn't a large man, but he carried himself with assurance.

I focused on the distant bush. I was more aware than I wanted to be that Arcus was watching, his silent presence doing nothing to help my concentration. But I closed my eyes and brought the heat within me to readiness, as Grandmother had taught me. Stoke the flames, then harness them.

My skin became hot. Sweat pooled in my armpits and between my breasts. I trembled with the effort. When the heat increased so much that I grew fearful of losing control, I let it out in a rushing torrent.

All the yellow grass between me and the bush caught fire and burned before fading to black. The shrub remained untouched.

I cursed under my breath.

"Control, Miss Otrera," said the monk. "You have power, but you need to learn control. If this had been a battlefield, you would have burned your own line of soldiers and left the enemy untouched."

"I have no interest in going into battle," I spit out, frustrated by my failure. "I just need to kill one miserable king!"

Arcus growled disapproval from behind me.

"And as for control," I continued, "that's what I'm here to learn, and *you* are supposed to teach it to *me*."

I poked my finger into the monk's chest on the word *you* and heard the sizzle of fabric. I jumped back and put a hand to my mouth. He waved a finger and his robe was instantly doused.

"As I said, Miss Otrera," he said calmly, if a bit frigidly. "Control."

Tears gathered behind my eyes, my sense of failure compounded by losing my temper. I turned away, blinking hard.

"Now," he said, "I have an idea of your process. You let the fire build inside you and then let it out in a raging flood. Cold is very similar in this regard. It can get away from you and cause much havoc if not focused on a target."

"But... I was focused on the target."

"Your eyes were. But was your mind? Once you learn to focus your mind, your fire will follow. Observe."

He raised his arm and brought it forward and back, lightning-fast. A tongue of ice cracked the air like a silver-blue whip. I jumped back reflexively as the ice flew past and clattered to the ground. He raised his hand again. A spiral of frigid air pulled dust and debris from the ground, creating a sort of funnel that swept from his hand, left and right, wherever he moved it.

"It takes great focus to control your power," he said. "At first, it will seem impossible. But you must learn to center your mind in stillness. Then you will learn to find that stillness at other times, even when there are distractions. Even in battle."

I glared into his stormy blue eyes. "It's easy for you. Frost-bloods are full of ice. I'm full of fire and heat. I can't just turn it off."

"Do not confuse frost with lack of feeling," he warned. "Frostbloods are fully capable of feeling in every way. The danger is that those emotions, while powerful and deep, may be covered with a layer of ice that prevents the natural expression of them. It is a painful state that I would not wish on you or anyone, Miss Otrera."

I was surprised by his vehement tone.

"But this is not about feelings," he continued more softly. "This is about training your mind. If you can't master your mind, you will never master your gift."

"Fine," I said. "I'll try again."

I took a shuddering breath and sat down.

"When you find the place of stillness," he reminded me, "it will feel like time has ceased to exist. First let the thoughts come. But always go back to the word I gave you. It will help you find the core of your mind."

Thoughts did come, fast and furious. Memories, images, worries. It seemed that as I willed my mind to calm, it became a raging torrent of jabbering nonsense, intent on irritating me into a state of fury. Finally, exhausted by the effort of pushing back, I let them wash over me. When there was a space, I came back to the word.

After a long while, there was a shift. I stopped being aware of anything.

I just was.

As I floated in that still space, something crowded the edge of my consciousness, no more than a breath of sensation. It was an awareness of cold. I poked at it with my mind, and it seemed to chuckle at my efforts.

No, it wasn't the cold that was chuckling.

It was—

I struggled to pull my mind out of the depths. It was like swimming in goose down. When I managed to open my eyes, I pivoted to look behind me toward the abbey, toward that awareness of cold. Arcus sat cross-legged on the ground a short distance away.

His eyes were closed, but a smirk tilted one edge of his mouth.

The world tilted. I slammed a palm against the ground to steady myself.

Brother Thistle spoke. "Arcus, is it too much to ask that you remain quiet?"

"I'm sorry," said Arcus, not sounding the least bit sorry. "But she was shivering so hard, I could feel it from here."

"I've been sitting on this frozen tundra half the morning," I bit out, pressing the heels of my hands against my eyes to clear my blurry vision.

"I thought Firebloods made their own heat."

"I was concentrating on other things, and that makes it harder. And I was distracted by—" I gasped. "I felt it. I felt your cold!"

Brother Thistle smiled. "You sense the cold on a physical

level, but the sensation is so slight, you would not be aware of it if not for the mental practice. Let me emphasize the word *practice*. It takes years to master this method. But even in its simplest form, a focused mind is a powerful tool. It will help you."

Help me kill the king, I finished in my head. Mastering these skills could mean the difference between success and failure.

"Why didn't I sense your cold?" I asked.

"I was repressing my frost," Brother Thistle said.

I turned to Arcus. "Were you deliberately making your cold stronger so I could sense it?"

He shrugged. "A little."

"Well, don't. Move somewhere else, and I'll see if I can sense you. And you, Brother Thistle, perhaps you can do the same. I'd like to see if I can sense you, too."

He shook his head, pushing up with his walking stick and stretching. "I must take my old bones inside for midday prayers. Arcus, will you continue the lesson? Miss Otrera, I expect all your attention when we train. Every morning, here, after prayers. Show me dedication and I will show you things you never dreamed you could do."

"And you'll tell me what you're training me for," I added.

He nodded, then walked toward the abbey. I hopped up and shook the cobwebs from my limbs, stretching tense muscles and wincing at the pins and needles in my feet.

"What do you think you're doing?" asked Arcus.

"Who says we have to sit on the freezing ground?"

He nodded. "You stand and I'll move."

"It'll ruin it if I can hear you clumping around in those boots."

His jaw tightened. "I know how to move quietly."

I closed my eyes and returned to the word. Thoughts came thick and fast. I took a deep breath and let them flow over me. As before, it took a few minutes until my mind began to quiet. This time, though, I stayed half in, half out of the still place. A part of me was searching. Searching for cold.

Nothing.

No, wait. There, on the edge, right *there*.

Slowly, poised in the middle of the endless universe, I raised my arm and pointed. I heard a harrumph.

"Very good," Arcus said, his voice closer than I'd expected. "But let's see how you do when I move farther away."

I nodded and breathed deep, centering myself.

Floating awareness. Searching.

Nothing, nothing, nothing.

A pulse of cold to my left. I raised my arm and pointed.

"Good. Let's try farther still."

I breathed, the thoughts fewer now. The world was empty. In that state, I was alone but not lonely. For a moment, I was whole. But a part of me searched for something outside myself. My heat longed for cold. Where was it? Where?

I raised my arms, palms out. Searching.

On the tip of one finger, then on my palm. A cool whisper. I moved my palm to the right, then left, then right until I sensed where it was strongest. Straight in front of me.

I pointed and earned a graveled laugh. "You're not half bad at this, Lady Firebrand. I was never very good at this game. Brother Thistle is teaching you well."

My eyes opened, but I couldn't reconcile the vision of my surroundings with the endless space inside my mind. The earth leaned to the right and I stumbled. I was caught by firm hands.

"Steady," Arcus said, setting me back on my feet. "You shouldn't come out of that state so quickly. Sit for a moment, go back into that place, and take your time floating up again. You could do yourself harm if you try to snap into awareness too fast."

I did as he said, letting my mind adjust slowly to the outside world. In a few minutes, I took one last deep breath and opened my eyes. Arcus sat facing me, an arm's length away.

"*Hmph*," he said in a thoughtful tone. "It's remarkable that you can do that with so little training."

My chest glowed a little. Maybe there was hope for me yet.

As we walked toward the abbey, Arcus put his hand under my elbow to steady me. I stiffened but didn't shrug it away.

"Your mind is progressing well," he said, "but it's your body that concerns me. You're still weak." He stopped and pushed my sleeve up to my elbow. As our skin touched, we both sucked in a breath at the discomfort of it. "You'll never hold a sword with those arms. Where are your muscles?"

"Yes, the prison was full of opportunities to build my strength." I jerked my arm away and shoved the sleeve back down.

"Well, you have them now. Starting tomorrow, I want you working yourself as hard as you can. The tower steps are steep. Up and down twice a day. Brother Peele in the kitchen has heavy pots to wash and bags of flour to move. Help him. Sister Clove in the stables can give you plenty of work, too."

It was all so sensible I had no cause to argue. But still, it annoyed me to be ordered around.

"And what will you do while I work myself ragged?"

"I'll be training, as I do every day."

"And what are you training for, exactly?"

He hesitated, then let out a breath. "To help you. It's my job to lead you through an entrance into the castle and, if we're both very lucky, to get you safely out again."

I realized my mouth had fallen open as he chuckled.

"What did you think, we would send you in by yourself through the front door? You wouldn't make it to the foot of the mountain without my help."

"What's the plan? Tell me everything."

"So impatient to ride to your death, Fireblood? You would make a good soldier." He quickly changed tack. "You favor your left shoulder. I had thought to teach you swordplay today, but I noticed you kept your left arm to your side and winced whenever you raised it."

I grimaced. Those cold blue eyes took in much more than I had expected.

"An old injury," I said, gently rotating my shoulder.

"From prison?" he asked softly.

I shook my head. "From when I was seven and fell out of a tree. I was trying to catch a squirrel. I wanted a pet."

He made a noise that sounded suspiciously like laughter. "And it still bothers you?"

"Only when I'm forced to spend hours with my backside planted on the freezing ground."

He smiled, drawing my eye. My heart fluttered at the way his eyes crinkled, the flash of his bright teeth. The scar that cleft his lip seemed to add to the attraction of that smile. Unsettled, I forced my eyes away and focused on the drab stones of the abbey.

"Why do you hide your face?" I asked.

A dark suspicion had crept into my mind. Arcus wore a hood and he was clearly scarred. He and Brother Thistle had said they were drawn to me because of what happened in my village. What if Arcus was one of the soldiers I had burned?

As soon as I asked the question, the temperature dropped. Frost spread underfoot, making dead leaves crackle.

"I don't recall giving you permission to ask me questions," he replied.

"I don't recall needing permission. What are you hiding?"

"I'm hiding nothing. I only cover what people don't wish to see."

I crossed my arms. He regarded me with a steady, unwavering stare. Perhaps I was wrong and he had simply lumped me in with all the small-minded fools who would ridicule someone for their appearance. I would never judge someone for their scars.

"At least I get to see your eyes today," I said.

"And why should you wish to see my eyes?"

"I don't know. Perhaps because I know so little about you and you know so much about me. Or, perhaps, to make sure you are a person and not a block of ice."

His expression turned guarded. I knew I was staring, but the blue of his irises was a mosaic of tones, not just one single color. I found myself straining forward in some unconscious, infinitesimal way, as if all those enchanting blues were calling to my blood, cooling it and heating it at the same time, leaving me in a state of restless confusion.

Something flickered in his eyes, which turned into a snowy sky, suddenly blank and cold. "I *am* a block of ice."

The words met my skin like a bucket of water drawn from a mountain stream. Dead leaves crunched under his boots as he turned and strode off, taking all the blues with him.

TEN

THE MIDAFTERNOON SUN DANCED
through the remaining library window, laying rectangles of
blushing gold on the stone walls.

"Sister Pastel, may I come in?" I asked from the doorway. In
the week since returning from my aborted escape, I'd seen Sister
Pastel, reportedly the finest illuminator in the abbey, hunched
over her work for hours at a time. I was fascinated by her work,
the precise, flowing letters and vibrant pictures.

She put her brush back into the cup and turned to me. "You
may enter, Miss Otrera."

I stepped forward, careful to keep my sleeves from catching
any of the delicate rolls of parchment lying on the tables.

"I had wondered..." My voice trailed off as my eyes caught

on a blackened table leg, reminding me of my show of temper during my previous visit. Surely the calm and careful illuminator wouldn't trust a Fireblood near all her precious books.

"I'm glad you came," she said, surprising me. Her mouth curved into something I took to be a smile on a face unused to the expression. "I have not thanked you for saving my life."

"No need," I said quickly. "Fire doesn't hurt me—at least not easily. I'm sure Arcus would have found a way if I hadn't."

"It was still a risk and shows character that you bothered. We were not friends."

"We weren't enemies. At least, not as far as I was concerned."

Her eyes fell to her hands, folded neatly in her lap. "I confess I saw you as one. The first day, when Brother Lack and I brought in your bath, I suspected you were a Fireblood. I was furious that Brother Thistle had allowed you to come here. I felt he was endangering us with your presence."

She paused, and I waited before prompting, "And now?"

"I see that you are trying to learn to master your gift with Brother Thistle's help. I ask your forgiveness for judging you wrongly."

I shifted uncomfortably. "There's nothing to forgive. I've been treated well here."

Her mouth curved again, and this time it was clearly a small smile. "Now, what brings you to my domain of smelly pigments and cramped fingers?"

"I was hoping you might show me your techniques. I don't want to interrupt your work, of course. But I would dearly love to learn how to do what you do, or at least whatever poor excuse I'm able to achieve. Your work is beautiful."

"Thank you. Sit at this table next to me and I will happily show you."

My cheeks heated with a joyful flush.

"But, ah," she added slowly, "perhaps take care not to let any frustration turn to heat. We would not wish another fire to start, especially not here."

My joy faded. "I didn't start that fire, Sister Pastel."

She paused, studying me closely. "I'm glad to hear that. Though it disturbs me to think one of my own order did, and that they didn't come forward to confess when you were accused."

I shook my head. "It could have been a fire improperly extinguished. We may never know what happened. But let me assure you, you can trust me. If I get frustrated, I'll find Arcus and ask for some extra training. He's always a good outlet for my wrath."

Sister Pastel chuckled and handed me a brush.

Over the next week, life at the abbey became a blur of routine. Even though I'd recovered, I continued to sleep in the infirmary. I was comfortable there, and Brother Gamut had confessed that not many rooms in the abbey were fit for occupation. In the mornings, I woke at the matins bell and dressed in my tunic and leggings. Then it was up and down the tower stairs twice before meeting Brother Thistle on the training ground.

I improved in uneven spurts, finally learning to burn the

detested shrub I had missed during my first lesson, and then any target that Brother Thistle pointed out, though my aim was, in his words, "rather unpredictable at times." He had me exert finer levels of control by starting the fire in the warming room every evening, drying wet robes hung out on wash day, even lighting a candle from a distance, which took hours and hours of practice. I was able to complete my tasks with increasing reliability. Still, the larger uses of flame often eluded me, much to my frustration.

After my lessons, I usually headed for the stables to help Sister Clove, who was in charge of the livestock. She had roughly hewn features and large hands that were gentle with the animals. I helped her muck the stalls, groom horses, and carry heavy sacks of seed or grain for the chickens and pigs and goats.

When I finished in the stables, I would head for the kitchen—housed in a separate building because of the risk of fire—and offer help to the cook, Brother Peele. He usually had me wash pots and carry buckets of water from the well. Occasionally, he asked me to gather herbs to season his pottage, which I had just done.

Strolling through the cloister on my way to the kitchen, I breathed the scents of crushed weeds and kitchen smoke. I gave the icy statue of Fors a saucy wink and clutched my robe tighter. After a few days of mild weather, a north wind had whipped up with a vengeance, forcing its way through my clothes and pulling at my joints.

As I passed through the reverent hush of the church, I noticed that some of the pews had been removed, no doubt burned in the fire, and the scent of ashes still hung in the air. My steps grew light, the soaring arched ceiling and large stained glass rendering of Tempus filling me with awe. On impulse, I walked down the central aisle and settled on one of the kneelers under the window. I gazed up at Tempus and he stared back, neither of us sure of the other. Maybe it would have been easier if it was Sud or Cirrus. But Tempus was almost as forbidding as Fors and more powerful, being the father of the four winds.

I pressed my hands together and prayed to Cirrus, watcher of the dead, to keep my mother safe in the afterworld in the sky. When I thought of my mother, my chest grew painfully tight. With chapped knuckles, I tried to rub away the pain at the back of my eyes before continuing to the kitchen.

"Sorry I'm late," I said to Brother Peele as I hung my cloak on a peg on the kitchen wall. "I was..." It seemed silly to tell him I had been praying. He prayed five times a day at set times, along with all the other monks. Fortunately, Brother Peele was too busy chopping potatoes to notice my half-finished sentence. The first time I had come to the kitchen to offer help, he had barely spoken, watching me as if I were a fox angling to steal his chickens. But he gradually became accustomed to me, and I'd found him to be quite loquacious.

"Rabbit's in the pot already," he said, motioning with his knife. He had an accent, having come from the northern hill tribes, and I liked the way he rolled his *R*s.

"I'll take care of the turnips," I said, pulling out a small cloth bag and placing it on a table. "I brought you some wild parsley I found by the stream yesterday."

"Excellent. We'll put it to good use. But take care you don't use so much salt this time. It's mined in Safra and nearly impossible to get these days, with trade closed off. You can't just go throwing handfuls into every stew. And keep your sticky fingers *out* of my bread. You're worse than a badger in a root cellar."

We were still peeling, chopping, and trading quips when the door burst open.

"Where the blazes have you been?" demanded Arcus.

"I was pestering Brother Peele for another biscuit," I said. "Unfortunately, I've found him to be rather stingy."

I received a playful whack from a grinning Brother Peele and a glare from Arcus.

"You were supposed to meet me for sword training an hour ago."

I gaped. "That's tomorrow."

"Today."

"But—" I cast an apologetic look at Brother Peele.

Arcus was completely unmoved. "You have ten minutes. Don't make me wait."

My hands shook as I drew my red tunic over my head and slid on my boots, my stomach twisting with nerves.

I had never held a sword, not even one of the wooden practice swords used by the boys in my village. Mother had said that weapons and hot tempers make a dangerous pair.

My fire was a weapon, but part of me. It could hurt, but it could also cook food, create life-giving heat, and boil water. The purpose of a sword was to maim or kill. Considering my plan was to kill the king, it was strange how the thought weighed on me.

Thick gray clouds seemed to hover over the spot Arcus had designated for our lesson. Instead of the usual training ground, he had chosen an area between the budding fruit trees and the river, where a fishpond sat dull and still under a patchwork of lily pads.

He wore his training gear, the blue tunic and black mask that covered his cheeks and nose but not his eyes, the color of frozen pools reflecting the sky.

He held out a sword. My hands chilled as they wrapped around the cold steel hilt. It was surprisingly heavy. Even after two weeks of training my strength, the weapon dangled from my arm like a broken branch.

"Why do I have a real sword and you don't?" I nodded to the wooden practice sword gripped in his hand. "Aren't you afraid I'll hurt you?"

"Your sword is blunted. And I wanted you to feel the weight of the real thing. Now, raise it like this."

I bunched my muscles and lifted the weapon.

"Higher!" he ordered. My arm trembled, but I raised it so the tip was level with my nose.

"Now, stand like this."

I mimicked his stance, feet apart, knees bent.

"You're off-balance," he accused. "I could take you down with one kick."

He came over to me, snapping out instructions as he put a hand to my back, my shoulder, the back of my knee, until he was satisfied. Although his hands were cold, they weren't bitingly so. It seemed the longer I stayed in the abbey, the more I grew used to the proximity of Frostbloods.

"Now, come at me."

I moved toward him, my sword held out. With one swipe, he dashed the weapon from my hand. It met the grass with a thud, sending up a spray of morning dew. Arcus still held his sword in the ready position.

"Is this the part where I beg for mercy?" I asked.

I was using light words to hide the fact that I was out of my element. Arcus seemed to think I wasn't serious about the lesson. His face darkened.

"You think the king's soldiers will care if you beg?"

Heat flared up my neck and into my cheeks. I picked up the sword, gripped the hilt, and went at him in earnest. He parried my stroke and disarmed me. I tried again, and my sword went flying.

After a third time, I picked up the sword and threw it as far as I could. It landed with a splash in the fishpond.

"You retrieve your weapon. Right. Now." The words were delivered from between clenched teeth as if he would rather have tossed me into the pond after it. Or perhaps just my severed head.

"You're supposed to be teaching me!" I shouted. "I already know that I'm useless with a sword. What are you trying to prove?"

Arcus looked away. "Brother Thistle is too easy on you. He wants to go slowly. He doesn't want to push. Meanwhile, war still rages in the Aris Plains. The land withers. Families starve. If this goes on, there will be no kingdom to save."

"And that's my fault?" I demanded. "For not being ready?"

He hesitated. "No, it's mine. For not teaching you fast enough."

"You think I'll learn faster when I'm out of my head with fury?"

"I'm trying to show you that losing focus in battle could mean losing your life. And you lose focus all too easily, Fireblood."

His words sank in slowly, like drops of rain. This lesson was a test of my temper. I had to show him I could keep it.

I slogged to the pond and searched until I saw metal shining under the surface of the shallow edge. As I touched the hilt, something brushed my hand. I jumped back, and the sword slipped from my fingers.

"What now?" Arcus asked tightly.

I shuddered. "Something cold and slimy."

"You're afraid of fish?" he asked in disbelief.

"I'm not afraid. I just...hate them. So cold." I looked at him meaningfully. "It's like touching a Frostblood."

"Indeed," he murmured. "Now, stop being ridiculous and get your sword."

I reached in again and grasped the hilt, gritting my teeth

in case I felt another slimy caress. Knees wet, I returned to our training area.

He demonstrated the various attacks and how to block them. He showed me how to protect my stomach, my flank, my thigh, my shoulder, my head. Some positions twisted my wrist at an awkward angle. My head spun trying to remember it all. If I parried too high or too low, he corrected me, making me repeat the moves until my arm ached.

As I was unlikely to overcome an enemy with power and size, he focused on teaching me to be light on my feet, using quick evasive moves to get out of the way, and how to block when I couldn't.

For a while, we went through the motions slowly; then the blows came faster. I panted as I tried to match his pace.

"Keep your sword up," he said.

"I'm trying, but we've been at this for hours. I'm tired."

"Watch your surroundings," he warned.

"Then slow down."

"This *is* slow."

I leaped backward, looking for a break from his constant advance. The earth was spongy under my feet. I stumbled.

"You're giving up solid ground," he shouted. "Watch your—"

My foot hit mud. Arcus threw down his practice sword and reached toward me, but my own sword slashed the air in front of me as I flailed. I fell backward into the pond. The water wasn't deep, but it was shockingly cold.

Arcus stood at the edge, shaking his head.

"You meant to do that," I gasped, breathless with cold.

"I didn't, but it's a good lesson." A smile tugged at his lips. "You look like a cat in a rain barrel."

I scrambled toward the bank, grabbing pond plants and water lilies to pull myself forward. My foot slipped and I dipped under and bobbed back up.

When I could see again, Arcus was shaking. It took a second to realize he was gripped by a fit of laughter.

"Shut up or I'll—" I slipped again, and my mouth filled with water.

"You'll what?" Arcus gasped. "Attack me with a fish?"

Recovering himself, but still smiling, he offered his hand. I grabbed it and yanked him toward the pond. He shot out his free hand and froze a section of the water around me, just in time to slide nimbly across its surface. He used my arm as a pivot point and swung back to the grassy bank. It was a controlled move and he'd been careful not to hurt my arm. A part of me admired the way he used his gift to alter his environment. The rest of me just seethed.

He offered his hand again, but I slapped it away.

"Always remain aware of your surroundings," he said, his voice low and serious, his grin fading. "Especially in battle. If you're quick-witted, you can use them to your own advantage. It may save your life."

"Let's see how quick-witted you are," I muttered.

I grabbed a handful of pond plants and mud and hurled it at

him. It caught him square in the chest, a long, slimy root wrapping itself around his neck.

"Maybe you should take your own advice," I countered. "That could have been my sword."

He brushed off the slimy green tendrils, the grin returning. If I hadn't been so angry, I might have enjoyed the way his eyes sparkled at me.

"Point taken, Lady Firebrand. Now, as you don't want my help, I'll let you get yourself out. We'll have our next lesson soon. Don't forget your sword."

ELEVEN

As Sister Clove's trust in me grew, she sometimes let me ride Butter all over the abbey grounds. Together, the mare and I explored the gardens, orchards, fields, paddocks, and the fragrant copses of trees used for firewood. On the northern edge of the land near the river, I found myself singing a song my mother had taught me, about enjoying the summer while it lasted, because winter would surely come and cover the world with snow once again.

Heading east, we rounded a cluster of apple trees and would have passed the orchard when I noticed a solitary figure leaning against a trunk. Although he was dressed in monk's robes, I knew from his broad shoulders and height that it was Arcus. I stopped singing and turned Butter away. I still hadn't forgiven him for my fall in the pond and had found excuses not to repeat our lesson, which was made easier by the fact that Arcus had left for a couple of days and only just returned. Apparently, he often left the abbey for a day or two at a time, though no one seemed to know where he went. If they did, they certainly weren't telling me.

"Ruby," he called. "Wait a moment."

I pulled to an abrupt halt. He had never used my name before. I waited as he came close, his hand lifting to pat Butter. He smiled at her soft nicker.

"That was a pretty song you were singing," he said. "Where did you learn it?"

I paused. "My mother taught it to me."

He nodded. "I liked hearing it today. I was...rather melancholy."

I felt my brows rise and struggled to smooth my expression. Brother Gamut had asserted that Frostbloods are fully capable of feeling deeply, but I wasn't used to thinking of Arcus as having feelings at all. Still, his confession at feeling melancholy was strangely disarming.

"Want to talk about it?" I asked, surprising myself. "My mother always said that sharing a problem halves the burden. Not that it ever took much prodding for me to share what I felt."

His mouth pulled up on one side. "That doesn't surprise me. No one is left in any doubt about how you feel."

I waited for him to continue. When he said nothing more, I shrugged and lifted the reins to ride away.

"Brother Thistle tells me you're making progress in your lessons," Arcus said quickly, almost as if he didn't want me to leave.

I made a dismissive sound. "Brother Thistle is very kind. And patient." Once the words were out, I regretted them. I shouldn't admit that my progress was slow. I wasn't sure what Arcus would do if he decided I wasn't worth his time. "I've mastered the smaller flames, though. I can pass fire from one hand to another without losing control of it. And my aim is improving."

He nodded, stroking his hand over Butter's neck. His hand was large and well shaped, with a sprinkling of dark hair and long, blunt-edged fingers. My attention was arrested to see how gentle he was with the animal.

He looked up at me. "You haven't had your second lesson in swordplay."

"One was enough, thank you."

His chin came up and I felt, rather than saw, the look he leveled at me from the shadows of his hood. "You don't get to decide that."

"So much for the freedom you promised."

"That's if you complete your task."

"If I survive it, you mean. And if I don't drown in a fishpond first."

He took a breath, his nostrils flaring slightly, and exhaled. I derived a twisted satisfaction from testing his temper. It was good to know he had one. It meant he felt something, at least some of the time.

"As for that," he said, clearing his throat, "I wasn't the best teacher."

I opened my mouth, then closed it, some of my resentment

fading. "No, you weren't." I let that hang in the air. "But perhaps I wasn't the most willing of pupils, either."

"I shouldn't have laughed at you," he said.

I remembered the way I kept slipping and bobbing back up. "I suppose I must have looked a sight." I stared at him, wishing I could see more of his expression. I thought the corner of his mouth twitched up a little, but he managed to control it.

"I know you're not keen to try again," he said seriously. "But it's important to know the basic maneuvers with a weapon. I ask that you trust me. This time I promise I won't laugh if you make a mistake."

I ask... I promise... Such phrases as I never expected to hear from the self-proclaimed block of ice.

I tilted my head. "Did Brother Thistle train you in the most effective methods of communicating with me?"

His head lifted and his lips curved. "He may have given me some advice."

"And you took it?" My brows rose.

"I'm experimenting with it. If it doesn't work, I'll go back to my tried and true method."

"By which you mean threats and orders."

His smile widened.

I pretended to look thoughtful. "Then by all means, I must make sure you find this new method rewarding. When do we resume lessons?"

"Tomorrow morning, after you're finished with Brother Thistle. Same place as before. If it pleases you."

"I'll wear ribbons in my hair if it'll keep your tongue so civil."

He grinned up at me for a moment before turning away. As he strode off, he hummed the song I'd been singing.

I blinked after him, feeling a strange fluttering in my stomach. Butter and I shook ourselves and continued our ride.

A sort of truce formed between Arcus and me.

Every day or two, he would give me another lesson in swordplay. I would do my best not to back into a bog or puddle, while he did his best not to yell at me or laugh when I tripped or lost my sword. I had little affinity for the lessons, though. The cold steel just felt so unnatural in my hand.

I said as much while Arcus and I walked back toward the abbey after a lesson.

"Don't think of it as a cold piece of steel," he said, touching my elbow and turning to face me. "Remember, it started out as liquid fire."

"Liquid fire?" I asked, meeting his eyes.

"Have you ever been in a forge?"

I nodded. "I visited the blacksmith's shop in my village sometimes to watch him make horseshoes or nails."

"I've been working on a new sword. Come by the smithy tomorrow morning after you finish with Brother Thistle and you can see what I mean. Perhaps if you can envision the steel in its nascent state, it won't feel so repugnant."

"Does that apply to Frostbloods?" I asked with feigned

innocence. "If I'd seen you in your nascent state, would you be less repugnant to me?"

A wicked gleam lit his eyes. "What nascent state do you mean, exactly?"

Realizing the other possible meaning of my words, I spun away. "Not that, you conceited icicle. I meant, if I'd known you as a child. Which, though impossible, is more likely than the scenario you're suggesting."

"Thank Fors. I'd hate to bare my . . . soul to you and be judged harshly."

Unwilling to let him get the better of me, I turned on my heel to face him and stepped in his path. He put his hands out reflexively, catching my upper arms. I let my eyes flick over him. "It might be worth the experience if I could take a chip or two out of that towering pride." I smiled the way I'd seen shopkeepers' daughters do with village boys.

He was silent, an unusual state for him. It was exhilarating, putting him off-balance, to the point where I felt a pang of danger. This was a game to which I could become quite addicted if I wasn't careful.

I turned away before he could see the flush that crept up my neck. "See you tomorrow, then."

"Just don't wear your cloak in the forge," he called after me. "With all the stray sparks, you're liable to catch fire."

But it wasn't the forge's effect on me that was worrisome.

The smithy, a long building to the southwest of the abbey, was dominated by a stone hearth filled with glowing coals and a large bellows in front. A variety of metal instruments hung from hooks on the walls. To the left of the hearth, a broad male back, uncovered but for a sheen of sweat, was bent slightly. He lowered a hammer with ringing force onto a piece of heated metal held with tongs on an anvil.

Luckily, the flush that swept over my skin was easily dismissed as a result of the heat of the room.

"I didn't think you were serious yesterday," I said between hammer blows, "about baring yourself to me."

Arcus stopped and turned, and I saw that a leather apron covered his chest. "It has nothing to do with you. It's hotter than the inside of Sud's volcanoes in here."

It was clear from his tone that his mood was a lot less playful than the day before, possibly because he was in a room that must feel excessively hot to him.

I moved closer, touching implements on a worktable along the way. "I thought you hated heat and flame."

"Necessary evils. I don't spend more time here than I must. Put on those gloves." He nodded to leather gloves that sat on a table along the wall. I noticed he also wore a pair.

"I don't need them."

"Put them on."

I did and joined him in front of the anvil.

"Take the tongs and put the blade in the fire," he instructed.

I took the tongs and held the long, crudely sword-shaped bit of metal above the coals. He put down the hammer and worked the bellows, making the flames leap higher.

"Ironwork is a dance of air and flame," he said. "To get the right level of heat, you need the right balance. Too little and you can't work the metal. Too much and you melt it. There, see that? That's the color we need. Put it on the anvil. Carefully."

I rolled my eyes at his imperious tone and did as he said. "I thought you wanted to show me liquid steel."

"You'll have to imagine that part. A few days ago, Sister Clove helped me heat the metal until it was pure liquid, then poured the liquid into a form and cooled it before starting to shape it. I've already refined the tip, but I need to add the bevel. Hold it steady."

He hammered the glowing orange metal, starting at the tip and working along the edge. "See how it glows? Think of it this way. Fire is at its heart, even when it has cooled and hardened. Without heat, there would be no transformation, just an unformed piece of metal."

I shifted position to give my arm relief. "So you admit fire is necessary."

Hammer, hammer, hammer. "I've already said as much."

"A necessary evil, I believe you called me. Hardly flattering."

He glanced up. "Do you need flattery?"

"I'd like you to admit the value of heat. And of Firebloods."

The hammer stilled. He met my eyes. "I do. Some of the best

weapons are forged in the Fire Islands. There is nothing here that compares to the beauty of a Fireblood sword."

My stomach made a peculiar dip. I couldn't find any words, so I nodded.

"It's cooled too much. Back into the coals," he said, and we repeated the process of fire, bellows, waiting for the right color, and back onto the anvil so he could work the metal.

"I should practice heating the metal myself," I said speculatively.

"No," Arcus replied, glaring. "Not until you have much more control. I'd hate to think what you could do in a room with this much fuel."

"Your confidence in me is inspiring," I said, rolling my eyes.

"Speaking of your unshakable confidence," he said, eyes narrowed as he inspected the sword's bevel, "had you any idea what your powers could do before Brother Thistle began teaching you? As you didn't grow up with other Firebloods, it's curious to me how much you actually know about your fire and your people."

"Most of what I know is from my grandmother. She was well traveled, knew history, and brought me books, some of them written by Fireblood scholars. You won't find those in Frostblood libraries."

"On the contrary, there are some here in the abbey. But by and large you're right. And I suppose you've answered my next question: how you learned to read."

"Yes, my mother and grandmother. But Grandmother was

the one who really challenged me to learn new words, memorize famous passages of prose and verse, expand my thinking."

He lowered the hammer and gazed at me long enough that I shifted uncomfortably. "Stop staring at me like that," I complained.

"Like what?" he asked, nodding to the hearth. "More heat."

I held the blade above the coals again. A stray spark landed on his arm. It hissed into oblivion instantly, but Arcus jumped back a foot. He sucked in a shaky breath and took the tongs from me, returning the sword to the anvil as if nothing had happened.

"You can go now," he said coolly.

"Oh, can I? Why, thank you, my lord," I said sarcastically. "And for the record, I already know how you feel about fire, so you don't have to be mad that I've witnessed one of your weaknesses. We all have them, you know."

He turned to look at me, his face completely expressionless. I tensed, waiting for a scathing response, but he mumbled something and looked away.

I left the smithy and headed toward the kitchen to help Brother Peele with dinner preparations, still puzzling over his parting remark. I must have misheard him. It almost sounded like he'd said, *I fear you are becoming one of mine.*

As Brother Thistle trained my mind, I became better at sensing the location of my Frostblood opponents. Arcus sometimes tested that ability by making me wear a blindfold. He was whisper-quiet as he advanced and moved around me, but I always knew where he was, my sword coming up to touch his. The problem was, I couldn't tell which position his sword was in, so I didn't know how to block. During one lesson, he finally let me use my fire to defend myself, confident, as always, in his ability to fight off every attack with his frost.

After our lesson, if the weather was good, we would find a spot under one of the fruit trees and unpack a snack of fresh bread, cheese, and crispy apples, compliments of Brother Peele. In between bites, I would ask Arcus questions that he somehow managed not to answer. His childhood remained a mystery, aside from his brief retellings of his nursemaid's stories, some of them surprisingly similar to Grandmother's. He was also willing to share combat techniques in great detail, but if I asked who had taught him or if he'd ever used the moves, and against whom, he would suddenly remember he had promised to help Sister Clove muck the stables or that Brother Thistle had requested his young eyes to decipher a bit of cramped script in some ancient book in the library. There was no surer way to rid myself of Arcus's company than by asking him personal questions.

I felt like something had changed between us, but I never knew if it was me alone who felt the difference. Once we'd exhausted discussions over my lessons, we strayed onto other topics. I started to reveal myself more, to tell him things I hadn't thought I would ever share, especially not with a Frostblood. Stories from my childhood, how I'd felt when I learned my grandmother had died, my guilt that she'd died alone on her travels, my secret envy of my mother's even temperament, my deep longing to fit in somewhere.

He never offered sympathy, which I would have rejected anyway, but he did listen attentively and ask questions, drawing things out of me that sometimes surprised me. Then I told him about the day the soldiers came, and my voice broke and I forgot whom I was telling, so lost in the fear and horror of that day. When I wiped my eyes and looked up, he was staring at me with such a profound look of rage that I jerked back in shock.

"Now I know why you hate us so much."

I blinked in confusion. "I don't hate you."

"Well, perhaps you should."

My mind raced with possible responses, but none of them seemed right, either revealing too much of how I felt or seeming insufficient in the wake of his strong emotion.

"I feel safe here," I finally said.

He swallowed and stood abruptly. "You've come as far as you can with a sword. Focus on your lessons with Brother Thistle from now on."

I watched, confused and hurt, as he strode toward the stables. I had worked hard on our sword lessons and had thought I was improving. It appeared he disagreed.

While I packed up the food to take back to Brother Peele, I saw Arcus on his horse, Alabaster, speeding toward the woods at a ferocious gallop.

One warm spring day almost two months since I'd come to the abbey, I dressed in my leggings and tunic and headed to the rocky training ground to meet Brother Thistle. Thin, curled blades of grass poked out of the dirt, and bud-laden branches rustled in a southwest wind. The air smelled of clean earth and yeast that wafted over the yard from the brewery.

"This maneuver is called the tail of the dragon," said Brother Thistle.

He demonstrated by putting his left foot forward as he leaned on his walking stick, then snapping his free hand forward and back as if he held an invisible whip. Frost swirled in a tight funnel that narrowed at the end and cracked against the ground, leaving it white.

"I saw the Fireblood masters use it to great effect in the Battle of Aris Plains," he said.

I put my foot forward and flicked my wrist. A spark leaped from my hand and landed on the ground with a fizzle. I cursed and tried again. This time, a thin blade of fire jumped out and squirmed on the earth before dying.

"You created fire arrows with ease just yesterday," he said with a hint of disappointment.

"I know. It's just...some days are better than others." I didn't know why my powers were so inconsistent. One day, my focus was sharp, my mind clear, and my gift obeyed my every command. Other days, I felt scattered, and it didn't seem to matter how hard I worked. There seemed to be something weighing me down, as if a wet rag were wrapped around my heart.

"I sense you have so much power, Ruby," he said, his voice full of hope and frustration. "What is stopping you?"

An image of my mother came to me. I thought of her often, remembering her calm and practical way of looking at the world, the way she was slow to anger and quick to forgive. I could picture her deft hands, which had been so clever at mixing new batches of tincture or salve. Sometimes an image of her face would flash into my mind, and I would find the spark in me dying.

"I suppose...it's the way I was raised. My mother hated violence of any kind. She would detest me plotting to kill someone with my gift."

"Is that why you struggle? Because your mother would not approve?"

"It's not only that."

I had always had this feeling that something was churning underneath my skin. Deep inside was a pot of boiling water, a forge fanned by endless bellows, a volcano waiting to erupt. And I had spent my whole life fighting these sensations. Now Brother Thistle wanted me to let them free.

"I was taught to hide my gift," I explained. "Never to use it. When I lost my temper, it was harder to control. My mother called it a gift but..." I shrugged, looking at the ground. "I know she thought of it as a threat as well. And it was. Once I was so mad I almost burned down our hut." I looked up at the monk a little sheepishly. "Firebloods like me are not meant to live in buildings made of wood and thatch."

A low chuckle came from behind us. I swung around. Arcus had approached at some point, quiet as a shadow.

"So if your temper brings out your fire," Arcus said, striding forward, "perhaps we can make you angry."

"Oh?" I asked, my pulse jumping with uncertainty, as it did every time I saw him since that day we'd last talked under the fruit trees. "And how will you do that?"

"Well, I recall you don't like being dumped in rivers or ponds. We could start there."

I crossed my arms. "It also weakens my power."

He looked thoughtful. "Then perhaps a milder version of the same." He lifted his hand high and waved it in a circle. The water in the air turned into tiny frozen droplets that fell on me, just as they had when he'd come to my cell. They melted as they hit my face, steaming slightly.

I gritted my teeth.

Next he sent a breath of frost into my face, freezing my eyelashes. My heart sped up, my breath quickening. I rubbed the melting crystals from my lashes and glared.

"Enough," I growled, the heat rising too quickly.

He flicked out a hand at my feet, and I was suddenly standing on the smoothest of ice. My soft-soled boots had no grip. I slipped and went down on one knee.

"I said enough!" I yelled, sending a blast of hot air at the ice, melting it. "Next time that'll be at you!"

"You may not find me so easy to burn," Arcus replied, his eyes grimly assessing.

"I would like to try," I said between clenched teeth, heat rolling off me in waves.

He nodded. "Burn me, then, my raging inferno."

I started with a simple blast of hot air, something that might singe his robes. He barely lifted a finger, and the air came back at me, followed by a chill wind.

I pushed out a hand, concentrating on the heat around my heart. A flame shot out from my palm and was quickly swallowed by a ball of frost.

I thrust both arms at him and summoned a wall of fire, larger than I'd ever been able to create before. A sheet of ice came up to meet it. I sent another gust of heat toward the ice, melting it. He snapped a blast of cold back at me, making me stumble.

Brother Thistle had restrained himself, I realized, allowing me gains and successes whenever we sparred. Arcus was giving me no quarter.

I steadied myself, changed my position, and threw a series of arrows of heat from various angles. With dizzying speed, he dodged or repelled all of them. They fizzled and hissed as they hit the cool ground.

We circled each other.

"Your task is weeks away, and this is the best you can do?" he taunted.

I breathed deeply as his barb struck home. It was exactly what

I feared, that I wasn't ready. With the hurt came a surge of anger. My blood heated and this time I didn't try to stop it.

Brother Thistle, who had been watching quietly, stepped forward. "Is this a good idea?"

"She won't hurt me," said Arcus. "She isn't capable of hurting me or anyone else. Including the king."

"Be careful," I warned, my voice low.

He sent a spiral of frost at my neck. I batted it away.

In an echo of my earlier move with fire arrows, he sent wicked shards of ice winging toward me. I parried, kicked, and melted them before they could connect.

"Better," he said. "Stop holding back."

We traded blows that increased in pace and intensity. As he parried all my attacks, I grew frenzied. I sent out a blistering wind that could have burned many an enemy, but my aim was wide.

"Focus!" he shouted. "Let yourself *go*, Fireblood!"

But I couldn't. A small part of me was still locked up tight, frightened of what I might do.

"She can't do it," Arcus said to Brother Thistle, who hovered, tense as a bowstring, on the edge of the training ground. "She'll fall at the king's feet and beg for mercy."

"I won't!" I shouted, blasting him with a wave of intense heat, which he deflected with a swirling cloud of frost.

"So scared of your own powers," he said, his voice heavy with contempt, pouring cold out in waves. "Too afraid to hurt anyone. Poor, weak thing."

Rage uncoiled itself inside my chest, a sleeping tiger that had been poked too many times. Since the attack on my village, I had pushed down so many feelings—hurt, fear, anger, grief. Now I was glowing with white heat. I whipped my hand forward and back, releasing a tail of the dragon. A thick column of fire with a wicked end shot toward his chest.

Arcus raised a hand to bring up a shield of frost. I thought I saw him stumble just slightly, but the flame hissed into a harmless cloud of steam.

He shook his head, and suddenly I saw that he was trembling with fury. He turned to Brother Thistle. "She'll never be ready. Our plan has failed already."

"We still have time," the monk replied.

Arcus slashed the air with his hand and turned to leave. "Not enough."

My fingernails bit into my palms. No matter how hard I tried, he was always better. He had all the power, and mine was nothing in comparison.

He was a Frostblood.

And like all Frostbloods in this land, he held dominion over me. In my fury, the gains I had made, the way I had come to see Arcus as an ally—all that disappeared. Pain lit my heart and spewed up hate, the way fire belches smoke.

I whipped my hand forward, aiming for his back. But instead it was his hood that erupted in flames.

Arcus cried out and fell to his knees.

For the space of a breath, I stood there, stunned, as Brother Thistle rushed forward. I couldn't believe I had hit him. Even mindless with fury, I hadn't been aiming higher than his loose tunic, which he would freeze in an instant. He had parried every other attack so effortlessly. He'd seemed invincible.

I stumbled toward him. The flames were out, the ruined hood smoking under his hands. He was on his knees, breathing hard, trembling.

"Stay back," Arcus hissed.

"I'm sorry," I whispered. "I'm sorry, I'm sorry. I wasn't aiming—"

"No," he said, his hands pulling off what was left of the steaming hood and tossing it to the ground. "You're never aiming, are you? For all your lessons in control, you are still wild."

Pain shivered in his voice. My heat was dying, and in its place was charred, blackened regret.

"That's not fair," I said, my voice pleading. "You deliberately goaded me. And I didn't think I could hurt you. You have your cold, your ice, to protect you."

He stood slowly and turned. His face was uncovered.

Oh, his face.

I rose and took an involuntary step back.

"Do I look as if I'm invulnerable?" he said, each word a well-aimed arrow, sharp and precise. "Do I look as if I cannot be hurt?"

I shook my head. My skin was cold with shock.

"What do you think the soldiers look like?" he asked. "The ones you burned?"

My mouth opened, but no words came out. Surely that wasn't what I had done.

"For all your talk of healing," he said, his words relentless, "you are the most dangerous person I have ever met. If I didn't need you so badly, I would have let you die in that prison."

His eyes bored cold hatred into mine. I stumbled backward.

Without another word, he turned and strode to the abbey, leaving me sick and aching, aching, aching with remorse.

TWELVE

I TOSSED AND TURNED THAT NIGHT. Whenever I closed my eyes, I saw the look on Arcus's face when he'd pulled off his hood: a mixture of stark pain and seething hatred.

Now I knew why he always wore a hood. His face had been burned cruelly. His ear and cheek on the right side were disfigured, the skin taking a new shape like wax that had melted and congealed. A scar ran right into his scalp, his hair growing white around it. The scar that cleft his lip curved over to the left. No part of his face had completely escaped damage.

It suddenly made sense, his threats when we'd first met, his paralysis when he'd tried to enter the burning abbey. He was terrified of fire, and for good reason.

And I had burned him.

Yes, his words had been harsh, but he'd just been trying to force me to give rein to my temper and unleash my powers. It was my own weakness that had made me furious, my inability to meet him or the Frostbloods who were exterminating my people on equal terms. And I'd lashed out. I'd burned him right where he'd already been hurt.

It made me realize that my feelings for Arcus had changed during my time at the abbey. At first, he had been just another Frostblood. But he hadn't used his gift to hurt me. He'd used it to help me master my own, to sculpt and mold me into someone stronger. Despite his cold demeanor, despite the fact that he'd baited me, I had grown to respect him, even to like him. And I felt more alive in his company than I'd ever felt with anyone.

I didn't understand how that had happened. He had threatened to thrash me, called me weak, and shamed me for my lack of skill. But I kept seeing something beneath the surface, a part of him I wanted to connect with if only he would stop freezing me out.

"Foolish girl," I cursed myself.

The worst part was the idea that he might think my mute shock at seeing his face had been disgust or horror.

I *was* horrified, but not for the reasons he probably thought. I was appalled that he'd endured so much and his face was forever disfigured, a constant reminder he could never escape. I was sickened at myself for forcing that reminder on him.

Dawn came. Orange rays of sunrise painted my eyelids and

burnished my hand as it lay on the floor next to my pallet in the infirmary. I rubbed my aching eyes and went about my morning wash, far slower than usual.

I was weak from lack of sleep and my ankle throbbed. Brother Gamut offered me his special tea, but I refused. I didn't feel I deserved relief just now. Instead, I trailed through the abbey like a ghost, silent and cold. Sister Pastel saw me pass by the library and waved a hand. I lifted mine in return but couldn't manage a smile.

I stopped when I saw Brother Thistle in the church. He was kneeling with his head bowed, his lips moving in silent prayer. With a final, adoring look at the stained glass image of Tempus, he pushed himself up with the aid of his walking stick and tapped his way down the center aisle, preceded by a cloud of frost.

"Brother Thistle," I said, making him start.

"Miss Otrera," he said, the words clipped.

I knitted my hands together. "I know you must be furious with me. I'm furious with myself. But please believe that I didn't mean to hurt him. I didn't even know I could."

He heaved a sigh. "I do not think it was intentional. However, it was—"

"It was uncontrolled and dangerous and...awful. I know. I'm sorry. I just want to tell Arcus that. And that I wasn't upset by his scars but by his words. Please, Brother Thistle. Can you tell me where he is?"

"He rode off early this morning. There was another raid, this time in Trystwater."

"That's only a day or two east, isn't it?" I asked in alarm.

He nodded. "Arcus wanted to see if he could find out more about why the soldiers were there."

"Do they know I'm nearby?"

"We have no reason to believe that. Arcus will be back in a few days to tell us."

My heart sank. "Oh."

His shrewd blue eyes softened. "If it will ease your conscience, I don't think you hurt him physically. Frostbloods with the gift are almost as hard to burn as Firebloods."

"But he has been hurt," I whispered.

"Yes. But not by you. He is powerful. His frost is strong. What you did was remind him of the worst moment of his life. That moment haunts his dreams."

I closed my eyes against the regret. "What happened to him?"

"It is not my place to tell you. Arcus can tell you himself if he wishes."

"Please, what can I do?"

He regarded me steadily. "Do what we ask of you. Learn to control your gift. Complete your task."

"I will. I'll learn everything you can teach me."

I might not gain Arcus's forgiveness, but I could earn back Brother Thistle's respect. I would bend all my focus to my training with Brother Thistle. I would control my temper, build my strength, and take every lesson to heart.

Because if the raids were moving closer, my time was running out.

It took three days for Arcus to return, a length of time that had seemed interminable. As soon as I heard he was back, I left the kitchen, where I'd been helping Brother Peele prepare for dinner, and went to see him. I tried to ignore the eager thump of my heart as I hurried along the dirt path between the kitchen and guesthouses, telling myself I was only anxious to apologize.

Arcus lived in a modest guesthouse separate from the main building. I had long wondered what he was doing in the abbey. At first, I'd thought him a mercenary, hired to help me kill the king. But hired by whom? I knew from Brother Thistle's nervous obsession with his ledgers that the abbey had no money. And the monk treated him more like a son than hired help.

I knocked on the door and received a curt "Enter" in reply.

Arcus sat at a small wooden table with two chairs, a book open in front of him. Candlelight warmed his soft gray tunic, half covered by a new black cloak with a hood that hid his face.

His room was bigger than mine and embellished with personal touches. A tapestry of sun-dappled woods covered one wall from floor to ceiling. A few musical instruments leaned against it. Books were piled in a corner. The table where Arcus sat was pushed to one wall. The other wall held his bed, which had a wooden frame and was covered in a blue quilt. A lamp burned on a little table next to it.

I broke the silence. "Your room is finer than mine. Clearly, some criminals are preferred over others."

He tilted his head. "I should let you know that I like apologies even less than I like gratitude."

I swallowed to ease the constriction in my throat. "I was furious with you, but I was aiming for your tunic. You had parried all my attacks so easily; it never occurred to me that I could hurt you."

When he made no reply, I said, "I'm sorry. Even if you don't want to hear it. I was miserable about it."

He nodded.

"And I hate that you went away. I couldn't even explain." I stepped closer. "I wish I could see your eyes."

He smiled bitterly. "But then you would have to see the rest of my face." The low, mocking words held a hint of pain. "And I would rather not see that expression of horror on yours again. Ever."

He said it as if it mattered what I thought of him. I moved forward and pulled out the chair opposite him at the little table.

"It wasn't horror the way you think. It wasn't—"

"I know shock and disgust when I see it." The words were sharp-edged and unyielding.

"Shock, yes." I shook my head. "Disgust, no. I didn't know that had happened to you and I felt—"

"Pity," he supplied.

"Regret. Horror at myself. That I could do that to someone. Everything you said was right. I am dangerous. To myself.

To others. My grandmother used to tell me my gift would save people someday. But I couldn't save anyone. Not myself. Not my mother."

"You can still save people."

"By killing the king," I supplied, blinking hard. "And what do you think of my chances?"

We sat in silence for a moment. I stared at my hands, which lay limp on my knees.

"Listen, Ruby." My eyes flicked up to find him leaning forward. "I do know you're much stronger than you were when you came here. Brother Thistle thinks you're more than just another Fireblood with a foul temper."

I smiled weakly at his attempt at teasing.

The oil lamp was burning low, casting the room in shadows.

"Why are you here?" I asked, staring at his lips, which had turned somber, and wishing again that I could see his eyes.

"Brother Thistle," he answered. "He took me in when I had nowhere else to go."

"What happened to your home?"

He shook his head. "Nothing. I left."

I waited for more, but there was none.

"Did you fight in one of the wars?"

"I've trained but never fought." There was something in the way he said it that indicated regret or shame, bitterness maybe.

"Were you caught in a fire?"

His lips compressed. "By which you mean, 'How did your face come to be so horribly disfigured?'"

"You won't talk about it, so I have to pry."

"You don't have to do any such thing. You don't need to know."

My hands tightened into fists, my earlier pleasure burned away like mist. It was always the same. The moment I drew close, he pushed me back with the force of a biting north wind. No one else made me feel so alive, but no one could make me so angry, either.

"No, I don't need to know anything at all," I said hotly. "Who you are, why you're here. Why you care about the king or the throne. I should just march off to my death without knowing why you sent me."

He stood so abruptly his chair tipped over and clattered to the floor behind him.

"You think I *want* you to die?" His chest rose and fell with agitated breaths. "That I'd happily send you to your death?"

My skin tingled. I had never seen him display such emotion. As always, his anger soon kindled mine. I shoved my chair back and planted my palms on the table.

"Yes! That is what I think. You've called me weak, threatened me, belittled me, and made me so furious I lost control and nearly hurt you. You'll probably celebrate a new festival around the day of my death." I threw my hands in the air, heat suffusing my face. "The Fireblood's Death Day. Good riddance to Ruby!"

He stepped toward me, his breath an audible hiss. "You are so—"

I stuck out my chin and stepped around the table, moving closer. "Reckless? Hot-tempered? Dangerous? I've heard all that before. Come up with something new."

"All those things," he said, his volume rising. "And blind. Some of us have to think of others. You only care about yourself."

A red haze settled in front of my eyes. The statement was so unfair. No part of my life had ever been my choice. As a child, I hadn't been allowed to get angry, in case I lost control of my heat. The only selfish thing I'd ever done was practice my gift, and I had been swiftly and mercilessly punished in the most agonizing and irreversible of ways. I'd drawn the soldiers who took the only living person I'd loved. I'd lost my mother and months of my life to the king. Now I was training morning to night for a task two Frostbloods had devised, a task that would benefit the kingdom but might cost me my life. Nothing I'd done was purely for my own benefit.

And Arcus and Brother Thistle didn't even trust me enough to fully share their plan.

"If that were true," I said, my voice thick with anger, "I would take a horse and leave. I would ride to the ocean and find my way onto a ship and never look at this cursed land again. Maybe I will!"

I whirled toward the door. His hand grabbed my shoulder.

"You won't. And you know why? You want to kill the king more than anyone. That's why you came back."

I turned and glared up at him, my hand itching to knock his hood off so I could pin his eyes with mine.

He was perfectly still, a statue carved of ice. I opened my mouth and closed it.

"You want to say something," he said. "Say it."

"Were you there the night my mother died?" I demanded, my voice thick with tension. "Were you one of the soldiers?"

Suspicion had wriggled up again into the shadows of my mind, only asserting itself when I was incensed enough to blurt it out.

His hand clutched my shoulder. His face was just inches away. "Is that what you want to hear? So you can hate me completely?"

He dropped his hand and stepped back, opening his cloak to show the thin tunic underneath.

"Kill me now if you're so keen," he said, his voice soft and deep. "Unless you want me to suffer. Maybe you'd like to have some sport with my face. Or would that be treading old ground?"

I was breathing heavily, my heart pulsing with simmering heat.

"Were you there?" I asked quietly.

He paused, his jaw rigid with tension. Finally, he replied, "No, but you'll believe what you wish. Why did you even come here?"

Some of the fight went out of me. I shook my head. "To say sorry and . . . because I want to know who you are."

Arcus let out a long breath. "This is the truth, Ruby: It doesn't matter who I am unless you win. If I die tomorrow, the world will be no different than it is now." He stepped closer. "Everything depends on you. If you fail, there is little hope for this kingdom. You matter." His hand lifted to hover inches from my cheek, seeming to freeze in midair, as if he couldn't bring himself to touch me.

"The world would be no different," I repeated, coating each word with scorn. "You say you don't want pity, and now I know why. You have plenty for yourself already."

His hand dropped. He stepped back.

I stepped forward, my hands in fists, suddenly furious that he was so easy to push away. "*I* would care if you died, you stupid goat's behind. *I* would miss you. Like I missed you when you left for days and I didn't know when, or if, you were coming back."

My voice broke, the veneer of anger cracking and letting my pain and longing through. I couldn't seem to help myself. I sensed on some level that he was as lonely as I was, and maybe he didn't have to be. Maybe *I* didn't have to be.

I stood close enough that the heat of my body met the cold of his. He smelled of soap and pine and woodsmoke and something enticing that was just him.

On impulse, I lifted my hand to the edge of his hood. As I slowly pulled it back, his hand came up and grasped my wrist. I stilled.

His lips were slightly parted, his breath cool against my forehead. Sometime in the past weeks, I had taken to wondering what it would be like to press my lips against his. I wondered whether it would hurt, whether it would sizzle, or whether our lips would just meld together like hot and cold air that make a mild summer breeze.

I lifted my forefinger and lightly touched his lips. He sucked in a breath but didn't move away. His lips were cold but not uncomfortably so. I ran the tip of my finger along the smooth corner, over the ridged scar of the upper lip, and over the smooth lower one.

"Stop," he whispered, the word tight, almost pained. "Stop."

The breath caught in my chest. It felt as if I'd been slapped, the hurt shuddering through me.

I dropped my hand and crossed my arms to hide my trembling. I searched the shadows of his hood for the smallest sign of emotion, but he was cold and still. The ice statue had been buffeted by a hot wind and had not even melted at the edges.

"A filthy Fireblood showing her feelings," I taunted, hurt and bitterness gathering into hard knots in my stomach. "You will have to beg Fors to wipe you clean, won't you?"

His lips tightened, but he said nothing.

"Well, don't worry. I'll be gone soon. You can absolve yourself then."

I turned, desperate to get away before I fell apart, and wrenched open the door. As I stalked out into the star-filled night, hot, shamed tears fell from my cheeks and landed, hissing, on the ground.

THIRTEEN

CLOUDS MOVED IN AND TRAPPED THE abbey under a canopy of rain. By unspoken agreement, Arcus and I avoided each other for the next few days. I was lucky to catch a glimpse of his hooded form through the window as he moved between the stables and his guesthouse. With a sinking heart, I realized he was probably embarrassed, perhaps even offended, though I doubted he could be as mortified as I was for my display. I had misread him completely and made a fool of myself when he clearly didn't feel the same.

I used my burning frustration at still knowing almost nothing of their plans to distract myself from my shame. Finally, one evening, I decided I would no longer tolerate their secrets.

After checking the refectory, where the monks ate meals, I

found Brother Thistle bent over his desk in the chapter house, a large square room with two columns leading up to a vaulted stone ceiling. A long table matched with velvet-upholstered chairs filled the middle of the room. Wooden benches lined stone walls under high, arched windows. The sun highlighted some faded gold leaf on the columns. The room was kept in better condition than the rest of the crumbling abbey because it was used to conduct business, where senior monks met with superiors from the Order of Fors.

"I should have known you'd be agonizing over your ledgers," I said, my shadow blending with that of the column I leaned against.

He started, his hand sliding over the pages as if covering the words. "Ruby, I didn't see you there."

"And calling me by my first name, too. Things must be bad. Do we need to start selling the silver?"

He cleared his throat and stood. "Perhaps nearly that bad, but not quite."

"Can you even see the numbers?" I moved to the desk and lit the candle with the tip of my finger. My eyes fell on a black book with gold lettering. *Gods and People.* "I was reading this book a couple of days ago." The persistent rain had given me some rare free time to read in the library. I read aloud from the open page. "'A fierce east wind will blow on the day the child of darkness is born, a child who will open the Gate of Light. And because Neb decreed there must be balance in all things, a west wind will blow when the child of light is born, a child who will fight the darkness and destroy it forever.'"

"Sit down, Ruby," he said, motioning to the bench. "How much do you know of the prophecies of Dru?"

I settled onto the bench and considered my answer. I didn't know much. My mother had hated prophecies. If my grandmother had even mentioned anything to do with one, my mother would have an uncharacteristic show of temper and say she didn't want my head filled with such drivel.

"With respect," I said finally, "prophecies are generally nonsense. Tales spun by self-proclaimed seers to make some coin."

"Perhaps. But Dru was different. Her prophecies were told to her followers some two thousand years ago from her home on the Gray Isles in the Coral Sea. And they were known to come true. Some of them are in that book." He motioned to his desk. "Some are in others. I have spent many years researching, seeking clues, eliminating false or corrupted accounts, finding lost ones. So let me assure you that I do not come by my conclusions lightly."

My foot tapped a rhythm on the stone floor. "Don't keep me in suspense. What did you find out?"

"You know of the god Eurus?"

"The sly and clever god of the east wind who was jealous of Fors and Sud for creating Frostbloods and Firebloods, and angry that his sister Cirrus sealed his Minax under the earth."

Brother Thistle nodded. "The book says that Eurus took his revenge with a kind of curse, and only a powerful Fireblood will someday rid the kingdom of it."

"What's the curse?" I asked. Although I didn't believe in the book or the legends, I enjoyed the details the way I enjoyed hearing a good story.

"If you've read that book, perhaps you know about the thrones of Tempesia and Sudesia."

"Yes, one was created by Fors, a 'throne of jagged ice that conferred great power.' And Sud created a throne of cooled molten rock. Let me think…'still glowing with veins of lava.'" I had read that part several times, fascinated by the idea of the fire throne.

"It's not just a story, Ruby. Many people in Tempesia still believe the Frost King's throne was created by Fors to help win wars. They believe it gives him immense power, amplifying what his strong bloodline already has."

"You're talking about myths."

"To me and my order, these so-called myths are as real as you sitting before me. Regardless, some of the accounts I have read say that Eurus corrupted both thrones, cursing the families who have sat on them since the ancient wars between Firebloods and Frostbloods."

"Ruling in an unbroken line doesn't sound like a curse to me."

"Until you consider that every ruler died tragically and often after a short reign."

I shrugged. "Tragic deaths are common whether you're a king or a peasant."

"Not only that. The rulers often went mad, hearing voices, carrying out terrible acts. King Ulrik drowned his first grandchild.

Queen Ecklin killed her husband in a fit of temper. King Askabar wiped out an entire province because a baron insulted his mistress, and that led to a civil war. There are far more stories of madness and strange deaths. Too many to relate."

"Horrible stories," I said, rubbing the goose bumps on my arms.

"I think some rulers were strong enough to fight the influence of the curse, and Tempesians and Sudesians enjoyed relative peace during those reigns. But they were only able to do so because the curse was not fully woken."

"And you think the curse woke?"

"Yes. After generations of calm, King Akur began showing signs of being overtaken by the darkness. The even-tempered king who had cared for his people suddenly sent troops to his southern border and started wiping out Firebloods. When Akur died, his elder son took the throne and tried to restore peace, but he only ruled for a year before he was assassinated. And now Akur's second son, Rasmus, rules with such open hatred for peace and fairness that the whole kingdom trembles."

I sat in silence for a minute, thinking. "It doesn't have to be a curse. People do terrible things. They make decisions that make no sense to anyone but them."

Brother Thistle pointed back to the book on his desk. "The text says that a fierce east wind will blow when the child of darkness is born, a child who will open the Gate of Light. When I was a young man, a terrible storm blew over Sudesia and Tempesia, a monstrous hurricane that wiped out towns and cities along the coasts. Very soon after, King Akur began showing signs of madness."

It took me a second to understand his meaning. "You think the child of darkness was born and that woke the curse?"

"I do. And roughly seventeen years ago, a similarly violent storm hit, but from the west. As you read, the book says that a west wind will blow when the child of light is born, a powerful Fireblood who will fight the darkness and destroy it forever."

The air in the room pulsed with a strange energy. "Well, shouldn't you be looking for this child of light if you believe the prophecies?"

He put his hands on his knees and sat back in his chair. "I have spent my life doing so. And I think I have found her."

It took me a moment to find my voice. "I've become quite fond of you, Brother Thistle. But if you're implying I'm the child of light, I must tell you frankly that I think you're touched in the head."

He smiled gently. "I know it will be very hard to accept—"

"Impossible."

"Why?"

"My powers are unreliable. I have a foul temper and I've hurt people. I'm more likely to be the child of darkness."

He wrapped his robes more tightly about himself. "Do not say that. You are no such thing."

"I think it's time for bed," I said, standing. I'd had as much as I could handle. It was more than enough to believe I was the last Fireblood in the kingdom. The idea that I was somehow destined to save the world from the curse of a god was far too much to accept. All I was supposed to do was kill the king, and that seemed impossible.

"Do not run from the truth, Ruby. Summer solstice draws near, the time when your strength is greatest. It is almost time for you to leave... and the time has come for me to tell you what we want you to do."

My heart kicked against my ribs. My palms grew damp.

"I am still researching the thrones and their connection to the ruling family, but I am confident of this: You need to eliminate the throne first. It protects the king and gives him power. If he could be overtaken by force, someone would have formed an army and done so already."

I raised an eyebrow. "And would people be willing to fight? To face torture and death if they lose?"

"The land is dying. The people are dying. They have nothing *to* lose."

"So you're saying, to have a hope of killing the king, I need to destroy the throne first. How?"

His light blue eyes bored into mine. "You must summon all the power you have. Everything, Ruby. You understand me? There can be no reservation. You must focus all your heat on the throne. Melt it. Destroy it."

I nodded. "What if I'm not strong enough?"

"You have to be."

Fear gripped my stomach. Things suddenly seemed so complicated, more starkly real. For everything to depend on me... it was unimaginable. I wasn't strong. I was volatile. Undisciplined. I didn't have the strength, the control.

I stared out the window. The dying sun left fingerlike streaks of purple as it slid from the sky. I rubbed my arms and tried to draw warmth from my heart.

"What if I do manage to kill the king without destroying the throne?" I asked. "What then?"

"Another ruler will take the king's place, someone who must be stronger than the throne and its dark appetites."

"And if not?"

"The curse will continue and the new ruler may become the same as the current one."

I crossed my arms and let out a breath. "You're saying if I don't destroy the throne, the kingdom will be no better off than it is now."

"That is very likely, yes."

I stood and started pacing the length of the room. "Why are you doing this? Why risk the abbey and...spend all this time training me? What's it to you?"

"I believe I came to this land for a reason. I cannot watch the kingdom fall into destruction. I am not even sure you, with everything you have gone through, understand the suffering that goes on all around us."

I came back to the bench and sat. I stared at the ice crystals under Brother Thistle's chair, shivering, trying to sort out my feelings, which were some combination of anticipation and dread. When a cold hand covered mine, I jumped so hard I knocked my head against the window behind me. Brother Thistle removed his hand, but I could feel his stare. His expression was almost forlorn.

"It was much easier to make these plans before I knew you," he said. "Before you came here, you were a tool to be used, a weapon to be wielded at our choosing. After all, you were slated for death anyway. If you died in the completion of our plan, it would be a worthy sacrifice. But now... please believe this is hard for me. You are a kind, feisty, headstrong, impulsive, generous young woman. I have grown quite fond of you."

"That's quite a list of virtues and vices."

"With the virtue playing the greater part," he said with a slightly sad smile. "It is much harder to send you into danger than I expected. And, I believe, even more difficult for Arcus."

I gave a harsh laugh. "I doubt that."

"You do not know him as I do. He is as gifted at concealing his feelings as he is at wielding frost. I believe I have come to know him better than anyone. The more he feels, the more impervious he seems."

"Really? And how does he show that he's impervious? I suppose by being passionate?"

"Ruby—"

"What happens when the throne is destroyed?" I asked, not wanting to hear any more about Arcus and his feelings.

"My belief is that when you destroy the throne, the curse will be destroyed as well. In that case, the king may undergo a transformation."

My brow furrowed. "What kind of transformation?"

"The curse has controlled him for years, but if the throne is destroyed, he may return to his senses and realize how far he has fallen."

"Or he'll be furious that I destroyed his source of power."

"True. But my hope is that by destroying the throne, you will cure him."

"Cure him? I'm supposed to kill him!"

"Well," he said, looking at me carefully from under his white brows, "I once told you that a reason we sought you out was because your mother was a healer. I have reason to believe that you will not need to kill the king. You might be able to save him."

I spoke slowly and carefully, struggling to keep a rein on my temper. "I've been training for over two months to kill the Frost King, and now you suggest I don't?"

He spread his hands. "I am only offering you another way."

"I don't want another way! My mother was nothing but kind to everyone, and they killed her in front of me! Can you even begin to understand—" I bit off the words as my voice broke. When I spoke again, it was low and calm. "No. I'm going to kill the king. That's what all this was for. That's...all I live for."

"Is it? Is that really all you have to live for?"

There was a long silence. Part of my mind chattered at me that I'd found friends, I'd found people to care about here. There was more to my life than hate. But another part said that I would never have peace. I clutched my hands together in my lap, my mind in turmoil. Brother Thistle leaned forward and cleared his throat.

"Summer solstice is barely three weeks away, Ruby. You'll leave us soon to attempt a task that has no guarantee of success. You need to decide what you're fighting for. Who you truly are."

Rage bloomed in my chest like a deadly flower. Pressure built behind my eyes and in my chest until it was too much to hold in. I wanted to scream and tear things apart.

"And you're saying I'm a *healer*?" I nearly spat the word. "After everything he's done to me, you think...I should try to heal him? I'd kill myself first."

I strode to the door and found my way blocked by a hooded shadow.

Arcus.

The thought of him listening to the conversation, silently agreeing with Brother Thistle, made my hands tighten into fists. I came straight at him, plowing into his arm with my shoulder as I bolted from the room.

FOURTEEN

SOUNDS WERE DROWNED OUT BY MY ragged breathing, my feet slamming the earth. I'd been so desperate to have a home again I had given up all thought of what I was doing here. They had brought me here to use me, and I had agreed, eager to die for them because I was getting what I wanted: revenge. And now they didn't want me to even have that.

The sun had set, but streaks of burnt orange still clung to the sky above the forest. I raced toward the trees, hoping the strong scents of pine and wet soil would calm my mind.

A sound like thunder rent the air. A wall of ice grew up in front of me, a glacier appearing suddenly as if it had risen from the ground, the reverberation knocking me off my feet and twisting my ankle. I cried out in shock, scanning the landscape.

A hooded figure stood near the abbey. Arcus had followed me.

Turning, I limped toward *him*, stopping a few feet away. The remnants of sunset transformed the lower portion of his face into a mask of beaten copper, dented strangely over his cheeks and lip. When I remembered the last time I'd spoken to him, my blood boiled in my gut like a fire fed with oil. I'd touched his lips, laid my affection at his feet, and he had shown me how repelled he was by my very touch.

"You promised not to leave," he said, his muscles bunched for a fight.

Of course he would assume I was leaving again. I pulled my arm back and cracked an invisible whip. Fire corkscrewed through the air, flying inches from Arcus's legs and spreading over the ground in a shower of sparks. He didn't even flinch. I lifted my arm again, this time aiming at his chest.

He was ready. A breath of frost met my spiral of molten heat, dispersing it in a cone-shaped hiss of steam.

My hands spun out a funnel cloud of blistering heat. I had never been able to do the move successfully during training. Now the wind howled as it bore down on its target. He lifted his palms but wasn't fast enough. The air hit him like a battering ram, slamming him to the earth. He lay on his back, unmoving.

I ran to him, torn by conflicting urges. I wanted to hurt him. I wanted to make sure he was unhurt. I wanted to leave him in the dirt and run away. I wanted him to stop me from leaving.

Shaking, I fell to my knees and put my hand to his chest. It rose and fell with each breath. A pulse beat at his neck. I had an urge to cup his cheek, to trace the scars on his face, to slide my fingers into his hair. He groaned and opened his eyes.

Relief coursed through me. I looked into the myriad of blues and then, unable to bear the cold, looked away.

"You lied to me," I said.

"When did I lie?" he asked.

I shrugged. "Maybe not outright. But you let me believe my task was to kill the king. That's the whole reason I did all this. You think it was easy? Learning to trust two Frostbloods to teach me how to master my fire. Taking orders, holding my temper, learning to quiet my mind. You think any of this was easy?"

"No. I don't think it was easy at all."

I kept my face turned away so he wouldn't see the pain I couldn't hide. "Fool that I am, I thought it would get me what I wanted. Revenge. And now I know that all you ever wanted me to do was destroy the throne. Do you know what Brother Thistle thinks?" I gave a snort of disgust. "Of course you do. Stupid, fanciful notions. I...I should have run away in the dead of night and never come back. I should have gone to the castle myself."

"So you could die in his arena like all the other Firebloods?"

"And the death you have planned for me is better? The one where the king kills me for destroying his throne? That's assuming I'm even strong enough. That's also assuming we even get past the castle guards. You'll be dead, too, by the way, if we don't. I hope the payout, whatever it is, is worth it."

Slowly, he raised himself onto his elbows. "If I could afford to be completely selfish, I wouldn't let you go after the king. I would take you far away from this land and keep you safe."

My lashes fluttered, pleased shock sending ripples over my skin. The red haze over my eyes began to fade.

I sat back and wrapped my arms around my knees. *I would take you far away from this land and keep you safe.* It had been so long since anyone had tried to protect me. A part of me longed to curl into his arms and warm him with my heat as his words warmed me. But the last time I had touched him, he had told me to stop.

He took a breath, and when he spoke again, his voice was steady. "But I cannot only think of myself. You know what's happening to my people. You know what's already happened to yours. It cannot continue."

I pressed my palms against the earth and focused on a spot in the distance. "Why me? You don't believe in prophecies. You said yourself I'm just another foul-tempered Fireblood."

He pushed up and sat forward, resting his elbows on his bent knees. His skin, where it wasn't scarred, was smooth and young, though I knew his eyes held the weight of experience many years older.

"Who else is there?" he asked. "What Fireblood will do this but you?"

"What if I do destroy the throne? When it's all over, are you just going to"—I waved a hand—"disappear into the air like mist?"

"From the time we leave the abbey until you're safely back again, I'll protect you with my life."

I looked at Arcus and remembered Brother Thistle's claim: that the Frostblood felt more than he showed. The pounding of my heart eased and the fog began to lift.

"And if I die there?" I asked. "Will someone take my body? Or will he put my head on a post at the castle gates?"

His fist hit the earth, making the ground reverberate. "You have to believe you can win. What happened to your rage? Your fire? Are you giving up already?"

"I'm not giving up! But you should have told me everything from the start so I knew what I was facing!"

"You want a guarantee," he said. "Assurances that nothing will go wrong. Ruby, there is no such thing."

I shrugged. He was right. I buried my nose between my knees and wished I were invisible.

"Please go," I mumbled against the fabric of my robe. "I want to be alone."

Arcus heaved a sigh, but I heard no sounds of him rising to leave. Finally, I lifted my head.

He looked south toward the road to the abbey, a silent silhouette. His profile, I couldn't help noticing, was nobly carved. How handsome he must have been before he was burned. Heat flared over my skin. How handsome he was now.

I turned away. I didn't want to think those kinds of thoughts about him, now or ever again. I was a fool to entertain them in the first place. It wasn't his fault that the fire in my blood made me feel things he couldn't. For once, I wished my blood were a little cooler, more like his.

"You asked me how I was burned," he said, his voice barely louder than the hissing of the wind. "A Fireblood master tried to kill me."

I didn't want to care, but I couldn't help it. In an instant, I understood Arcus's initial fear and animosity toward me. I had threatened to burn him so badly his mistress would run from him in terror. I curled my nails into my palms to ward off the guilt that welled up at the memory.

"He caught me unawares. I was lured to a place where I was alone. I was a fool for not taking better care. After all my training with weapons and combat, I didn't even get in one hit before I was on the ground, my throat so raw I couldn't even scream my agony."

It took a minute to find my voice. "Where did you live?"

"In the king's court."

My head jerked up, my eyes widening. In the fading light, he was little more than a silhouette.

"After my father died and I took his title, I made some powerful enemies. Men who wanted me gone."

My heart pounded in my ears at the realization that Arcus was a titled lord. "Why?"

One broad shoulder gave a slight shrug. "I wasn't what they'd expected. They wanted me to be like my father and I wasn't."

"And . . . you think these men sent someone to kill you?"

He nodded. "I believe my death was meant to get rid of me and to stir up hatred toward Firebloods, to look like an attack."

"Why are you telling me all this?"

"You said I never tell you anything. I'm trying to change that."

Warmth fluttered in my chest. He was finally trusting me with answers.

"Why would anyone want to stir up hatred when there was so much already?"

"The king at the time had plans to make peace with the Firebloods in the southern plains. There are barons who had laid claim to that land, whether it was theirs by right or not. Killing off or driving away the Firebloods benefitted them."

Nausea twisted in my stomach. "That's monstrous."

"Yes. The king thought so, too."

"So he didn't hate us."

"He had every reason to. His mother, you remember, was killed by a band of Fireblood rebels. But when he was a child, his tutor told him other truths. Fire and frost used to be allies. Long ago, one of our kings married a Fireblood queen. King Ilaien and Queen Rosamund. Have you heard of them?"

"I thought it was just another one of Grandmother's stories." As a child, I hadn't believed that a Fireblood would want anything to do with a Frostblood.

"It was a very long time ago," he said. "Hundreds of years. No one wants to remember times of peace now. But the king did. He'd seen his father do things that were wrong. He wanted to change the kingdom. But he was killed, and Rasmus took the throne."

I shook my head. "You knew them both?"

"I grew up in the castle. Rasmus wasn't always the way he is today. Though his personality was always...changeable, I'm convinced the throne corrupted him."

"So you believe that nonsense about a curse?"

"I didn't used to. But I've read the books and heard Brother Thistle's evidence, and now I do. The throne has to be destroyed, and the king might be cured."

My spine stiffened at the implication: *Don't kill the king. Heal him.* "And why does Brother Thistle care so much? What made a monk of the Order of Fors turn against his own king?"

Arcus cleared his throat. "He was once part of the Frost Court, a decorated warrior after the Battle of Aris Plains. When he took his vows, King Akur chose him as the official representative of the order. But eventually he wouldn't tolerate Brother Thistle challenging him over his treatment of Firebloods anymore. The king sent him away to this abbey, where Brother Thistle dedicated himself to researching the prophecies and educating the brothers and sisters. He truly believes that a Fireblood will determine the outcome of an ancient rivalry between the gods. And he was affirmed in his belief in divine influence when I came here."

"How so?"

"After the attack, I was left for dead. I felt the life ebbing out of me. And then..." He waved a hand in the air, sending a cool breeze over my face. "It sounds fanciful. A woman with golden hair and golden eyes stood next to me."

My scalp prickled. She sounded just like my vision in the woods.

Arcus continued. "Suddenly, my agony was gone and I was in the abbey. I don't know if she was real and brought me here or if I was...spirited here somehow. But many of my burns had begun to heal. Brother Gamut worked tirelessly to heal me completely. It took many months."

Although his suffering horrified me, my heart warmed when I thought of Brother Gamut's gentle hands and kind heart, as well as Brother Thistle's determination that the order would always help those in need.

"Did anyone here see the woman? Did she give you her name?"

"No. She said only one thing."

He paused.

"What was it?" I asked.

He sighed. "She said that the Fireblood girl would be the key to peace. It seemed to hurt her greatly just to say that much, as if something choked the words. I...I think it was Sage, the one gifted with the sight."

"You said you didn't believe in the old stories," I reminded him.

"I said I didn't believe in the prophecies. I don't believe they all come true. I believe we always have choices. Even Sage can't tell us what is going to happen. Only what might happen. And sometimes prophecies are just wrong."

"So that's why you took me from the prison."

"That was part of it."

I sat silently for a while, sifting through the details of what he'd told me. Arcus wasn't a mercenary but a displaced noble, looking to heal the king he had known as a child. It made sense now that he had wanted to destroy the throne rather than kill the king.

But that didn't mean I agreed with him.

"I wasn't leaving," I admitted. "I was just upset and I wanted to be alone. I wasn't going to break my promise."

I changed positions and let out a pained sound as my swollen ankle pulsed with the stab of a hundred needles.

"You're hurt," said Arcus, shifting toward me. "I'll take you to Brother Gamut."

"Don't!"

But he didn't pull me up. He blew out a breath that encased my fevered ankle in blessed cold. The throbbing calmed instantly.

"I think you have a bit of the healer in you, Arcus."

"Let me carry you to the infirmary," he said as he crouched next to me. "I have grown accustomed to holding this particular bundle of crackling firewood."

My chest warmed a little at the hint of fondness in his tone, but I hesitated, struggling with my anger, my bitterness, and my sense of betrayal. He had shared things with me I never thought he would, though, and I couldn't help the feeling of closeness that came from that.

He was careful not to touch my ankle as he slid his arms under my knees and behind my back. For once, the cold that seeped from his body into mine didn't bother me.

"Damned ankle," I muttered. "Always a trial and a burden."

"Much like the girl to whom it is attached," he mused.

I opened my mouth to say something biting in return but completely forgot the words as I felt his lips press gently to my head.

Heat flared over my skin. I told myself it meant nothing. It was a gesture of friendship. But a feeling of contentment persisted, calming me as much as the sound of his footfalls and the beat of his heart against my ear.

He pulled me tighter to his chest, and I let my suddenly heavy eyes close as he carried me back to the abbey.

FIFTEEN

THE NEXT MORNING I MADE MY WAY
to the library, intending to lose myself in the dip and swish of
brushes and ink. Sister Pastel had said I was making progress in
the art of scribing and would likely be waiting for me.

Instead, I found the hunched form of Brother Lack writing
furiously at one of the tables.

"Come to start another fire?" he jeered, rolling up the page,
which then disappeared into the folds of his robe.

"You know I didn't start it. Because you did." The accusation
was a gamble, a suspicion I'd had since the night of the fire. But I
hadn't had the courage to voice it before.

My gamble paid off. He looked startled, guilt written clearly
on his face. "How dare you even *imply*..." When I gave him a

disbelieving look, he took a shuddering breath and drew himself up. "I merely wish to protect my order, as no one else here is prepared to do so! I've seen the way he looks at you, a Frostblood warrior undone by a Fireblood girl. It's disgusting. You went to his room, alone, and then just last night I saw him carrying you in his arms, a foolish look of... of *adoration* on his face."

I was breathing hard, my temper fraying. "Not that it's any of your business, but I care for Arcus as a friend—"

"Spare me your lies. If you cared for anyone here, you would relieve us of the danger of your presence."

I made a disgusted sound. "There's no reasoning with you. You're not like Brother Thistle or Arcus or Brother Gamut. Your mind has been poisoned against me because of my gift. You say I'm dangerous, when it's your people who have wiped out mine."

"And what came before that? I lived in the South, where Firebloods rained terror on my people. I will not stand here while you twist things to make yourself the victim. Get out of my way," he said, his chest rising and falling rapidly.

"No." I moved to block the doorway. "What were you writing so furtively when you should have been at morning prayers?"

My hand darted out and snatched the letter poking from the collar of his robe.

"You dare to put your filthy hands on me!" he railed, coming at me with a raised fist. I dropped the letter and sent a blast of heat at his arm, but momentum carried his hand forward. His fist slammed into the side of my face with a blow that knocked me soundly out of the room to sprawl on the floor of the corridor.

"You burned me," he said in shock, holding his singed wrist. His face turned red. He brought his foot back. I curled into a tight ball just before the sharp toe of his sandal met my back.

When he pulled his foot back to kick me again, I grabbed the other foot, yanking him to the floor. I used my elbows and knees the way Arcus had taught me when he gave me a lesson in close combat, then finally managed to shove him across the floor.

"Do not make me use the full force of my heat on you," I said, cupping my hands together and letting fire build between my palms.

His eyes rounded as he stared at my hands. With jerky movements, he pushed himself up and stumbled away. His sandals slapped the stone floor as he disappeared around the corner.

A few minutes later, I was on my pallet in the infirmary when Arcus came in. His eyes gleamed like bleached sapphires. He looked furious.

"How badly are you injured?" he asked.

"Not badly at all. How did you hear?"

"Sister Agnes saw the commotion and came to me for help."

He fell to his knees beside me and examined my swelling cheek, his nostrils flaring with veiled rage. I shivered with a pleasant chill at his nearness. He took the cloth I had used to wash, dipped it in the basin, and blew on it to make it cold. He held it against the swollen skin of my cheek, and I sighed with relief.

"Brother Lack had some sort of letter," I told him. "He didn't take kindly to my attempt to read it. I wonder if he means to complain to the order about my presence here."

"Brother Thistle is checking on his whereabouts right now," Arcus answered.

He put the cloth back in the water and wrung it out. I grabbed his wrist to guide the cloth to my cheek, and he sucked in a breath. I let go instantly.

"Sorry," I muttered, clasping my hands in my lap. "I burn you without even meaning to."

He raised the cloth and put it gently to my cheek. "It...does burn in a way. But I don't believe I would ever get a wound from touching you." He took a deep breath. "The heat seems to seep under my skin when I would prefer to remain cold. It's...easier that way after what has happened."

I wanted to ask so many questions but wasn't sure which he would answer. "And my touch threatens that somehow?"

"In a way. I brought you here to prepare you for a huge task," he said, dipping the cloth in the water and touching it to my cheek again. "An enormous weight rests on your shoulders."

I sighed, irritated at the reminder of what made me truly important. I wanted to mean more to Arcus than a way to melt the throne.

"And now I wonder if I can let you go," he added quietly.

I searched his face, shadowed by his hood, for signs that I'd misheard. The space between us seemed to crackle with energy, his words repeating themselves in my mind.

"It doesn't matter, does it? There is no other way."

"Someone else could kill him," he said, his voice tight. "I could."

"And the throne would take the next king, and the next. We'd never be free."

"That is truer than you know," he whispered, his fingers finding and clutching mine.

His hand was cold, but it made my skin tingle and my heart beat strong and fast. I didn't want to do anything to make him move away.

"What is the truth, Arcus?" I asked quietly. "You're full of secrets, and I would like to know one or two."

He paused for a minute, then opened his mouth to speak.

"Only I wish to see your eyes while you tell me," I added quickly. "You showed me your face before."

"To scare you," he said, drawing away from me. "To punish you for what you'd done. I don't want you to be scared of me now."

I looked up at him, taking in his stiff posture and tight jaw. "I'm not scared of your scars."

He took a shuddering breath and I held mine, waiting, wondering what he would do. Slowly, his hands went to the edges of his hood and pushed it back just far enough that I could see his deep blue eyes and ravaged cheek. My heart kicked into a gallop, its echo throbbing in my temples. He was trusting me. Choosing to let me see.

"Is that enough?" he asked, his voice endearingly uncertain.

I nodded and he exhaled a deep, relieved breath.

"No part of you is frightening or unappealing to me." I

paused to let that sink in. "But I understand that's as far as you are comfortable."

His hand gripped the quilt on my bed, the other hand squeezing the cloth that now dripped, forgotten, in his other hand. "You don't know the effect your words have on me, Lady Firebrand. It took years to build up this ice. You will melt it and then I will be broken."

He stood abruptly and paced the room.

I shook my head. "Just when I think I understand you, you say something to confuse me. First you seemed to detest me, then you treat me with kindness. Then you tell me you wish me dead. Now you fear I will somehow break you. Which is it?"

He paused. I stopped breathing, half regretting that I'd pressed him. I wasn't sure I could handle being pushed away again.

"I promised you a secret," he finally said, his eyes glittering in the candlelight, "and I can't think of any way to tell you plainer than this."

He took two strides toward me, fell to his knees, and turned my face up to his.

His lips moved over mine, the scar on his upper lip feeling pleasantly rough. His touch was tentative, but a shock of pure, toe-curling excitement shot into me. I returned the pressure eagerly. His lips were cooler than mine, but not painfully so. His temperature must have risen. I knew mine was up.

His arms slipped around my back, pressing me to his chest.

My hands curled around his neck, my fingertips greedily tangling in his hair. I pressed myself closer. His fingers dove into my hair, pulling the strands free of the string that held it back.

He broke the kiss to press his lips to my temple. "Gods, how I have been dying to touch your hair." His voice was low and gritty and hoarse. Just hearing it made my skin burn.

His eyes met mine and I marveled again at the myriad of colors. They were a cold winter morning and an evening on the lake, a crisp mountain stream and a blue starflower, crushed underfoot at the end of summer.

"Am I frightening you?" he asked roughly, his hands moving to my shoulders. "Only tell me to stop and I will. You must trust me, Ruby, that I would never hurt you."

"I trust you," I breathed, drawing him back to me. His cheek slid across mine, the slightly hair-roughened skin a tantalizing abrasion against mine. I moved my cheek to feel it again. He made a sound low in his throat and found my lips, brushing them back and forth, tasting me.

Part of my mind couldn't believe this was happening. I'd had dreams, but this was so much better. I hadn't known the feel of his skin against mine, the way it would make my heart leap, the joy of being wanted and being able to show him that I wanted him, too.

I longed to touch his face, to get to know those scars that he tried to hide. For whatever reason, they were fascinating, irresistible to my hands, which wanted to soothe and mend them, if only touch could do so. I risked moving my hands to his cheeks and he let me. When my fingertips drew near his ruined ear, he grabbed my wrist.

"By Fors," he breathed, trembling a little as he held me. "The gods are testing my control."

"And mine," I agreed, smiling wider. "But then we both know that's severely lacking. I've been waiting for you to kiss me for ages."

He chuckled and then sighed, placing his forehead against mine, his eyes closed.

"I shouldn't have done that," he said softly.

"You should have done it a lot sooner," I corrected.

He smiled. I angled my head for another kiss, but the door suddenly burst open and Brother Thistle stepped in, his walking stick trembling in his hand. Arcus pushed himself away.

"Brother Lack has left," Brother Thistle said. "The stable boy was made to saddle one of the horses and he heard Brother Lack muttering threats. Something about going to Greywater—"

"The garrison," Arcus said.

Terror gripped me. "He was writing a letter to someone in the library. He said he wouldn't allow me to corrupt the abbey anymore."

Brother Thistle turned to Arcus. "You need to find him. I didn't think it would come to this, but he would do anything if he believes his actions protect the order."

Arcus glanced at me. A pained look passed over his face.

"I'm sorry," he said in a low voice, and he was out the door and gone.

Brother Thistle sucked in a deep breath as frost flowed around his feet in a swirling, chaotic pattern. Though he looked in my direction, I had the sense his mind was somewhere else.

"This is not how it was supposed to happen. All our careful plans." His eyes flickered. He finally seemed to see me. "Your face is bruised. Are you hurt?"

I took a breath. I couldn't even feel the bruises. I wanted to run after Arcus and find out what was happening. But I knew my ankle wouldn't let me get far.

"I always seem to be, don't I?"

"I will send Brother Gamut with his tea," said Brother Thistle, turning to the door. "Stay here."

After a long while, I went out in search of news. The abbey was unnaturally quiet. Finally, I found Brother Thistle in the chapter house leaning on his walking stick, staring out the window.

"Any word?" I asked.

He shook his head. His face was wan and stiff and seemed more heavily lined than usual. We sat together, each minute crawling past.

The sun was halfway down the sky, the heat of late afternoon warming the seat under the window. A cloud moved over the sun, making me shiver.

Suddenly, Brother Thistle sat up straighter, his brows snapping together. He leaned forward.

"Is that? Yes. A horse." He tapped his stick on the floor in excitement. "Oh, praise Tempus. Arcus has returned."

Although frustrated by the abrupt end to our conversation, I looked out, eager to see Arcus. A distant figure rode toward the abbey, a dark smudge against the gray road and hazy trees. As it came closer, the shape split into two, then three, then more.

"There's more than one rider, Brother Thistle." Trepidation crept along my skin like tiny spiders. "Are you expecting visitors?"

He pushed his face closer to the glass, his eyes trained on the distant specks.

"What color do they wear, child?" he asked, an uncharacteristic tremor in his voice.

I shook my head, squinting. "It's hard to make out."

As the shapes drew closer, Brother Thistle's hand went to his heart. "By Tempus, no."

In the bright midday sun, the riders had become clear. Blue tunics with a white arrow in the center.

The mark of the Frost King.

My heart raced. Time seemed to stop and then rushed forward.

Brother Thistle cursed under his breath and pulled a key from the folds of his robe. Pressing it into my palm, he said, "Give this to Sister Pastel. She will take you to the catacomb tunnels that lead to the woods. Only the senior members of the order know where the tunnels come out."

"I'm not going to hide," I argued, my voice rising.

I was scared, more scared than I'd been since being in Blackcreek prison. But the need to protect my friends was greater than my fear.

He put his hand on my shoulder and pushed me backward, surprising me with his strength.

"This is no time for a show of stubborn temper," he said, more forcefully than I'd ever heard him. "If they find you here, there is no telling what they will do to us all."

His reasoning penetrated my defiance. Staying to fight could do more harm than good. I couldn't risk the monks and Arcus just to show myself that I wasn't that same scared girl in the village. But it felt wrong to cower in the dark while they faced the soldiers without me.

There was no indecision in Brother Thistle's eyes or hands as they took my shoulders and shook me.

"Go!" he yelled.

With an agonized backward look, I went.

SIXTEEN

AS THE OTHER MONKS PREPARED TO present an open, innocent face to the soldiers, Sister Pastel hustled me down the steep stone steps that led into the bowels of the abbey. Bones were piled in ossuaries and on shelves, neatly stacked rib cages and spines covered in a thick layer of dust. I gagged at the invisible bits of bone and sinew in the air, the final exhalations of the dead.

No sooner had we descended than the clank of steel and thumping of boots came from above.

"Not a sound, child," she whispered.

I needed no reminder. The crowded catacombs were so silent that any noise seemed like an explosion of sound. Not that the crowd minded. They were all dead.

"What will happen to the others?" I asked softly.

Sister Pastel shook her head. "Tempus willing, the soldiers will not find anything and go away."

Anything, meaning me.

"This way," she whispered, motioning me away from the entrance.

The walls were carved from the rocky earth. The ceiling was so low that even my head brushed it in spots.

Every few feet, a recess in the wall formed a kind of shelf that served as the final resting place for a pile of dusty bones. I kept my eyes trained on the torch. The sight of them was disquieting, as if the noise of my passage might wake them into chattering complaint.

As we walked, the ceiling grew lower and there were no more bones, just a dim tunnel twisting and turning away into nothingness.

"I can go no farther," said Sister Pastel, panting from the exertion of bending her spare frame so low. "If the soldiers are looking for you, they're sure to find the catacombs eventually. You must go to the end and find the way out. It's hidden in a cave among a pile of stones that look like a natural rockslide at the bottom of a hill. When you're out, head west. There's a path that leads up the mountain, where you'll find many caves in which to hide. We'll come get you when it's safe."

When I had first come here, I had wanted a way to escape the abbey. Now I'd grown used to the safety and familiarity of it. I wanted to spend my mornings training with Brother

Thistle, helping Sister Clove in the stables, and gathering herbs for Brother Peele. I wanted to sit in the library with Sister Pastel with the late-afternoon sun caressing the thin parchment, making it glow. I wanted Brother Gamut to bring me tea in the evening to warm my insides while we discussed the day's events.

And Arcus...

What if the soldiers had him? What if I never saw him again?

But there was no time to fall apart. A bittersweet confusion of gratitude and sadness closed my throat. I pulled a startled Sister Pastel into a swift embrace.

"Thank you for everything you taught me," I choked out.

"No need for that, child." She patted my shoulder. "We will see each other again soon enough. And then perhaps I'll let you try a bit of color on your paper."

"That would be wonderful. Please, please be careful."

"I will. Now go. The torch will be of no use to you as the ceiling is so low. There is only one narrow way forward and you will still have some light to guide you once you're out."

She was right that the torch would have been a hindrance. I was soon on my knees, crawling through the narrow black space.

It seemed like hours of silent, dusty stumbling. Rocks tortured my knees and shredded my leggings. The long trek had taken a toll on my ankle. I tried to forget my pain and concentrate on putting distance between myself and the soldiers, inch by inch.

The tunnel started to rise and widen. My heart quickened.

After some twists and turns, a shaft of grainy, dim light

streaked the wall. Another turn, and a spill of rocks half blocked a gap in the tunnel.

My way out.

I clambered over the rocks, anticipating the first lungful of clean forest air, when my tunic caught on one of the jagged stones. I grunted and reached back to tug it free. It made a slight ripping sound as it came loose.

Triumphant, I reached up to launch myself from the musty tunnel.

Something stopped me. A tickle in my brain. A flutter of warning.

I froze. I had caught a hint of some scent. Sweat and horse.

I scrambled backward to lose myself in the cool darkness of the tunnel, but a hand flew out and wrapped itself around my wrist, dragging me forward over rocks.

As soon as I gained my feet, I threw my head back. My skull thudded against something, a nose or a chin, drawing a surprised grunt. I lashed out with my foot and heard another satisfying grunt as I connected with a shin. A heavy fist came down on the space between my shoulder and my neck. My hands and knees smacked into the packed earth.

"Filthy Fireblood," a man's voice said.

I was in a cave, a space the size of the library at the abbey. Light filtered in from an opening just ahead. Four soldiers surrounded me, all wearing the blue tunic with a white arrow.

Focus. Find your heat.

My teeth must have cut my cheek. The metallic taste of blood on my tongue helped me focus. I swallowed and closed my eyes, letting pressure build in my chest to send out a blast of heat.

"Oh no, you don't!" A boot landed on my back, sending me sprawling onto the earth. "Empty your casks!"

Cold water sloshed on me from all sides, enough to shock my senses and make me lose focus. It dripped over my neck and pooled under my cheek in the dirt. I squeezed my eyes shut, furious that my heat had been counteracted so easily.

"Is that her, Captain?" one of the soldiers asked.

"It is," said another voice. "That monk was as good as his word. A wisp of a Fireblood girl with black hair, just like the one who escaped."

I pushed upward onto my elbows. A solidly built figure blocked the sunlight from the cave opening.

"I've been searching for you for a long time, Firefilth," he said softly.

I blinked and his features came sharply into focus. The blunt nose, sharp cheekbones, and beard-roughened chin. The face that I had made myself remember over and over every day since I had landed in the king's prison. The one I had imagined scarred and burned and begging for mercy I would never show.

It was the captain who had killed my mother.

"Last time I saw you, you were soaking wet and half dead on the floor of Blackcreek Prison. How did you escape, I wonder?"

I started to shiver, that terrible night coming back to me in waves. I tried to focus on my heat, but fear and cold weakened me.

The soldiers closing in, the villagers retreating. Mother and I ringed by blazing torches...

Panic seized me. I put my hand out and sent a blast of heat at the soldier's face. He brought his leather-covered arm up, and it darkened with the blast. He snarled a command, and another splash of water covered my head.

"I'm not who you remember," I warned, wiping rivulets of water from my lips. "You captured a scared girl that night. I'm not scared anymore."

It was a lie. My stomach churned and my chest ached with the pounding of my heart.

I pressed my hands to the ground, heat spreading to cover the packed-earth floor of the cave. Some of the men cried out and lifted their feet in a comical dance, the thin, worn soles of their boots little protection from stinging heat. The captain, though, wore thick leather soles.

His mouth thinned. He grabbed my hair and pulled my head back, making me suck a pained breath through my nose. More water sloshed over me and I started to shiver.

"You Firebloods think you're so powerful, but all we need to defeat you is a little cold water."

I leveled him with my eyes. "I will kill you all with my dying breath."

His smile dimmed, but he recovered quickly.

"As much as I would love to choke the life out of that poison-ous throat, we have our orders. All the strongest Firebloods are taken directly to the king. He wants to decide the fate of your kind himself."

With every twitching muscle in my body and every wild flicker of heat in my soul, I wanted to blacken his skin and watch him wither and come apart.

But then Arcus's words came back to me: *Who else is there? What Fireblood will do this but you?*

If there was even the slightest chance I could still complete my task, I needed to try. I didn't know where Arcus was now, whether he was coming back or if he himself had been captured. Without him, I had no way of gaining entrance to the castle. Meanwhile, the soldiers would take me directly to the king. At this point, allowing myself to be captured was the best option.

I made a show of bowing my head in defeat. The captain rocked back on his heels, grinning at my trembling form. He clearly thought I was terrified and defeated.

"His Majesty was none too pleased when he found out a Fireblood had escaped his prison," he said. "It would have meant my life if I hadn't found you by the solstice."

"Then it's a pity you did," I said, meeting his eyes.

He leaned in to whisper in my ear. "After a few days in the keep, you may find yourself wishing we'd killed you now."

PART

TWO

SEVENTEEN

HE TRIP DOWN THE MOUNTAIN WAS almost as painful as the trip up. I was trussed and tied onto the back of a horse. Layers of wet linen were wrapped around me to keep me cool.

As we left the mountain behind, I ached with longing for the abbey, almost as much as I'd once ached for my cozy little hut near my village. I kept turning to look back, half expecting to see Arcus gallop up in pursuit. Everything was different between us now—he wouldn't just let them take me. But after a day or two, when Mount Una grew hazy behind us, I started to give up hope.

The land was barren on the ride north, and many of the dwellings were empty. The few people who peered out of windows as we rode past were sallow-cheeked and thin. I wondered how so few would manage to plant and reap the crops they so desperately needed.

After a week, we reached the rocky foothills of Mount Fors, broken by winding paths. The sun was low in the sky when the king's castle came into view, perched like a ragged stalagmite on the mountaintop. To the west, streaks of molten gold and bloody purple floated in the air like radiant scarves thrown into the sky. One side of the castle was lit brilliantly, the sunset reflecting and refracting off the ice in a dazzling display.

"Beautiful, isn't it, Firefilth?" said the captain as he rode alongside.

My jaw clenched. "If you like ice."

The lower portion of the mountain clutched at trees and scrub between gray rocks. As we climbed, the green became sparser and the ice dripped and oozed, first in pockets and patches, then thick, broad strokes. I was soon shivering, not only from the cold, but also from the sensation of being closed in on all sides by increasingly sheer, high frozen walls, as if the road had been cut out of the ice with a colossal knife.

We turned a corner and I was reduced to the size of an ant, for the road was lined on both sides by icy statues of enormous men. They were the Frost Giants I had read about in the old myths, symmetrical and perfect, formed of ice and given life by Fors. But there appeared to be no life in these statues. No movement, sound, or breath. My neck prickled as I passed, as if they watched me from somewhere inside the icy prison of their bodies.

We neared a huge iron gate embedded in the mountaintop.

Soldiers lined walls and held bows at the ready. It wasn't the arrows aimed at me that scared me, though. It was the frost wolves, white fur bristling, peering over the edge of the parapet. I'd heard stories of these keen-nosed creatures hunting Firebloods, for which they were specially bred.

One of the wolves raised its head sharply, sniffing the air and turning its twitching black nose in my direction. It fixed me with its icy eyes, wide and empty of anything but hunger, then raised its head and began to bay like a hound. The other wolves then went into a frenzy of sniffing and howling, voicing their fury that I was too far away for them to rip into and taste my hot blood.

The cacophony brought guards to the gates with swords raised.

"Name yourself!" called one wearing a steel helm.

Our party halted except for the captain, who rode forward. "Captain Drake, formerly of Blackcreek garrison. We have a Fireblood for the king."

The guard assessed me with thinly veiled hatred. I wondered if he had fought in the border wars and how many men he'd lost to Firebloods. I returned his look with equal animosity.

After a thorough examination, the guard waved us through. We crossed a stone bridge over a wide moat with chunks of ice floating in the water. Every now and then, a scaly white fin could be seen. I shuddered and trained my eyes forward.

We passed into a wide courtyard dotted with statues carved of ice. We dismounted and grooms rushed forward to take our mounts, all of them careful to keep their distance from me. As we moved on foot toward a tunnel that led to a massive door, there was a commotion from the right.

"Kill the Fireblood!" a voice screamed from the crowd that was watching nearby. A woman in a simple, faded dress hurried toward us, her white hair covered by a kerchief, her eyes wild. Her lined face was twisted into an ugly blend of pain and malice. "She killed my Cam, my only son!"

The captain stepped forward and gently stopped the woman as her long-fingered hands took swipes at me like a cat trying to reach a mouse. She turned her furious stare on the captain.

"How can you protect this murderer?" she shouted.

"I'm no murderer," I said shakily, disturbed by the intensity of her hatred. Likely, her son had died in battle and I was just the convenient face of her grief. "But your captain is."

He backhanded me across the face. "Shut your mouth, Firefilth."

I put a hand to my stinging cheek and blinked away the tears that pricked my eyes at the blow.

He turned back to the woman, his expression smoothing. "She'll be dead soon enough."

"Let me do it," she begged, her hands opening and closing. Seeing the vengeful hatred in her eyes, I had a strange moment of recognition, like I was looking at a grief-crazed version of myself. It chilled my soul.

"The king decides how she'll be punished," said the captain, his voice steady and persuasive. "Leave her to him. Leave her to me."

After a few panting breaths, she nodded, her shoulders slumping. She shot me one last hostile glare.

"Die slowly, murderer," she said, loud enough that the air echoed with it. "Die in pain."

I could feel her eyes boring into my back as the guards led me up wide white steps to the castle's massive iron door. My steps faltered and stopped as we entered, so overtaken with the grandness of the place I'd entered.

The interior of the castle was a monstrous ice cave. Here and there the ice came down to meet the floor in smooth, natural-looking columns. The ceiling was cold blue with repeating curves but with a smooth-looking surface, like a toad's skin. Light seemed to shine from it and through it, creating thousands of fractal patterns on the walls. In the center, where the ceiling rose up to form a dome, stalactites clustered in a sharp, strangely elegant chandelier.

In a few spots, gray stone walls were visible beneath the blue sheets. The castle must have been built of stone and then augmented and covered with ice.

The massive scale, the intense blues, the delicacy of the stalagmites and stalactites that reached for each other in various corners—the sheer, sweeping boldness of the room—pinned me in place and stole my breath.

"Move," the captain commanded, shoving me between the shoulder blades. I stumbled and shivered violently, my hands and feet aching with cold as they took me down a series of corridors, some wide, some narrow, all of them a mixture of stone and ice, to a wide archway.

Here the floor was made of colored stones set in an intricate mosaic of shapes that formed pictures. There were birds with berries in their beaks, horses with flying manes, frost wolves chasing a fire fox, fantastical creatures I had never heard of, gods and goddesses and mortals playing out the scenes of every myth I had ever read and many I hadn't. I was so immersed in it all that I barely noticed we had stopped.

I pulled my attention from the floor. About twenty paces away sat a massive throne of ice, its back soaring almost to the ceiling. Ice spread out from its base and up the walls like veins connected to a heart. It was a hulking monstrosity of thick, jagged ice that thrust upward like sharpened swords. Though the ends of the icicles were sharp, the texture of each was smooth, as if they'd been polished with merciless attention until no bumps or snags remained, all of it blindingly bright in the setting sun, which entered through a large window behind the throne.

Shadows cavorted inside the ice like wisps of black smoke.

This was no simple block of ice. It was *the* throne, crafted by Fors and pulsing with dark power.

Excitement surged through my body. I was in the presence of the throne. If Brother Thistle was right, its destruction would mean the healing of the kingdom. My people, whoever still lived, could return or come out of hiding. Perhaps a new ruler would take a new throne untainted by the curse.

But that depended on the imposing man currently seated on it. His robes were midnight blue, his hair and skin so pale they almost blended with the ice. His eyes were polished onyx. His hands rested on either side of him, a large sapphire glinting on the ring finger of one hand.

He was much younger than I'd expected, with no lines marking his glowing complexion. He couldn't be much older than I.

"We have a Fireblood for you," said the captain, his low voice echoing around the massive room.

Some invisible force seemed to take hold of me, as if the throne itself beckoned and repulsed me at the same time. A rough shove from behind sent me to my knees, my palms meeting the cold stone floor with a dull slap.

Dimly, I registered several people near the king turning to look at me, a tall man in fine robes to the right of the throne, a young woman in a plum velvet gown to his left, a cluster of what must have been courtiers in conversation.

The king stared down at us with perfect indifference. It was as if I were part of the floor, one of the birds with a berry in its mouth or one of the foxes being chased by a wolf. If it weren't for the movement of his eyes, I could have mistaken him for a statue.

One of his fair brows rose. "She's nothing but a skinny girl." No one could miss the crackle of scorn in his voice. "Your orders were to bring me the strong ones."

The captain cleared his throat. "This is the Fireblood who escaped Blackcreek Prison. She burned a dozen of my men without trying. I don't believe she is weak, Your Majesty." Though it seemed to hurt him to admit it.

"Where did you find her?" the king asked.

"In Forwind Abbey on Mount Una. We don't know why

worshippers of Fors would hide a Fireblood, but one of the monks was loyal to Your Majesty and sent word to our garrison. We're questioning the leader."

Choking ribbons of fear closed my throat. The thought of Brother Thistle being tortured for information about me was unbearable. I struggled to my feet.

The king's eyes narrowed on me. Goose bumps broke out on my flesh and my breath made puffs of mist. Even a look from the king was enough to half freeze me. I shuddered at the strength of his power.

"So, you care about the monks," he said, rubbing his jaw thoughtfully. "They must have been good to you, which suggests they were willing hosts."

I stumbled over my words a little as I tried to offer an explanation he might accept. "I claimed to be a refugee. They didn't know I was a Fireblood."

The captain gave a disbelieving snort. "The monk called Lack told us everything. They knew, and the old monk healed you anyway."

The old monk. *Brother Gamut. No.*

It was one thing to hurt me, but that gentle monk had spent his life among herbs and plants, his only goal to learn better ways to heal, just like my mother. Heat covered my skin.

I heard Brother Thistle's voice in my head. *Good. Now let that anger build....*

I focused on my heart but was shocked to find only tepid warmth. It was as if my fire was being pulled from my body, sucked away by an invisible siphon that left me cold and weak. My eyes widened and my throat closed.

If I couldn't access my heat, I was lost. The king. The throne—the destruction of both depended on my gift.

"Is there a problem, Fireling?" the king asked, his eyes narrowing to dark points, his lips twitching. "You look…a little cold."

As he said the words, my limbs went stiff. My feet wouldn't move. I realized they were mired in frost up to my ankles. My heart still beat hard in my chest; my breath came in panting bursts. But when I opened my mouth, whether to plead or threaten, my jaw was too stiff for speech. Sheer blind panic flooded my veins. I was completely and utterly at the king's mercy.

"You're accustomed to frost having little effect on you, aren't you?" He smiled, looking satisfied, like a well-fed cat. "Well, I'm no peasant. My power comes from the throne of Fors. It absorbs your heat."

The cold reached my stomach and was creeping toward my chest. My breathing slowed and my vision dimmed. So this was how the king killed Firebloods. As if through a fog, I saw his smile, felt his raw pleasure in the act of making me hurt.

I tried to force words from my frozen throat. Stars burst in front of my eyes.

The young woman in the plum gown stepped forward. She gave me an intense look from thickly lashed violet eyes before turning to the king.

"Pardon, Your Majesty," she said in a soft, melodious voice, "but would it not be a fine idea to let her fight? We haven't seen a Fireblood in the arena for several weeks. Perhaps it would raise the spirits of your soldiers to see your champions defeat a Fireblood, to remind them of our great victories. It could be an auspicious way to start the summer season of games."

Annoyance flickered in the king's eyes, but the woman's expression was patient, inquisitive, and hopeful. Her wheat-gold hair, lit from the window behind, was braided and twined on her head in an elegant style that suited her delicate features. I had the sense that if anyone else had been so brazen, they would have been frozen on the spot. But the king seemed to consider her words.

"My arena is for warriors and champions, and she is neither," he replied. "Fighting is a privilege that must be earned through a show of strength."

He tapped his fingers on the icy throne, the sapphire ring glinting in the light. The shadows in the ice shifted.

"She must be tested," said a voice that resonated in my head like a thousand chiming bells, excruciatingly loud. From what I could see, no one in the room showed signs that they had heard anything at all. The king's head was cocked slightly.

"She must be tested," the king repeated. He lifted his hand and made a careless gesture in my direction. The cold rushed away, leaving me boneless. "Take her to Gulzar. If she survives the beast, perhaps I'll consider allowing her into my arena. If not, at least my pet will have a hot meal."

The captain laughed and bowed low, then put a hand to the back of my neck and pushed me down.

"Your benevolent ruler just spared your life, Firefilth," he hissed into my ear. "Show your gratitude."

I stared at the floor, my mouth tight. There wasn't a scrap of gratitude in me.

"Thank him!" he ordered. Although I wanted nothing more than to blast the captain with flames, there was still the sense that my heat seeped from my body, dripping to the floor like blood. My head grew light. If I stayed much longer, I would lose consciousness. The king would declare me weak and I would lose any chance to prove myself.

"Thank you," I forced out through clenched teeth.

I was yanked up and spun around, then half marched, half dragged toward the arched doorway.

"There is something different about that one," said the voice of a thousand chiming bells. I spun around to see who was speaking and saw only the king, his eyes blacker than tar. I turned away, but I felt his narrow-eyed stare press on me as I was led from the room.

EIGHTEEN

"THE BEAST HAS LONG ARMS," SAID one of the guards in a glib tone, his face pressed to the steel bars above my head. "Best to stay out of reach."

I had been thrust into a dark underground space, a roughly round room made of stone. Ice coated one wall. The only light came from an opening overhead. The smiling faces of a cluster of guards stared down.

"And should I stay away from its mouth, too?" I mocked, struggling to cover my fear. "Or curtsy and welcome it to pick its teeth with me?"

"You do look a bit like a toothpick," he said with a wide grin.

The heat that had been suppressed in the throne room rose

to the surface. I lifted a hand to roast him with a carefully aimed spiral of fire when the floor shook.

Then another sound, quieter but far more alarming. Great puffs of air, as if they had come from a large bellows.

Breathing. Sniffing. The shuffle of feet.

Terror sharpened my senses. I crouched in the ready position that Brother Thistle had taught me. In my mind, I heard him say that fighting is first about calming and focusing the mind. I took several long, shuddering breaths.

A hook high on the wall held four long chains. I ran to them and pulled myself up using footholds in the wall. I managed to get several feet off the ground. Relief pulsed through me. Much better than being on the floor.

The beast came into view, a lighter shadow in the tunnel beyond the gate. Its body was shaggy and thick with a dirty, ragged coat that might once have been white but was now a muddy gray. Here and there, tufts of matted fur formed ridges that stuck out at odd angles. Its nose traced the floor, its humped back reaching halfway to the ceiling, each padded foot leaving an oval of sparkling ice in its wake. It sniffed and shuffled, following an invisible line of scent to the spot where I had just stood, then lifted its huge head and looked around.

I wasn't high enough on the wall, not nearly. Even the ceiling wouldn't be out of its reach. A long arm with razorlike claws took a tentative swipe in my direction.

A rough chuckle came from above my head.

"I warned you about its arms," said the guard cheerily.

"Shut up," I snarled, pushing off the wall with my feet while holding the chain and flying toward the beast's outstretched paw. It was like kicking a boulder. I yelped and fell to the ground, rolling out of reach.

The beast turned and lumbered after me, huge and slow but determined, plumes of frost curling from its open mouth. There was nowhere to go, nowhere to get momentum or to take a breath of rest. I backed toward the open gate.

The guard's voice came down again. "There's nothing back there unless you fancy a pile of bones."

I believed him. There would be no way out.

I laid a wall of sizzling flame around myself. The beast reared back onto its hind legs, its loud exhalations mixed with my own jagged breathing. But the cold stone floor put out the fire. If I didn't wrest some control back from the wild fear, I would be dead.

I connected with the concentric rings of heat around my heart, pulling it forward into my hands, and sent a spiral of flame at the beast's chest. The flame sizzled off bits of ice that clung to the animal's fur. The beast kept coming. I threw a handful of fire at its face, catching it on the nose. It roared in pain and shook its massive head a few times before fixing its eyes on me again.

"You don't want to eat me," I said softly. "I would bubble and boil in your stomach and make you hurt. You don't want me."

It cocked its giant head.

"I'm a poor meal. All skin and bone. I would catch in your throat and choke you. I would burn your throat."

It moved slowly now, stopping to listen every time I spoke. If I could just get it near its lair, maybe I could use my fire to drive it back and pull the gate closed. I walked toward the gate, talking the whole time, the beast slowly following me.

"Aw, this isn't any fun," said one of the guards.

"What do you think we should do?" said the other. "Throw water down on her?"

I kept my eyes on the beast, my heart pounding, and threw an arrow of fire upward at the grate.

The guard yelped. "Well, she doesn't seem to want to play with us. We'd better let her get some rest. She'll feel better in the morning. Good night, Firefilth."

I heard something sliding as the room dimmed. The guard was covering the opening, my only source of light, with a board.

"No, please!" I screamed, all determination not to show weakness wiped away by dread.

A muffled laugh echoed as the board scraped into place. The room was black and silent but for the breathing of the beast in the dark.

My heart raced. My breath came in gasps. A scream built at the back of my throat. I jammed my fist against my mouth.

Stop. Think. Remember your training.

I took a breath and tried to find the quiet place in my mind.

I calmed a little and remembered something that could help me: the beast was a thing of frost. I could sense its cold.

I'd spent hours practicing this while wearing a blindfold. And the beast wasn't as silent as Arcus had been. I had two senses to help me.

The thing was sniffing the floor. I could hear its nose scraping the stone as it came closer. I sensed its frost, felt its cold breath on my face as it opened its mouth.

I dove out of the way, feeling it brush past me as I rolled on the floor and came to my feet. A draft brushed against my back. That must be the tunnel to the beast's lair. I didn't want to back myself in there. I moved away from it, my hands out.

Sniffing. Cold breath.

I threw myself to the right as a breeze from the leaping creature brushed past, my hand slapping the wall. Cold to my left. I moved along the wall to the right, sliding my hands along the stone. I paused, my senses on alert, and realized the sniffing had stopped. It was silent. The beast couldn't be smart enough to realize I could hear it. Could it?

A rush of cold built in front of me. I threw myself to the side, but not fast enough. A blade-sharp claw sliced my leg, cleaving a gash into my calf. I sucked in a breath and kept scuttling to the right. The beast sniffed and roared, clearly excited by the smell of my blood.

I sensed it was a few feet away to my right, coming closer. I moved quietly, slowly, but it moved with me. I raged silently against the blood dripping from my calf. The beast could smell me now, no matter where I moved.

Arcus had told me to be aware of my surroundings, to use them to my advantage. Where were those blasted chains? Maybe I could use them as a weapon, catch the beast in the eye.

I moved along the wall, stopping when I came to the drafty tunnel. If I crossed that point when the creature came at me, I might be driven back into that hopeless space. I hovered, unsure what to do.

The cold came at me unbelievably fast. I had no time to do anything but curl into a ball as its teeth grazed my back and arms.

Without thinking, I pulled my arms free and threw fire behind me from my open palms and into the creature's mouth.

Something sizzled and popped, liquid exploding around me like a burst bubble. Bones snapped and the body collapsed on me in a shocking flare of cold. I stayed still for a minute, dazed by the suddenness of the attack and the strength of my own inadvertent response. When my head cleared, I struggled out from under the dripping carcass, gasping as the freezing liquid soaked through my clothes and slid down my back.

"Get me out of here, you idiot guards," I shouted, relief making me light-headed and a little giddy. "I killed your foul beast."

The board scraped back, letting in a sliver of light.

"You're still alive, Toothpick?" asked one of the guards, his voice high with disbelief.

"What does it look like?" I said shakily. I motioned to the body, squinting as the light hit my eyes. The sight was revolting, a steaming pile of burned and smoking flesh. But it was a welcome sight.

"Looks like a melon exploded in there," he said gleefully, pointing to the dark blue blood dripping from the walls.

"By Fors, she did it," said the other guard. "You did it, Firefilth, I'll give you that. But the king won't be happy that you killed his pet."

I panted, looking up at him for a few seconds. "I'd have been less happy if I were in that stomach right now."

A hint of a smile lifted the guard's lip.

Elation and shock numbed my fingers and toes. I'd done it. I had beaten incredible odds and defeated the beast. Despite my bravado for the guards' benefit, I couldn't quite believe it. For several moments, I felt invincible.

A shadow shifted in the ice on the far wall, moving like black smoke. It had a vaguely human shape, a head with horns and two pointed shoulders. Wisps of something like hands floated at its sides. A chill far colder than ice rushed through my veins. Then it slipped away, faster than my eye could follow.

The captain's face came into view above. His voice rang out, ordering his guards back to work. He took a long look at me through the bars.

I wiped my hands on the stone. "This thing stinks almost as bad as your soldiers."

His eyes narrowed. "Nothing stinks worse than a Fireblood."

He dusted off his hands before turning away, as if speaking to me had sullied him.

Alone again, I slid until my head met the floor, huddled into myself, and closed my eyes.

I was so cold. I searched my memories and found one that

made my heart clench: the look in Arcus's eyes just before he kissed me, his cold lips warming under mine, his ice-chip eyes shining as he looked at me between kisses, like I was something precious and rare and beautiful.

Warmth flickered in my chest. I clutched the feeling to me even as I was hauled up and led to a cell in the king's keep.

NINETEEN

THE CELL IN THE KEEP WASN'T SO
different from the one in Blackcreek Prison. Same stone floors,
a bed of straw in the corner, a small window. An old man in
stained, stinking robes came in and bandaged my leg. His hands
were rough and he used no healing herbs, so different from
Brother Gamut with his gentle touch and miraculous tea.

I closed my eyes and asked Sud to protect those dear to me:
Arcus, Brother Thistle, Brother Gamut, Sister Pastel, and every
monk whose name I could remember, listing them again and
again until I fell asleep.

In the morning, I was given a basin for washing, then dressed
in sturdy clothes: a brown tunic and leggings. From there, I
was taken by guards and presented to the king. As I entered the

throne room, something again snatched my heat in an invisible fist and held on tight. I trembled with the effort of keeping myself under control and my face blank.

The king was resplendent in robes of deep blue with gold trim. The sapphire ring glinted on his hand, echoing the color of his eyes, which had seemed darker the day before. Bright morning sunlight poured through the window behind him. He lounged in the throne with an air of ease. As I halted, a spark lit his eyes, a little glint of anticipation that made him seem even younger somehow. If it had been anyone else, I would have thought him attractive.

The throne looked clear today. No shadows moved in its depths.

The same bearded man and young woman stood to the king's right. As my eyes slid over the golden-haired girl, who wore a long-sleeved turquoise gown, I judged her to be roughly my age or a little older. She returned my look and her cheek dimpled as if she was holding in a smile, not mocking but warm, almost friendly. I blinked in surprise and looked away.

"You killed my beast," said the king, his voice echoing off the icicles hanging from the ceiling. "Seven men were killed and seven more maimed to get that creature here from Mount Sarcassa. And now you've destroyed it."

He seemed to wait for a response. I worked to keep the hatred out of my voice. It would do no good to get myself executed for insolence. "That was the task you gave me, Your Majesty."

"Nevertheless, you've taken away a source of pleasure, a

favorite in my arena. I wonder what compensation you can offer for that loss." Although the words were accusing, there was an almost playful quality to his tone.

I blinked, trying to adjust to his change in demeanor from the day before. "You find pleasure in watching your champions killed?"

"I enjoy watching two powerful creatures fight, and so do my people. Isn't that right, Lord Ustathius?"

The bearded man agreed, stepping forward, his chin taking on an arrogant tilt. "Just so, Your Majesty. It is always a curious thing to see who wins. The champion may be ferocious or disciplined, ruthless or principled, but they all die in the end. It provides a critical lesson: There is no security but in power. Power always wins."

The king nodded almost reflexively, as if he were used to agreeing with this courtier. It reminded me that the king was much younger than he seemed with his cold, cruel eyes.

"Power matters," the king agreed. "All other qualities are merely decoration."

So in their eyes, people like my mother who were gentle and spent their lives healing others didn't matter at all. Heat bubbled up in my chest, but the throne whisked it away so quickly it made me ache. I struggled not to put a hand to my chest.

"Well," I said, "by your measure, I'm worthy because I defeated your beast. I was more powerful and should have a chance to win again."

He regarded me for long seconds, his eyes slightly narrowed.

"Yesterday, I was certain you were weak." Another pause. "I don't like being wrong."

"No one likes being wrong," I replied, forgetting to hide the scorn that burned my throat.

Something glittered in his eyes. Primitive fear tightened my spine and sharpened my senses. But I held the king's gaze. The room seemed to narrow until it contained only the two of us.

"You speak with reckless freedom, Fireling," he said in a low voice. "And yet I could kill you with very little effort."

At his words, the shadows in the throne sprang to life, swirling up behind the king in a thick, smoky cloud. He suddenly looked older, harder. His eyes darkened.

I had nothing to bargain with, no leverage against the king. I needed to show him I had value to him. And the only thing he valued was strength.

"Yes," I said. "You could. But then you would never know how powerful I am."

A smile lit the young woman's face. The bearded man next to the king took a step forward. "This will not be like facing a witless beast. His Majesty's champions have fought their way to the arena and will stop at nothing to kill you."

"You can't win against my champions," the king agreed. His tone was dismissive, his conviction so strong, as if the matter was already decided.

I changed tack, attempting a tone of brave unconcern. "If you kill me now, you'll miss the pleasure of watching me lose in your arena. My death might be the most spectacular you've ever seen.

Surely you can't resist the prospect of watching my blood spilled for your entertainment."

Something dark flashed over his face. His gaze swept over me in the pulsing silence.

If I wanted to destroy the throne, I had to live. To live, I had to win. And to win, he had to give me a chance to fight. I waited, barely breathing.

The young woman with wheat-gold hair gave a light laugh, breaking the thick tension. "She argues well, Your Majesty. There is nothing worse than a quick, boring death in the arena. She would give a champion good sport, I'm sure."

The king relaxed visibly, his eyes glittering blue with mirth and making him look younger again. He addressed the guard. "Put her in the room reserved for a challenger."

I clenched my muscles to hide my shaking relief, though I knew I would have to face highly trained and merciless enemies. No matter how much I had trained at the abbey, I wasn't prepared to go up against that level of skill.

"And, Fireling," the king added with a glint of steel in his eye, "I will hold you to your promise of a spectacular death. Don't succumb too quickly. The sport is in watching the struggle."

I curtsied low. "I will do my best to die slowly to please Your Majesty."

As the guards turned and took me from the room, his dark laughter followed me.

The guard led me to a windowless room with a simple wooden bed and a washstand. So another prison, albeit a more comfortable one. When the door shut behind me, I turned and knocked on it experimentally. It was thick, but it was made of wood. I could burn my way through. Then again, even if I managed to escape and somehow made it past the guards, my goal was still to destroy the throne. And I had no idea how.

I lay on the straw-stuffed mattress and stared at the stone ceiling, trying to recall everything Brother Thistle had told me about the throne. But I couldn't remember anything about it stealing my power and how to overcome that. Maybe he hadn't known.

The door swung open and two guards stepped in. One put a tray of food on the floor, then they swung out. On the tray, a large wooden bowl held a thick stew with a hunk of bread on the edge. I rushed over and took a bite, closing my eyes in pleasure to find it piping hot.

I was back on the straw-stuffed mattress when the door opened again. I slid off the bed and found my feet, my limbs moving automatically into a pose of readiness, knees bent, fists raised to defend myself.

A woman swept in, her full, deep plum satin skirts swishing around the door before she closed it behind her. Her eyes widened as she took in my stance, her wheat-gold eyebrows lifting.

"Ready to fight, I see," she said in her elegant voice. "Good. But save your strength for the arena. You'll need it."

It was the young woman from the throne room, the one who

had helped persuade the king to let me fight. Forcing the muscles to relax, I lowered my fists.

"Who are you?"

Her gaze swept my room. "A little rustic, these quarters. If you win enough matches, they might find a nicer room for you. That's some incentive. Also, you'll be alive. That's reason enough to come out swinging."

"I thought you wanted me to die a spectacular death."

"That is what I said." She paused, assessing me. "My name is Marella. My father, Lord Ustathius, is the other man who spoke today, the king's most trusted advisor, serving three kings in succession. You'll find I'm a valuable ally."

The arrogant old man who had droned on about power being the only thing that mattered. I couldn't see how I, in my current position of powerlessness, could matter to him, or to his daughter.

"And what did I do to earn your..." I hesitated, not sure how to describe what this young woman offered.

"Friendship?" she supplied. "It's simple. Stay alive. Win your matches. Be faster and stronger than your opponents."

I raised my arms. "I'm hardly going to be the strongest."

"Not your muscles, perhaps. But your fire. Use it to its fullest. Be ruthless."

"I didn't expect anyone here to encourage me to be ruthless with my fire, especially against one of your own."

"That's the only reason you're still alive," she said. "To provide sport by trying to kill one of the king's champions. If you lie down and welcome death, I've troubled myself for nothing."

"How have you troubled yourself?"

"I've risked the king's displeasure by suggesting he let some-one else kill you, for a start."

"Was that really such a risk?"

"The king is volatile and highly unpredictable. He isn't in control of himself. He yields to the whispers of…others…who urge him to fill his appetites for bloodlust and cruelty. Say the wrong thing and you may find yourself in the keep, or in the arena. Or killed at his own hand. So yes, Ruby. It was a great risk."

I startled a little at the sound of my name. She could have called me Fireling, as the king had, or Firefilth, as the captain so enjoyed doing, but instead she chose to give me the honor of my name.

"You dare say such things about the king?" I asked, barely above a whisper.

Her brows rose. "Are you going to tell anyone?"

I shook my head.

Her lips curved at the edges. "Of course not. You're intelligent. And we both want the same thing. For you to live."

"Why do you care? What does a Fireblood mean to you?"

"We have more in common than you think. I want to be, if not a friend, precisely, then at least an ally. If you can't accept me as that, perhaps think of me as an enemy who shares a common goal with you."

"And that goal is?"

She spread her hands and smiled. "For now, your goal is simple: stay alive. That will be difficult enough."

"And you want nothing else from me?"

She paused thoughtfully. "A few answers, perhaps. How old are you?"

"Seventeen."

Her eyes lit with triumph. "Brother Thistle must have been ecstatic to find you."

I felt the blood drain from my face. "You know him?"

"Of course. He used to serve here in the castle before he was sent to the abbey at Mount Una. And speaking of the abbey, who is the mysterious young man who lived there with you? The one who always wears a hood?"

I barely stopped myself from asking how she knew about Arcus. Then I remembered that he had grown up here, in the king's court. Marella must have known him. How tempting to ask her questions about him, what he was like as a child, what had happened to him. But I couldn't risk revealing anything to this stranger.

"All the monks wear hoods at times," I said.

"Not a monk. A handsome young man who bears scars. A Frostblood with a gift unequaled by anyone but the king. Does that sound familiar?"

I shook my head, my pulse raging in my ears. "No."

Her lips curved again. "Very well. Trust is built slowly. I can be patient."

She went to the door and knocked. A guard opened it immediately.

"Remember, Ruby," she said over her satin-covered shoulder. "Don't hold back tomorrow and you have every chance to win."

She swept out, as graceful as a young doe, leaving the scent of some exotic flower in her wake.

A thousand questions crashed through my thoughts, like waves breaking over each other in a gale. What did Marella and her father want? How did she know about Arcus and Brother Thistle? What was her intention toward the king? She was clearly full of plans and saw me as a vehicle for their execution. What would she ask in return for keeping me from death in the throne room? What help would she yet give?

I threw myself back on the bed. I had one day to rest. Tomorrow I would fight. It didn't matter that Marella intended to help me outside the arena. Inside its walls, I would stand alone.

I couldn't help but remember what Brother Thistle had said when I'd asked him and Arcus if Firebloods were ever champions.

We have never heard of a Fireblood coming out alive.

TWENTY

THE NEXT MORNING, A SERVING woman entered carrying a bundle of clothes. She wore a simple brown dress and a matching kerchief over her brown hair, which was plaited and hung down her back. She was several years older than I, with a slim build and delicate features: a heart-shaped face and large, frightened eyes.

"I'm to help you dress," she said, her voice quavering slightly.

"What's your name?" I asked, clasping my hands together to hide their shaking. I had slept badly.

"Dor-Doreena," she replied, her eyes flicking up to meet mine before returning to the worn wooden floorboards. "I serve the champions."

I sighed. "Are you afraid of all Firebloods or just me?"

Her round eyes grew even bigger. "I'm sorry, my lady. I don't mean to offend."

"You don't offend me," I replied. "And I have never been called 'my lady' in my life. Call me Ruby."

She shook her head. "I couldn't, my lady."

Her hands trembled as she laid a tunic and leather armor on the bed. It was strange to realize that while I was terrified of what would happen in the arena, a servant was afraid of me. No doubt she'd heard stories about Firebloods being merciless killers or some such thing.

I kept up a constant chatter, partly to put her at ease and partly because her nervousness made my own worse. I talked about my village and how strange it was to be in such a grand place when I'd grown up in a thatch-roofed hut, and how I'd never worn armor and would have no idea how to put it on without her help. Anything to make me seem more innocuous.

She was silent, but her hands no longer shook as she held out the bloodred tunic. She was very careful not to touch me.

As I adjusted the tunic, I decided I was tired of my own voice and asked her a question. "You said you serve the champions, Doreena?"

She nodded.

"Is there anything you can tell me that might help in the arena? Anything at all?"

She picked up a leather breastplate and held it in her hands for a few moments before speaking.

"You have a better chance if you win the crowd," she said in her quiet voice.

She lifted the breastplate and I put my arms through. I felt a little dizzy at the hard feel of it against my chest. Wearing armor made the impending fight seem much more real, the thought that it was to protect me from blows or blades.

"Has the crowd ever been won over by a Fireblood?" I winced as she closed the straps at my back. "Ow, a bit too tight."

She loosened the straps and then stood in front of me, her rosebud lips pursed as she examined me. "I've never heard of any Fireblood who was loved by the crowd. Perhaps you will be the first."

It didn't seem likely. The Frostbloods had come to watch me die, in payment for all the parents and children they had lost in conflicts with my people before we were wiped clean from the kingdom. My fear and anger must have shown on my face because Doreena stepped back.

"How do you know so much?" I asked with a forced smile.

"I have served the champions for two years. I hear them talk."

"And what else have you heard that might be of use to me? Do you have any tips?"

She blinked in surprise and gnawed her lip before answering. "It's difficult when I don't know who you'll be facing. I suppose all I can offer is that everyone has a weakness. Try to pay attention. Many of the champions have injuries—some part of their body they protect, something they favor. If you spot their weakness, focus all your attacks on that spot. And…well, you're small. Keep your distance. If they get hold of you, you don't stand a chance."

If I hadn't been so nervous, I would have laughed. "At least you're honest."

"Honest to a fault, I'm told. Perhaps I shouldn't have said anything."

"No, I'm grateful for your advice."

She held up a piece of soft calf leather, dyed black. "Here is your mask."

It had openings for eyes, nose, and mouth. It reminded me of the mask Arcus wore during training.

Thinking of him at all was painful, but remembering the way I had burned his hood and mask and the way he'd cried out in shock was terrible. My throat closed up and I blinked hard.

Instead, I concentrated on what he had said to me, that I was the most dangerous person he had ever known. My only chance at survival depended on my ability to be deadly.

When Doreena put on my mask, it covered everything but my eyes, a small triangle under my nose, and my mouth. I hated it instantly. It choked me, the idea that I was some faceless body sent to die for the king's entertainment. I whipped it off and threw it to the floor.

"Sorry," I said to Doreena, her wide-eyed look making me embarrassed by my sudden rage. "I can't breathe in that."

"It's either wear a mask or a helm," she said, twisting her hands together. "You must have your face covered. It's tradition that opponents meet on even ground, noblemen and peasants alike. They're only unmasked once they're dead."

A cheerful thought.

"Well then, find me a mask that allows me to breathe, because I'm not wearing that. And a helm would be too heavy."

She nodded. "I will find you something."

In a short while, she returned with a mask that covered my eyes. It was overly ornate, decorated with red feathers and seed pearls. When I asked her where she'd found it, she blushed a deep shade of pink.

"It's from a mistress of one of the noblemen," she said. "She had a secret to keep and I have kept it. She owes me."

"What kind of secret?" I asked, curious what could cause such a blush.

"It's not uncommon for nobles to desire a night with the champions. I'm valued for my discretion."

I smiled, looking at her with new interest. "I do believe I like you, Doreena. You're a survivor."

"And so, I hope, are you, my lady."

As I fell into step with the guards, our booted feet made the rhythm of a battle march that echoed the susurration of blood in my ears. We passed from the castle and into the courtyard and from there, through a tunnel that led into the great arena. The guards left me in the shade of an alcove reserved for those about to fight.

My heart pounded so hard my vision blurred. I closed my eyes and took deep breaths and then forced myself to assess my surroundings.

There were fighters of all kinds: mostly men in ragged clothes and others in steel breastplates, some with gleaming sword hilts above decorated scabbards, some with no weapons at all. There were a few women, though it took me a moment to realize that, as they were broad-shouldered and armored and looked as imposing as the men. I wondered how they'd fought their way here and what their lives had been like to bring them to a place like this.

I'd never seen so many people in one place. The arena was built of ice, the smooth circular walls giving the impression of a huge bowl. Tier after tier of seats grew out of the inner wall, curving around the arena on all sides. The excited noise of a thousand people produced the hum of an immense hive, disconcertingly loud and incoherent.

Balconies jutted out at intervals, holding spectators who were finely dressed, with puffs of frosty air coming from their mouths. Few clouds of frost rose from the folks packed into the regular seats. Apparently the nobility were more likely to have the gift than the common rabble.

As the guards left, they pointed out a woman called Braka, a tall, broad-shouldered warrior with steely gray eyes who was moving from fighter to fighter, sharing pointers and encouragement. Icicles hung from her metal shoulder-guards and clustered over her thick salt-and-pepper hair, which was arranged in a plethora of braids. I gathered she was responsible for training the Frostblood champions, though no such training had been offered to me. Not that I expected it. I clasped my hands behind my back to hide their shaking.

Before I could decide what to do next, or where I should be, a rotund man with short white hair and deep indigo robes stepped into the center of the arena.

"Good people of Fors," he boomed over the buzz of the crowd. He raised his hands and the noise quieted. "Today, for your edification and enjoyment, we present a variety of fighters, from lowly thieves and traitors to beloved champions. We bring you marvelous beasts, exotic animals from near and far. And as always, we bring you spectacle, entertainment, and feats of strength and daring that will leave you breathless with delight. You honor your king by cheering for his champions and cursing his enemies. May the deaths be honorable and the fights be bloody!"

My legs twitched with the urge to run. I gripped the icy wall, hoping the cold biting into my hand would help focus my mind. Instead, I found myself doubled over, a hand to my stomach, breathing shallowly as I fought to stay upright.

The pounding of hooves reverberated through the ground. Riders on white horses poured out of a wide opening at the other end of the arena, the morning sun glinting off polished armor. They wore bright helms and carried long spears topped with points of ice, sharp as steel. The riders were followed by champions on foot, their appearance drawing adoring cries from the crowd. Next, a procession of animals pulled against leather leashes held by muscular handlers. Snarling frost wolves, hulking white bears, a wide-faced tiger with white-and-blue stripes, even a massive white bull with gray horns and a yoke around its neck held by two men on each side.

The next animal was very strange. It was a large bird with crimson feathers, long legs, and small wings. Its beak looked deadly sharp. It writhed and pulled against its handlers, at one point pulling its face loose from the harness and breathing a cloud of fire. I gasped with the crowd.

A creature of fire, here in the city of Fors.

The bird was lovely, elegant, wild. It was dangerous and impossible and unlike anything I had ever seen. It hurt my heart to see such strange beauty leashed and so out of place. The animal thrashed so hard against its handler that I feared it would snap its delicate neck.

A strong urge to run out and free the animal flashed through me. But a moment later, the animals were led back through the door. Only the frost wolves were left in the arena, their mouths emitting puffs of cold mist that danced in the sunlight.

A man was brought out by two guards, his hands bound. The purple-robed announcer introduced him as a traitor to the realm. The crowd answered with shouts of fury. The wolf handlers gave a command, and the wolves all sat, their bodies trembling with anticipation as the handlers took off the leashes and left the arena. The prisoner backed slowly toward the edge of the ring.

From the doorway, one of the handlers shouted a command, and the wolves shot forward like arrows from a longbow, their haunches rippling as they closed in. The prisoner screamed and I cried out with him. In a blink, he was out of sight as the wolves fell over one another to get at him. The man's cries were almost drowned out by the roar of the crowd. Almost, but not quite. I stumbled into a dark corner, my stomach heaving over and over until it was empty.

The announcer introduced more animals and more traitors. More cries of pain, more growling and snapping and cheers. I was dizzy and sick and no longer comprehending things clearly. When I looked up again, a blue-and-white-striped tiger was lifting its bloody muzzle from a prone body as its handler threw a harness over the animal's head and led it from the arena.

"And now, good people," said the announcer, his voice cheerful and clear, "for a rare treat, the Firebeak will face our most seasoned champions."

Six armored warriors entered the arena. The bird was pulled out by two handlers, who struggled to keep it controlled. The creature's eyes rolled wildly, its talons clawing the dirt as it bucked against the leash. The handlers released it and ran for the arena door as the bird shook off its harness and breathed a cloud of fire, the flame making orange light dance along the ice.

The champions raised their shields and sent out streams of frost from their hands. Ice formed on the bird's feathers. It breathed another cloud of fire that faded to a puff of smoke. The men retreated.

Streams of frost and fire shot back and forth. The champions kept moving back. They were clearly afraid of the fire. Hope expanded in my chest. The bird was fast. It whipped back and forth, spewing fire in thin streams aimed right at the men's faces. It seemed like the bird would never run out of energy or fire.

But my hope didn't last. The champions spread out in a wide

circle until the bird was in the center. As soon as it breathed its fire at one man, another came at its back, too quickly for it to block. The bird was wily and tried to avoid the frost, but there were just too many men and eventually it was hit from all sides and fell. The warriors rushed forward as a group. A stream of fire erupted upward as six arms were raised and six spears came down. A second cloud of fire, smaller this time, floated upward, followed by a puff of smoke. More raising and lowering of spears and more cheers from the crowd. As the champions left the arena and the dust settled, the bird was still. It looked so small, its beak too delicate, its feathers incongruously bright against the dull ground. Its long neck was bent strangely, bringing to mind another memory of a delicately bent neck surrounded by dark hair.

Everything came into sharp focus. The pain and suffering of the animal cut me deeply.

The Firebeak was dragged from the arena, and the regular matches began, each more brutal than the last. At first, raggedly dressed men with short swords or knives faced each other. When it was too much, I closed my eyes, but I could hear the crowd cheering, the pained cries as sharp metal pierced flesh. The healer's daughter in me ached with helpless fury at the cruelty, the needless waste.

By the third match, I was leaning against the wall, my legs completely numb. I finally let myself sink to the floor and realized my face was wet with tears.

"Get up, girl," said a harsh voice. I looked up at Braka and her icy braids. "You're a challenger now. There's no room for tears."

"You saw what they did to the Firebeak," I said, my voice hoarse and cracking. "Is that what they plan for me?"

"You're being allowed a fair fight against one champion," she said, her eyes as steady as her voice. "You have as much chance as any other challenger. Don't let them see you crying. Face them all like a warrior, whether you are one or not."

Gathering my will, I pushed up and leaned against the wall as Braka walked away. I wanted to tell her that I didn't care about honor, but instead I said a prayer to Sud and went back to the doorway, watching as the fighters went from raggedly dressed peasants to men in leather armor with gleaming swords.

The fight that drew the most excitement was between two gifted Frostbloods with no weapons but their hands and their ice. I tried to take in the attacks and parries, hoping it might help me somehow. When one of the Frostblood fighters finally slipped and fell, the other one finished him off with a shard of ice through his throat. I turned away as the champion basked in the crowd's approval.

"You're next, Fireblood," said Braka in a low rumble. "The names have been drawn and you're to fight Gravnach...one of the most favored champions."

From the opposite side of the arena, wooden doors opened and out walked a bear of a man. He was dressed in black leather with bright steel armor covering one arm from shoulder to wrist. And here I saw what Doreena had meant about winning the crowd. This man knew how. He walked in wide circles, stopping to raise his arms and roar in a theatrical way. The crowd responded with wild cheers.

"At the sound of the gong, you fight," Braka said. "Once it begins, it won't stop until you're dead. Die with honor, Fireling."

It didn't escape me that she no longer claimed I had a chance. I turned to look her in the eye, determined to show strength.

"You mean until Gravnach is dead."

She smiled, showing a missing tooth, and gave a small dip of her chin before turning away.

I moved into the shadows near the arched entrance to the arena. Every contraction and release of my heart seemed to last a hundred years, the moments stretching into an eternity of agonized anticipation. The gong sounded and the moment snapped into focus.

I stepped into the arena, squinting into the glare. The shouts of adulation turned to a chorus of hoots and jeers. My chest grew tight. I fought a dizzy, overpowering need to run.

As my terrified gaze swept the crowd, the sun caught a bright flash of gold: the king in a raised viewing box bounded by elaborate filigree railings carved of ice. He wore a gold crown set with sapphires. If it weren't for the searing cold in his dark eyes, I might have thought him beautiful, a warm golden idol sitting among the endless shades of blue. He had an air of lazy expectance, as if ready for some diversion but not sure it was worth his attention.

I lifted my chin. I thought I caught the hint of a mocking grin in return.

Marella stood next to him, her brows drawn together, her jaw tight. As our eyes met, her brows smoothed and she gave a slight smile. She mouthed one word: *Win*. At least I had one person who believed in me.

A chant started in one corner of the stands and built like a gathering wave that crashed over the crowd, the whole arena throbbing with the pounding beat.

"Gravnach! Gravnach! Gravnach!"

The massive champion had his back to me, as if the presence of a challenger was beneath his notice. The chant beat its way into my skull, sapping my energy. I had to do something, anything to shake off the paralyzed fear that was seizing hold of me. Raising my hands, I sent a blast of fire rolling along the ground. When it reached Gravnach's feet, he jumped and wheeled around. The crowd hissed and called out, "Kill the Fireblood!"

I expected their hatred, but the intensity of it shocked me.

The crowd faded out of focus as Gravnach pounded toward me in a long-legged run. I waited for him to stop, expecting we would circle each other the way other fighters had. Instead, he kept coming, like a huge fallen tree rolling down a hill, and me no more than a patch of weeds to be crushed in his path. I fought the urge to run.

When he was close enough that I saw the whites of his eyes, I threw myself to the side and swirled a blast of fire at him. He blocked it with two raised forearms and an explosion of cold that stung my face.

Breathless and frustrated, I sent out a series of arrows, aiming for the openings in his defenses. Most of them fell away from him with a sizzle, but a few found their mark, landing on his mask or on his skin with a hiss. He took a step back, and I had a moment of triumph.

Then he bellowed and sent a wave of frost along the ground that slid under my feet. I slipped and landed on my back. The sense of vulnerability was terrifying. For a second, I was motionless, but when he threw himself toward me, I snapped into action and rolled out of the way, sliding to my feet. I sent bolts of fire behind me to gain some time, then whirled and faced him again. *Don't stop moving*, I told myself. *Don't think; just move.*

The crowd grew louder. "Gravnach, Gravnach, Gravnach!" The chant hit me over and over like a blacksmith's hammer, pounding my nerves thin.

My opponent circled me slowly. His small black eyes were full of annoyance beneath his mask. I had failed to beg for mercy or whatever it was that most opponents did within seconds of fighting him. At least, that was what I told myself: I was stronger than all the others. I would win.

Faster than I would have thought possible for such a large man, he stepped forward and swept two curving walls of ice on either side of me. I extended my arms and sent out spirals of heat, stumbling backward as he advanced. He threw thin streams of ice over me, making a loose cage. My face must have shown my panic because he smiled at me through the icy bars.

Don't think; move.

I threw out a hand and blasted a hole. As I slipped out, he

threw up a wall of frost behind me and slapped me with frigid air. I stumbled backward and slammed into the wall he'd created before scrambling away.

There was a pattern here. His moves were like little tests, almost playful in their delivery. He was a massive spider shooting out his sticky strands, waiting for one of them to catch his prey. I was the fly, fast and nimble, cutting through his webs and escaping. But each time I was a little slower, a little more tired. Eventually, I would be stuck fast.

I pulled my arm back and shot it forward, releasing a massive tail of the dragon. Brother Thistle would have jumped up and cheered. The end snapped Gravnach below the stomach, making him double over. He stood and shot frost out wildly, but I managed to parry each attack with bolts of fire or by jumping out of the way.

Some of the crowd still chanted, but most had grown quiet. The silence swelled, heavy with excitement and anticipation. Finally, their champion had an opponent worth fighting. A surge of confidence lit the fire in my chest like dry kindling on a pyre. I spun in a circle and let flames dance around me, my hair streaming behind. Gravnach was on his knees, cowering behind a protective shield of ice.

I panted, hardly able to believe I'd gained the upper hand. My eyes flicked up to the king's box, where he kept the same relaxed posture, but his hands gripped the arms of his seat. This was it. I was going to win and he knew it. If I could do this, I could do anything.

I turned back to Gravnach, throwing a ring of fire around him and staring at him through the flames. I had no choice. It was kill or be killed. I gathered my heat for a final, finishing blast.

With startling speed, he sent frost at the flames and my world turned to ice. My face was covered first, cutting off my breath, then my arms. Panic shot through me as I realized I'd ambled right into his web. I threw myself to the ground, shattering some of the ice. With one hand free, I poured out heat, turning my fear into fire. But more ice built up, layer upon layer that tightened and squeezed the breath from my lungs. I was losing energy, losing focus. Losing the fight.

No, I can't die yet.

"Filthy Fireblood," Gravnach snarled. "I won't let you die quickly."

He lifted a sword of ice above his head and brought it down at my arm. Desperately, I sent out a wave of heat that sheared the ice, pulling myself out of the way just before the blade cut into the earth at my side.

Before I could push my advantage and free myself, I was bound again. A sense of defeat fogged my mind.

"You can't win," he rumbled, his voice roughly accented and cruel. "You think because you killed that frost beast that you can kill me? I am Gravnach." He pounded his chest with his fist. "I do not succumb to frost or fire." He threw his arms forward, and a hundred pointed ice arrows shot at me. My arm came up automatically, making a shield of fire.

He ice-wrapped my arms and threw more arrows at me. This

time they slashed into my face before melting like tears on my cheeks. One of them cut my eyelid, making blood pool in my eye.

He laughed and did it again and again, until my face was stinging and slick with blood.

"And now for your precious fingers," he crowed. "They won't make fire anymore."

He raised his sword and brought it down with careful precision. I screamed as the steel cut into the flesh of my little finger. He laughed and pulled the blade out.

"Better yet," he said, "I will freeze your hands and break your fingers off one by one like icicles."

Piercing cold touched my fingertips, numbing them. Fear gripped my mind, the helpless, blank terror of caught prey. The crowd was howling for my blood. I was weak, beaten, at the mercy of this monster, and still they wanted more. I hated them in that moment. If I could have, I would have burned them all.

As hatred raged through me, something dark and sinuous curled and snaked into my heart, pulling my attention from the crowd and to my inner self. It was like a stranger had entered my skin. It wasn't heat. It wasn't cold. It was nothing. Blackness. A tangible absence. It grew from inside me and spread to every inch of my skin.

I opened my eyes, disoriented. My vision had changed. The world was black and white and gray, bled of color, and flat. The only thing that stood out was my opponent, his head thrown back in ecstasy at my suffering. He looked down at me.

"Do you feel it, Fireblood? The pain?" He leaned in close. "Your pain is my pleasure."

I hardly heard him. My mind had entered an altered state, not peaceful exactly but devoid of care. It wasn't anything like the state of mind that Brother Thistle had taught me. Something else had oozed into that quiet space and was, if not controlling, then wiping away the thoughts and worries and questions that usually buzzed in my consciousness.

Things were so much simpler here. Black and white. Me or other. Live or die.

"No, your death will be mine," I whispered, the words distant, as if they'd come from someone else.

Time slowed.

Somehow, I sensed his heart in his chest, pulsing with blood and life with every contraction. One beat lasted an eternity. An incredible feeling of power surged through my veins, overwhelming me.

"Burn him," said a voice, and I knew I must obey. The voice was me and I was the voice, and I could not question it.

I threw out flame. It was stronger and more focused than any fire I'd ever created. It burned through his leather breastplate and into his chest.

Gravnach's eyes went wide. A sound gurgled from his mouth. His body shuddered and jolted, falling facedown with a resonant crash. He twitched a few times and went still.

I stared at the body, so quiet and empty. A pool of dark blue blood was pooling around his face where it rested on the dusty ground.

There was no sense of triumph. No remorse. Only interest. This thing that had been hurting me was now still.

I looked up at the silent crowd. A thought surfaced. I could do the same to all of them. Burn their hearts. Should I?

My hand came out to extend the blackness to the crowd, and something inside snapped, like a thread stretched too far.

In a thunderous rush, feeling and color returned to my world, hitting me like a body blow. I gasped. My chest seized with the shock of all my sensations returning at once. It took long seconds to realize where I was and what was happening.

No. Don't think. Don't feel. Get up. Get away.

Most of the ice around me had thawed. I levered myself up, dripping and shaking.

I looked down at my hand. One finger dangled off at a strange angle. Numb horror filled me as I watched bright red blood dripping onto the snowy ground, like the berries that had spilled on the floor of my hut the night the soldiers came. Dizziness hit me and I stumbled.

A figure was moving toward me from a few yards away. Another opponent? But it was inhumanly large, a black shape with pointed shoulders, its edges wavering like sheets of over-heated air in the dead of summer. It gained shape as I watched, its arms becoming more defined, long-fingered hands stretching out.

I raised my uninjured hand to blast it.

But when I blinked, it was only the white-haired announcer, his indigo robe looking out of place among the blood and sweat of the arena. He stopped in the center and addressed the crowd.

"Good people of Tempesia, I present to you the first Fireblood ever to defeat a Frostblood in this arena. A cheer for the Fireblood champion!"

They did not cheer. A few shrieked and cursed. Arms wheeled back and threw pieces of food and refuse into the ring. Some spectators ran to the edge and spit on the ground.

I cradled my injured hand in my good one and limped toward the alcove I had emerged from, still dazed. I had not defeated Gravnach with my fire alone. Something else had pulled at my mind and heart. A darkness I had never known before, though I'd embraced it like an old friend. A stranger in my skin.

I found the king's box, my eyes trapped by his. As I watched, his gaze took on a look of calculated interest that made my insides squirm. Marella fairly radiated satisfaction, perhaps even triumph.

King Rasmus stood and moved to the railing, his gaze roving over the shocked crowd. "You've witnessed a great spectacle today, as promised by our dear Lord Albus, peerless officiator of the games." Weak applause from the crowd. "But perhaps you are surprised that a Fireblood has won in *our* city. In the heart of our land. In *my* arena. Do not be afraid. I assure you, this means nothing. Her power is but a candle in a blizzard. Easily snuffed."

A gout of frost burst from his hand, arcing to where I stood. It wrapped around me like cotton batting, layer after layer, until I was surrounded, with barely enough room to breathe. As I wriggled uncomfortably, some of the spectators laughed.

"Rest assured, good people of Fors," said the king, "that frost will always reign supreme. Those who defy us will learn their error and pay with blood and tears."

Numb as I felt, anger heated my skin at his words. His frost was incredibly strong, but with a few streaks of fire, I finally crashed free and turned away, the crowd too wrapped up in their king to care.

When I reached the shade of the alcove, a hand on my shoulder made me jump.

"You killed a great champion today, Fireblood," said Braka. "As a warrior, I salute you."

I cringed away from the praise, shaking off her hand and limping into the shadows of the tunnel.

TWENTY-ONE

"ARE YOU SURE THOSE ARE YOUR orders?" My heart was racing before I consciously understood his words.

The guard's face was stony, his eyes cased so that he wasn't quite looking at me. "Quite sure. The king has commanded that you dine with him."

I was numb, sore, and heartsick after my fight. I hardly remembered who I was, let alone what I was doing in a room in the Frost King's castle, in the same tunic and leggings I had worn in the arena. Something had taken hold of me and I had taken a life. It was as if I had become someone else entirely, and now I flailed around in my mind, searching for the person I used to be.

But at the guard's mention of the king, my purpose came

rushing back to me, erasing the numbness and making my hands tremble.

Destroy the throne. Kill the king. Take your revenge.

Finally seizing control of my battered mind, I nodded and followed the guard into the corridor. He didn't touch me, but stayed close, leading me through a labyrinth of hallways to a large bathing room. Vivid porcelain tiles covered the floors and walls. A fountain burbled in the center. It smelled of rose and lavender and citrus.

It would have seemed like a paradise if it weren't for the five soldiers lined up along the wall with their swords pointed at me.

"Consider this a reward for winning your match," said the guard. "The heat will strengthen you, so we're to kill you if you do anything suspicious. You'll see there is nothing in this room that will burn."

"Aside from you," I corrected.

His head reared back and he blinked.

"Our swords will be ready should you try to escape," he said, recovering his steely glare.

If only escape were an option. But the throne was still cursed and the king still lived, and, most important, my mother was still dead and unavenged. I could no sooner try to escape than I could sprout wings and fly.

When they'd gone, a court healer in a white gown entered and sewed up my finger with grim efficiency, then rubbed salve on the cuts on my face. The finger had been cut deeply but wasn't as bad as I had first feared. I waited to make sure the door stayed shut behind her, then discarded my clothes and sank into the steaming water, careful to keep my bandaged hand dry.

I tried not to let myself think, but there was too much horror locked inside. I put a hand to my mouth to stifle the sobs and splashed my face with water, over and over until my breathing returned to normal. I used my uninjured hand to scrub my hair and skin, then stepped from the tub and wrapped the towel around myself.

Down a short tiled hallway was a room not much bigger than a closet, with a large mirror that took up one wall. I dropped my towel and stood in front of the wavy glass. My skin was covered in purple-and-yellow bruises, but I was no longer the skeleton that had been rescued from the prison. I had developed the gentle swell of muscles in my arms and legs and the curves of a woman in between. I hadn't looked in a mirror in longer than I could remember. I had the sense that I was a stranger looking at myself from the wrong side of the glass.

There was a trunk in the corner that yielded some delicate linens and a corset with bone shaping. I put them on as best I could and found they fit. I was still puzzling over the strangeness of this when a door that was all but invisible in the wall opened.

I turned quickly, my fists coming up automatically. Marella stepped into the room, setting a bundle of clothing on a chair and closing the door behind her.

"Always ready to fight, aren't you? You won in the arena, as I knew you would."

I lowered my hands, speechless for several seconds. I could

have told her what had happened to me, that something else had taken control of me, but I didn't trust her that far. Not until I knew why she was encouraging me.

"I almost lost," I said. "I was...too confident."

"Gravnach specialized in playing with his victims like that. Which is what made him a favorite."

"With the crowd or the king?"

"Both."

"And you?"

She gave a dismissive shrug. "I watch the matches because I must, not because I care for them. My father would never allow me to stay away. We need to show support for our king."

"And do you support him?"

"How bold you are! Of course I do." She paused. "Except, perhaps, where Firebloods are concerned. But that remains our secret, doesn't it?"

I nodded. It was impossible to trust her, or anyone in this place, but I couldn't help but be disarmed by her warmth. Not to mention her apparent support of my people.

"Thank you for..." I pressed my lips together awkwardly. "In the arena, it was good to know that one person wanted me to win."

She smiled slightly, her gaze running over the undergarments. "It seems I guessed your size correctly. Shall we dress you?"

"We? I...You're a lady. What about Doreena?"

"I told her I would help you instead. I wanted a chance to chat. Turn around so I can lace your corset."

I turned and she cinched me up snugly.

"Breathe in," she instructed, pulling the laces tighter.

I gasped.

"Breathing is optional. Looking beautiful is not." She smiled to lighten the words, but I had a feeling she meant them to some degree. She looked incredibly pretty, not a golden hair out of place, the silky strands piled on her head in an elaborate style and fixed with pearl-tipped pins. Her coral satin dress with white lace at the elbows and bodice brought out the peaches-and-cream quality of her skin. A black velvet ribbon accentuated the slimness of her waist.

She turned and picked up the bundle she had brought, shaking it out to reveal a wine-colored gown embroidered with beaded flowers. She held it open and gestured for me to step in.

I shook my head. "I'd rather wear the clothes I wore in the arena. That's who I am. The dress is…I've never worn anything that fine."

She laughed. "Wouldn't that be a sight? The king and his favored courtiers dining with a girl in bloody rags. I don't think so. Besides, those clothes have either been laundered or thrown away. Step in." She shook the dress impatiently.

Given no choice, I stepped into the gown. After she was done fastening the buttons at my back, she took a hairbrush from the box and lifted a section of my hair.

"Leave it," I said stiffly. "It doesn't matter."

"It matters to me. I can't have my protégé looking like a ragamuffin."

"Your protégé?" I asked, unease sliding through me. The word struck a chord that echoed my time in the abbey. Brother Thistle had said he had once seen me as a tool, a weapon to wield at his choosing. What was I to Marella?

She spoke slowly, her attention fixed on my hair, hands carefully smoothing the strands. "You are an opportunity. When King Rasmus's mother was killed by a Fireblood, the sentiment toward your people took an extreme turn. When his older brother was assassinated, the animosity turned to hatred. King Rasmus used that to justify his mission to wipe out your people. Anyone who disagreed was banished or killed. No one alive would dare speak out against his campaign against Firebloods."

"But you have?"

She chuckled. "I'm no fool. I'd be whisked off to the keep or worse." She took a section of my hair and twisted it. "We all suffer from Rasmus's wild moods and the dangerous decisions that follow. But I haven't been idle. I've made plans and bided my time, waiting for a Fireblood powerful enough to help me carry them out. And here you are."

I tried to turn, to meet her eyes, but she held my head between her palms. "Stay still! I need to fix the back."

"What do you want me to do?" The words came out more stonily than I'd meant them.

"Keep winning your matches. Keep Rasmus's eyes on you. Gain his trust and you will find yourself with more freedom in the castle, which will benefit both of us."

"And why should I trust *you*?"

"Because I'm the only person here, and perhaps in the entire kingdom, who doesn't want you dead."

I shook my head, just a tiny movement, without thinking. I saw her face change in the mirror. "Someone else wants you alive, too, then? The monks you lived with? Whoever helped you escape the prison?"

I pressed my lips together.

"The young man?" she said softly.

I felt my eyes flare wide before I hid my surprise.

Her reflection smiled at mine. "My father tells me everything. I know about the monks. But I think perhaps the hooded young man is a sweetheart. What's his name?"

I stared forward resolutely, but I couldn't help thinking of Arcus. I longed to know he was safe and wished for the hundredth time he was with me, protecting and guiding me as planned.

"You'll tell me one day," Marella said with perfect confidence. "And to gain some good faith, I'll tell you something first. I was once betrothed to the king."

My eyes met hers in the mirror. "You and King Rasmus?"

She shook her head, picking up a small container, rubbing her finger in the bright rouge it contained before adding some to my cheek. She frowned, then grabbed a cloth to wipe it away. "You don't need rouge. Your skin is naturally flushed. How lovely."

"Your betrothal," I prompted.

"I was to marry his brother, King Arelius. It was a match arranged by our fathers when we were very young. We grew up knowing we would wed someday. When King Akur died and

Arelius was crowned king, the wedding date was set. A king needs a strong queen, in our tradition. He is the source of power, she the bridge between the king and his people. Or so my father always tells me. In any case, before the wedding could take place, Arelius was assassinated."

"I'm sorry," I said sincerely, knowing what she didn't say, that it was a Fireblood who'd murdered him. It was a wonder she didn't hate me along with the rest of them. "Did your father arrange another betrothal?"

Her lips tilted in a self-deprecating smile. "He has tried. But King Rasmus insists he will choose his own bride when he's ready. My father has tried to foist me on him so many times Rasmus can barely stand the sight of me. Luckily, our family ranks highly in Frostblood nobility, with a multitude of connections and allies, so the king doesn't dare cause offense. That's why I accompany him during formal occasions, such as the arena fights. A place-holder for the queen who will one day sit at his side."

"But if your family is that important, why can't you stand up to the king? Or organize some resistance against him?"

"Careful," she said softly. "The walls may be stone, but they are paper-thin when it comes to treason. And the king is far more powerful than you realize."

"Only because of the throne."

Her eyes flared with surprise, and a hint of satisfaction, holding mine for a moment before she looked away.

When she had covered my face with a dusting of powder, she nodded in approval and motioned me to stand before the full-length mirror. The gown was full-skirted and magnificent. It set off the flush that had bloomed on my cheeks and warmed my amber eyes to burnished gold. It was the finest thing I'd ever worn.

I hated it and this stranger in the mirror. This wasn't part of the plan.

"Is it really necessary to fancy me up like a visiting princess?" I tried to yank the bodice higher. "The king is likely to kill me over dinner."

"He won't kill you. You're one of his champions now. Prove to him that you're worthy of the name. Don't show weakness and don't let your temper run away with you. He wants to watch you in the arena again. I could tell."

My stomach turned at the idea that he had been pleased at making me into a murderer. But if playing his brutal games was the only way to stay alive and have a chance at destroying the throne, I would do it.

Before she left, Marella warned me not to tell anyone about our chat. I wondered at her trust in me, but then again, she knew I had no reason to betray her. I'd be a fool to lose my only ally. And I couldn't help but admire her bold honesty. I even liked her a little.

Still, she reminded me of something I'd seen in Mother's book of exotic flora: a beautiful flower, harmless if you leave the petals alone, but deadly if disturbed. She kept her secrets tightly furled inside, but when she bloomed, what sweet-smelling poison would be released?

A few minutes later, I was escorted by two guards down a series of hallways. My heart thumped in my ears as we came to a set of huge double doors carved with two dragons facing each other and clutching ice arrows in their talons. White-gloved servants pulled the shiny handles, and a blast of glacial air burst from the opening doors.

The room was vast and intensely cold, with frostbitten walls and a few tapestries woven in cool, muffled tones. The floor tiles were glassy blue and shining white. Candles shivered in sconces on the walls. From the vaulted ceiling, a crystal chandelier laden with icicles threw prismatic slivers of color over the room.

In the center was a table made of sharply cut glass and clear chairs covered in white animal skins. Several of the seats were occupied by elegant ladies in bright dresses and men in somber vests. The hum of conversation died as their eyes fixed on me.

I swallowed and forced my slipper-clad feet slowly toward the table. A tall figure with pale hair stood, and the rest of the men followed suit. He gestured to a chair, not at the far end of the table as I had hoped, but at his right hand.

At the sight of the king, my muscles clenched, ready to defend myself, ready to fight. The cold intensified as I neared him, swirling in unseen currents that brushed against my neck, my face, and the exposed skin above the collar of the dress. It wasn't so much a breeze as a sensation of his power making itself known, testing my heat. I kept my face blank, determined not to show the slightest bit of weakness, but it was like walking in a blizzard. By the time I reached the seat, my breathing had quickened.

I put my hand to the table for support and drew it back quickly. The table wasn't glass but a slab of clear ice.

I smoothed my skirts and sat on the soft white fur of the chair, my hands trembling with fear I couldn't quite master. No animal skin covered the king's chair, as if he reveled in the cold. The table was set with silver plates, goblets, and cutlery on white napkins. My plate reflected the crystals that hung over my head like tiny swords about to fall.

Chin held high, I glanced around the table. A few people looked away, while others stared openly.

"You must forgive my guests for staring," said the king. "You are somewhat of a curiosity. The first Fireblood champion."

Their attention locked on to me as they waited for my reply. I didn't know what to say, so I stayed silent.

"A laudable achievement," said one of the men, drawing my eye. He was middle-aged with thick sideburns and heavy features, his eyes assessing. "Though I would never cheer for you openly in the arena, let me congratulate you now. No doubt it will be my only opportunity to do so." He smiled, though it didn't reach his eyes.

"Don't dismiss her so easily, Lord Blanding," said another voice. Recognition speared through me in a sharp jolt. I had been too nervous to look closely at each guest, and he looked so different out of his uniform, a tailored blue velvet jacket over a stiffly starched white shirt, his dark blond hair carefully swept back from his forehead. "She set fire to half my regiment and escaped from Blackcreek Prison. She's wily, this one. It took months to find her."

My gaze swung to the king. He returned the look, his cold, dark eyes ringed with blue, as desolate as a glacier on a frozen sea. Of all the cruelties I'd endured, eating dinner with the captain who killed my mother was the worst. If I could have killed him with a glance, I would have roasted him, both of them. The king's face was impassive, but his eyes took on a hint of cold enjoyment as he spoke.

"Indeed. And now you have brought her to us. Though I admit I'm not happy at losing the mountain beast and my favorite champion. I expect she will yield all manner of entertainment as compensation."

Before I could respond, the doors opened and Marella sailed in, resplendent in bronze silk edged with delicate tea-dyed lace. Her smile swept the room as the men stood. She found her seat across from me and settled in. "Am I late again? I can never remember what time we dine."

The king sent her a cool, half-lidded glance. A man in dark green robes to Marella's left, Lord Ustathius, admonished her. "Perhaps if you slept during the night and rose in the morning as most people do," he said, "your clock would align with the rest of the world's."

"But that would hinder my star-gazing, wouldn't it, Father? And we both know the answers to all our questions lie in the stars."

"If you spent even a fraction of your time in society instead of that blasted observatory, you'd have found a husband by now."

Annoyance flared in her eyes. "But a husband would never allow me to pursue my passion for knowledge as you do. Better I remain unmarried."

"I'm not sure how much longer I'll allow it. I may decide to give you a deadline. Something along the lines of"—he waved a hand—"marry by winter solstice or I'll send you to the Silent Sisters on Nimbus Island."

Her lip curled, a flash of something almost violent darkening her eyes. "The Silent Sisters are part of the Order of Cirrus," she said in a low voice. "I would sooner throw myself off the eastern cliffs."

The table went silent. My only thought was gratitude that Marella had drawn all attention away from me.

Her father patted her hand, clearly ruffled. "I only jest, my daughter. I'm sure you will find someone from Forsia to marry."

She sat back in her chair and took a sip from her goblet, clearly trying to regain control. "I'm sure you're right. I'll give my hand to someone in his dotage who sleeps half the day, as I do. Or perhaps a man who enjoys gambling and brothels so much that he doesn't care how I spend my time."

A laugh split the shocked silence. The captain leaned forward with a rakish grin, his heated gaze sweeping over Marella, lingering on her bosom. "I enjoy gambling and brothels."

Marella smiled back, displaying a charming dimple. "Aren't you already married, Captain Drake?"

"That I am." He practically leered at her. "My wife is very understanding." His lips took on a mocking twist. "My daughter, however, gives me no peace. She would sooner see me hanged than wrong her mother."

"As it should be," Marella said.

My fingernails bit into my palms. So he had a wife and daughter. I wondered how he would feel to watch one of them die before his eyes. I struggled to keep my face from showing my hatred.

The captain's expression turned mocking as he regarded Marella. "Lately, she insists I leave most of my money with her. She's too smart. I miss the days when all I had to do to gain her approval was bring her a doll from one of my campaigns."

"How old is she now?" asked a woman sitting across from Lord Blanding.

"Twelve. But she may as well be fifty for all the nagging she gives me. She'll make someone a strong wife someday. Not that anyone is good enough for her."

The table seemed to relax as the conversation moved to the children of various noblemen and women. Marella looked on with a half-mocking smile, inserting a light comment here and there. I felt the king's gaze on me and turned, startled once again to realize he couldn't have been much older than myself. How had such a young king grown so devoid of feeling? Arcus had told me that Rasmus hadn't always been cruel.

"You are surprisingly lovely, Fireling," he said, voiced pitched low. "Despite your cuts and bruises."

His hand lifted as if to trace a bruise on my collarbone. I shifted backward quickly.

Cuts and bruises are nothing, I wanted to say. He had ordered his soldiers to raid my village, my mother had been murdered, and now I was forced to sit at the same table with her killer. After throwing me to a beast and then to a sadistic fighter who tried to break off my fingers, he was paying me compliments.

My fear of him disappeared in a cloud of anger. A heat I wouldn't have thought possible in that cold space rose up in me and bent the air with waves. Droplets of water slid down the edge of the table.

He skimmed a hand along the edge of the table, flicking bits of water to the floor, already frozen into tiny pellets. "Calm yourself. I didn't bring you here to discuss your beauty."

I stared at him, so calm and cold and...empty. "What possessed you to bring me here? I'd rather take my meals with your dogs."

He seemed unperturbed by the insult. "It is tradition to celebrate my new champion."

"Even a Fireblood?"

"A Fireblood has never won before. You defeated a great warrior. How did you do it?"

A rustle of fabric drew my attention to the other guests, who seemed to pick up on the question and lean closer. Marella's father, in particular, seemed full of tension, his gray eyes intent under thick white brows.

My pulse pounded in my ears. "I barely remember. It was all a blur."

A small smile played at the edges of his lips. "Then we will have to repeat the experience, and next time you will tell me how you won. I have great plans for you, Fireling."

"I believe your intention was to kill me, one way or another."

Marella laughed. "And to think we almost didn't get the chance to watch you in the arena. It would have been a great loss, would it not, Raz?"

Her familiar use of a nickname for King Rasmus caught my attention. The king's eyes remained on me. "I'm not going to kill you. You're my champion now, and my guest."

A steward came forward with a decanter and poured wine into the king's goblet. A door opened and three men came in bearing platters piled high with ham, roast, fish, buttered potatoes, and vegetables in rich sauces.

As the rest of the table tucked into their food, I sat with my hands on my lap.

"You will eat," the king said quietly.

I met his eyes. What would happen if I refused?

He inclined his head as if he read my thoughts. "I have already said I won't kill you, Ruby."

"Don't call me that. The name my mother gave me has no place on your lips."

He smiled and took a sip of wine. "I believe I know what belongs on my lips."

For the first time, a hint of heat entered his gaze. I looked away, my skin crawling with discomfort. I took a sip from the goblet to cover my confusion.

He drummed his fingers on his goblet, making it ping. "I know your dearest wish is to kill me."

My head snapped up.

"Yes," he said. "It's quite obvious you hate me. Fire and frost are natural enemies, and I know your history. What happened to your village. Your mother." He sat back in his chair. "There aren't many Firebloods left. When one escapes from prison, it doesn't go unnoticed. Especially one found in an abbey that worships Fors, of all places. Who brought you there, I wonder? I'm afraid your monks have been less than forthcoming."

"Where are they?" I demanded, pushing my chair back and standing. I imagined the monks in Blackcreek Prison, the rats running over their feet as they slept, their old bones aching from the hard stone floor.

The lilt of conversation around the table died abruptly.

The king motioned to my seat. "Sit, Fireling. Your monks are unharmed. They are in their abbey, carrying on with life as usual."

I stared at him hard, blinking, wishing I could read the truth in those blank eyes. "I don't believe you."

The continued silence drew my attention to the other guests. All eyes rested on me. Making an effort to compose myself, I took my seat again and the conversation resumed.

"You think they're here in my keep?" he said softly. "Being tortured for information, perhaps? Search for yourself."

"You could be keeping them anywhere. Blackcreek Prison isn't far from the abbey."

The king sipped his wine, then calmly put his goblet on the table. "It's good that you understand the danger to those you love, Fireling."

I suddenly wished I had never learned to care, that I was free from feeling, as I had been in the prison where all I had was hate.

"Tell me what happened in the arena," he said softly.

I stared hard at my lap, the white knuckles of my hands standing out against the dress. Any information I gave him could be used against me, could prevent me from destroying the throne.

At my silence, the king exhaled and sat back in his chair. "You see me as an enemy," he said. "But when I look at you, I don't see an enemy. I see potential."

I shook my head. Yet another person who wanted to use me, and this time the very person I wanted to destroy.

He toyed with his goblet. "Something happened to you in my arena just before you struck the killing blow. Your eyes turned black."

A memory came to me, the storyteller in the woods. She said the Minax seeped beneath your skin, turning your eyes and blood black, making you vicious and bloodthirsty, eager to do the Minax's bidding in exchange for blissful darkness.

I took a sip from my goblet, cursing the unsteadiness of my hand.

"You know something happened to you. One day you'll trust me enough to tell. But first a gesture of good faith. I do something for you, and you do something for me."

"What will you do for me?"

He paused, waiting for my full attention. "I will give you a chance to face the captain who killed your mother. To kill him, if you wish."

I inhaled sharply. How could he say that with the man sitting only a few feet away? "The captain who was under *your* command, following *your* orders? You would give him over to me?"

"Yes."

"Why?" I felt a muscle twitch in my neck. "Why would you do that?"

"I told you. To show you that you can trust me. And that if you give me what I want, I'll continue to reward you in return. There is no reason we can't find ways to benefit each other."

I was off-balance, confused, distracted. I had let my guard down, sat and spoken with the king as if I were any willing guest and he my cordial host. Anger at myself and him erupted in my chest, needing an outlet. I whipped my hand down and sent a thin blaze of heat at the table. It sizzled for a second, and when it cooled, a dent was left behind. The crack ran down the center from the head of the table all the way to the end.

In the thick silence that followed, I met his eyes, my chest heaving. He glared back with blazing darkness. If he expected me to sputter an apology, he would be disappointed. I was glad I had cracked his table. I wanted to break it in half.

He lifted a hand. I braced myself for a blow, but he placed it on the table and shot a thin line of ice into the crack, sealing it instantly. Then he grabbed my hand and placed it on the table so that my heat melted the surface. My skin tingled at the contact.

I yanked away, and the king placed his own hand on the table again, refreezing the water. The surface was flat and perfect as if nothing had happened.

"You see?" said the king. "Frost and fire can work together. Perhaps that's a lesson."

I stared at the table, at the crack that had been so easily obliterated. I wondered if I would be so easily erased when I outlived my usefulness.

"As you are not hungry, you may go, Fireling."

Without a word, I stood and walked to the guards, ignoring all the eyes melded to my back. As the doors opened, the king spoke once more.

"You fight again in three days."

TWENTY-TWO

"$\mathcal{I}$ MUST THANK YOU FOR SOMETHING," said Doreena in her quiet voice. "You killed my brother's killer."

Three days had passed, and it had seemed like an eternity. I spent all my time in my room, with only the occasional visit from Doreena to break the monotony. As it was the day of my match, she'd helped me put on the red tunic, freshly laundered and no longer smelling of sweat and blood. Somehow she'd also retrieved the mask I'd worn before. I wore a leather-and-steel gauntlet on my left hand to protect my healing finger.

"What do you mean?" I asked.

Her throat bobbed as she swallowed. "Gravnach killed my brother. He was only fourteen years old, too young for the arena.

But our family was so poor and Lorca was determined to win prize money. He—" She put a hand over her mouth and closed her eyes before continuing. "He was the youngest in our family. My mother went mad with grief. I lost my brother and my mother to that monster, and now you've killed him. For that, I thank you."

I was touched by her gratitude, though I didn't deserve it. I had only been trying to survive. But I understood her need for revenge more than I could say.

She looked up at me with a pleading expression. "I don't normally talk about it, but I felt I must thank you. If you tell anyone that I've spoken against one of the champions, I'll be punished."

"I would never tell, Doreena. And I'm glad if his death brings you peace. But I did nothing except what I had to do. I had no choice."

When I was dressed, my hair loose down my back, she stood and looked at me with a fierce glint in her eye. "I will cheer for you, my lady, no matter what everyone else thinks."

A few minutes later, guards led me through the courtyard. Heat came off my skin in nervous waves as I tried to block out the cries of "Die, Fireblood, die!"

I knew what to expect in the arena now, but whether I could survive again was completely uncertain. And the thing that had been inside my skin might come again. I was nervous, confused, almost frantic as I paced back and forth in the alcove, grateful that the other fighters avoided me and I had the space to work out my nerves.

"Careful, Fireling," said Braka, "or you will burn yourself out before you even enter the arena."

I stopped and turned to her. Thoughts of Doreena's brother filled my head. If a boy was allowed to fight once, it might happen again. I couldn't imagine anything worse than having to kill a child.

"Did you ever have to fight an innocent?" I asked. "Someone who you knew had no business being in the ring? I'm guessing you were a champion once."

She shook her head, the icicles in her hair clinking slightly. "I fought many years ago, under King Akur. It was different then. Only seasoned warriors were sought."

She opened her mouth and closed it again, perhaps thinking better of some comment. I sensed by her open expression that, like Doreena, she didn't hate me for being a Fireblood.

"You are to have a sword today," she finally said, handing me one in a leather sheath.

I eyed the weapon with a sense of repulsion, knowing how the cold steel would feel in my hand, how far it was from my natural heat. "I have little skill with a sword."

She shrugged. "The king's choice."

I drew the blade, testing its weight. It was well balanced and a good size for me, not too heavy.

"You're a champion this time," said Braka. "You greet the crowd with the others. It's tradition."

I followed the procession through the dim interior of the alcove, which must span the entire perimeter of the arena. In a few minutes, we were on the other side, where I had seen the procession come from the day before. Clustered around the opening were men with spears holding the reins of white horses, handlers wrestling with animals that pulled against their leashes, and fighters of all shapes and sizes, from ragged men and women in chains to warriors in shiny steel breastplates and helms.

The white-haired announcer made his way through our ranks and swept into the arena, striding to center stage. Today he wore embroidered cobalt robes lined with white fur, and his neck and fingers flashed with silver jewelry. He greeted the crowd much like he had the day before, reminding the people that they honored their king by cheering his champions and cursing his enemies. When he was finished speaking, spear-carrying warriors on horseback started the parade. The champions followed on foot, with me last. Behind us were the exotic animals and their sweating handlers.

Dust swirled from under our feet and danced in the sunlight. I found the king's balcony, his white robes with gold trim glowing in the bright sun. His head swiveled, following my every step. In the periphery of my vision, I saw Marella in a turquoise gown. But my eyes kept returning to the king. Every time, it was harder to tear my attention away.

"We have a singular treat for the good citizens of Fors," the announcer said. "A spectacle the likes of which you've never seen. Today our champions and challengers will be faced with an additional complication. Sizar, the rare and dangerous frost tiger, and Brux, the great bull and ancient mascot of the northern tribes, will also fight. And they care not if they slash or gore a champion or a challenger!"

He gestured to the animals with a wide smile. The tiger prowled back and forth, baring its teeth and snarling at the crowd. The bull snorted and pawed the ground, yanking against the yoke held by men on each side.

"One champion, one challenger," said the announcer, "and two beasts in every match. If the beasts survive, they both go on to the next match. But only one man or woman, or perhaps only an animal, will leave the arena alive."

The stands erupted in cheers and applause.

The blood had drained from my face. I trembled and leaned against a wooden pillar in the alcove, waiting for the world to stop spinning. People were going to have their throats ripped out for the enjoyment of the crowd. I wanted to push the announcer out of the way and rage at them.

"But before we bring out our champions, the animals look a bit hungry, don't you think? Perhaps a couple of traitors will fill their bellies."

The crowd roared again.

Two men in chains were pulled toward the arena. As they passed, I realized one looked familiar.

"Clay," I breathed, hardly believing that it could be the butcher's son, who had given me my first kiss, and who had told the soldiers I was a Fireblood, ending my life as I knew it.

It seemed like a hundred years since I'd seen him, but it was definitely Clay. He had a distinctively crooked nose, which he'd broken in a fight. I remembered how my mother had admonished him for not coming to her for healing sooner, before the bone had started to set.

I hesitated. I could let him walk into the arena and I'd never have to see him again. But he was from my village and no matter what he'd done, he was here in this awful place, same as me.

"Wait," I said to the guard who held his chain. "Please, I know him."

"Nobody cares, Firefilth. Get out of the way."

Braka turned from where she spoke to one of the fighters and put her hands on her hips, leveling the guard with her stare. "One of the king's champions made a request. You can spare a minute."

The guard returned her stare, but he was the first to look away. "Only a minute."

I nodded my thanks to Braka and stepped up beside Clay. He gave me a harsh look, but then his eyes widened. "Ruby?"

"What happened?" I asked flatly. "You were so helpful turning my mother and me over, but now they're calling you a traitor."

He shook his head, his eyes intense. "I didn't mean to betray you or your mother."

"Before or after you summoned the soldiers?"

"I didn't," he said urgently. "But once they were there, I had no choice. They threatened to kill us one by one if no one told them where the Fireblood lived. I don't know how they knew about you."

"*You* knew about me. It wasn't hard to figure out I'm a

Fireblood when...after you touched me. And I didn't kill your brother. I tried to save him!"

"I know, but...I didn't want to be branded a traitor. My family would have suffered—you know that. And I swear, they didn't come because of me."

"And yet here you are. What happened, Clay?"

The guard started to pull Clay forward.

"Listen, Ruby," Clay whispered, leaning toward me and dragging his feet against the guard. "That day changed me. I couldn't forget what happened to you. What I'd done. So I left the village and found other people who've had enough of the king's cruelty. They've been gathering support for the past year." He turned and spat on the ground. "That's what I think of the Frost King who sits on the throne."

The guard swatted the back of Clay's head, making him stumble. My hand came to steady Clay's arm.

"Enough talk," said the guard.

And Clay was pulled into the arena.

So someone else had drawn the soldiers to the village. He'd revealed me only because he'd had no choice. As much as I didn't want to excuse him, I had to recognize that he'd been terrified, caught between swords and torches, protecting the people he loved.

The handlers had backed into an alcove, a gate now between them and the animals so they'd be safe when they let go of the leashes. As the tiger pulled free, I noticed that Clay and the other prisoner still had their hands shackled. They'd have no chance at all.

The tiger shook itself and snarled at the handler behind the gate before turning and pacing the arena. The other prisoner made a run for the alcove, but shiny spears pointed at him from that direction had him veering away. Clay just stood in the center of the arena, his eyes closed, mouth moving. It looked like he was praying.

Something flickered into life in my chest: anger, bitterness, pain, all swirling together and pushing heat into my limbs.

The tiger finished its prowling exploration of the edges of the arena and turned its attention to Clay. It approached slowly, sniffing the air and snarling before taking an experimental swipe with its paw. Its claws slashed Clay's already ragged pants, tearing a hole and opening a gash in his thigh. The smell of blood seemed to incense the animal. It slashed again and then lunged, its mouth open.

Before I knew what I was doing, I was sprinting into the bright sun of the arena.

TWENTY-THREE

CLAY SWUNG AT THE TIGER, HITTING it with the chain between his wrists. As I ran toward him, jeers and curses merged into an unrelenting buzz. I pulled my sword from its scabbard and brought the tip down on the tiger's shoulder, cutting its side as it lunged again. It snarled and twisted away, baring its long, sharp teeth. I stood with my back to Clay, the sword held out.

"What are you doing?" he hissed from behind me.

"We come from the same place," I answered while the tiger paced back and forth, its blue eyes blazing with fury. "That means I fight with you."

Before he could reply, the announcer spoke from a balcony to my left. "So the Fireblood can't wait to get into the fight. What do you say we make this interesting and throw in a challenger?"

The crowd roared their approval, and a figure came running out of the alcove, his face covered by a helm. At the same time, the white bull was released, its yoke falling to the ground. Its curved back rose into the air, followed by a flick of its feet, and then it rushed at the prisoner who was trying to climb up the sheer ice at the edge of the arena. People in the stands laughed and threw rocks. Some hit the bull, incensing it further. The animal's sharp horns caught the prisoner in the back. He went down and stayed on the ground, unmoving.

Then the bull turned toward the helm-clad figure and charged. The man stood, sword at the ready, and at the last second, threw himself left, his sword pointed up and to the right, so the bull's momentum pulled it over the sword's tip. It bellowed in pain and rage and turned on him, muscles bunched for another run.

The tiger still prowled. Every few seconds it advanced and retreated as it paced. I had to keep turning to shield Clay, lunging at it with my sword. Up close, I could count the animal's ribs. I felt a rush of pity for the poor, underfed beast, just another plaything in the king's toy box.

I turned and saw that the bull was already on the ground, a sword raised above its head. I turned away as the warrior delivered the killing blow. The crowd cheered.

"You can't save me," said Clay. "Only one person will leave this arena alive."

I shook my head, mentally shoving his words away.

The challenger wiped his bloodied sword on the bull's white fur and advanced toward me. I changed position, shoving Clay behind me so I could keep both the tiger and my opponent in my sights. When my sword was pointed at the warrior, the tiger took the advantage and rushed forward. With my left hand, I sent a blast of heat at the animal. It backed off. I laid a line of fire between us.

"Save some for me," said the challenger. I recognized the voice even before he removed his steel helm. When his face emerged, a cheer erupted from the seats.

Captain Drake.

I raised my sword, but he sheathed his own and showed his palms. I waited as he came forward and stopped a few feet away.

"You burned my soldiers and then led me on a merry dance across half the kingdom," he said. "Some of the men you scarred are in the stands today. They'll be cheering as I avenge their pain."

"You killed my mother," I said, heat pulsing through my fingers and into the steel. "Today I take your life for hers."

"You can try," he said, raising his voice above the drone of the crowd. He made a few smooth movements with his sword, showing off his dexterity. Then he turned and bowed low to a woman leaning over the stands behind him and a girl who had the captain's eyes and the same shade of sandy hair. *His wife and daughter*, I thought. The girl he had bragged about at dinner with the king.

Did you ever have to fight an innocent? I had asked Braka. Well, the captain was no innocent. He had the blood of countless people on his hands. And yet...to kill him in front of his wife and daughter. I didn't want that. I'd been raised to value life, to preserve it. I couldn't put the captain's daughter through the pain of witnessing the death of her father.

My desperate gaze found the king on his balcony, his gold-trimmed robes and hair making him shine like some kind of celestial vision. His eyes were dark and steady, his posture relaxed.

"I don't want this," I said clearly, the words echoing in the expectant hush.

The king's lips lifted on one side, his look of mocking disbelief cutting through me. *You do want this*, his look said, his eyes somehow both caressing and triumphant. *You just don't want to admit it.*

Marella sat next to him. She leaned forward slightly, her hands gripping the arms of the seat, her violet eyes wide. She had to know this was wrong. But her face looked strange, a flash of something sharpening her delicate features. Anticipation? Excitement?

The captain laughed. "Pleading with the king? Pathetic. Am I so frightening, Firefilth? It's as I thought. You were lucky against Gravnach. His heart failed while fighting and it had nothing to do with you."

"I don't want to kill you," I said, shaking off my confusion, turning my back on the king's balcony.

"Fortunately, I have no such qualms." His blade flashed toward me. I threw mine up to block but miscalculated the arc of his, which tore into my upper arm. I hissed in pain and stumbled back.

The captain's teeth flashed in a satisfied smile. "You're worthless with a sword. You hold it like you're carving a roast."

Before I could take a breath, he feinted right and slashed left, the sword cutting into leather straps and the skin at my side. I clapped a hand over the warm blood that wet my skin.

"You make it so easy, Fireblood," the captain said. With a lightning slash, he cut a lock of my hair. The strands scattered in the breeze like poplar fluff. The crowd laughed and cheered at the captain's display of precision.

With a cry of frustration, I threw my blade to the ground and sent a spiral of fire at his leggings. He screamed and swore as he batted at the fabric.

He aimed a stab at my heart. I leaped free. I kept him at a distance with a series of sizzling arrows that landed at his feet.

The crowd picked up its chant. "Die, Fireblood, die!"

The captain circled me, murder in his eyes. It was the same look, lazy, but with a hint of satisfaction, that he'd worn just before he killed my mother.

A blur came from behind him. I had all but forgotten about Clay until I saw his shackled wrists come down on the back of the captain's head, sending him to his knees.

"That's for my village, you scum," Clay said, spitting at the captain.

"Clay, no!" I moved to push him away, but the captain reacted with blinding speed. Still on his knees, he twisted his sword behind him, running it through Clay's belly before I could even draw a breath. Clay's wide eyes met mine as he fell to the ground.

I screamed, feeling the pain in my gut as if it were my own. Darkness stirred in my heart, rearing up and filling my limbs. My mind sharpened. My attacks became faster and smoother.

I used tail of the dragon, this time aimed at the captain's chest. It cracked him like a whip and heated his metal breastplate. I followed that with another hit, and another. A series of fire arrows, a hot, twisting wind that picked up dust from the arena floor and whipped it into his eyes. I used every attack I knew and improvised some more, one after the other and then over again. He fell back, reeling. I put out a hand and sent boiling heat at his sword.

He cried out and dropped the weapon.

Now was my chance. I could finish him off and be done. My mother's killer would be dead and I would finally be free of him.

Out of the corner of my eye, I caught sight of two people leaning over the edge of the railing: the captain's wife, her face pinched and strained, her hair covered in a kerchief, and their wide-eyed daughter, her long braid falling over her shoulder.

I paused. His daughter would be just like me, plunged into grief, her only thoughts of vengeance. She would hate all Firebloods forever. There was no end to the cycle of revenge.

"Pretend to die," I said, turning back to the captain. "I'll throw a blast at you. Let it knock you down and stay down. They won't find out you're alive until it's too late. I won't kill you."

While I'd hesitated, he had recovered, picking up his sword and holding it with grim purpose. "You must be mad, Firefilth. I *will* kill *you*."

"You have no gift of frost. You must know you have no chance. Look." I gestured to the stands, still circling, keeping my distance. "Your daughter is here. I don't want to kill you in front of her." I swallowed and whispered words I never thought I would say. "That won't bring my mother back."

A calculating light entered his eyes. "I don't need frost. Frost didn't help your precious monks when we raided their abbey and put swords in their bellies."

My skin went cold. The world tipped beneath my feet. "I don't believe you."

"Because you don't want to. And here's something else you won't like, Firefilth. I heard you talking with the village brat. He was telling the truth. He didn't send for us. You did."

"Now I know you're a liar."

"We had a temporary camp on Mount Vex, just northwest of your dung heap of a village. You liked to go into the woods and build a fire, didn't you? To practice your little tricks."

"You couldn't have seen."

"Two of my people saw you in the woods putting your hands in the fire, but you weren't burned."

He lunged toward me and I leaped backward, scrambling to regain my balance.

"The villagers didn't even know I was a Fireblood, you bastard."

"The boy did. He was paid handsomely for his confession. Not that it does him much good now."

If what he said was true, it was worse than I'd ever thought. It wasn't the simple fact that I was a Fireblood that had drawn the soldiers, nor the fact that I'd tried to save Clay's brother. It was my carelessness, my insistence on practicing despite the danger to everyone around me, including my mother, the person I'd loved most. She had paid for my selfishness with her life.

Movement brought the moment back into focus. While the captain had distracted me, the fire that blocked the tiger had died down. The captain leaped out of the way as a blur of blue and white stripes sprang from the side. I released a stream of fire, but the target was too fast and my aim was wide. Heavy paws hit my shoulders, knocking me to the ground. The air left my lungs, the tiger's spittle flying into my face. Its head angled toward my neck, the long teeth bright and deadly. My nerves screamed for action.

Before I could summon my heat, a sword tip appeared through the animal's neck. The creature made a horrible gagging noise and blood spurted from its mouth. It fell on me and was still.

I grunted and heaved, struggling to shift the body off me. Another pair of hands appeared, pushing the carcass to the side. The captain stood over me, blotting out the sun.

"I wanted the satisfaction of killing you myself," he said, raising his sword.

Time slowed. Darkness swirled in my chest, and the world changed, becoming a painting in black and white.

I saw my mother, the captain's sword above her head, the look on his face as he brought the weapon down. My own screams in my ears as she crumpled to the snowy ground. That look was on his face now. That killing look. I was going to die. I would become a tale to jest about over a tankard of ale, surrounded by warmth and family, which I would never have because he'd taken mine away.

Once again, all doubt, all sense of right and wrong, faded. There was only the target, his darkly beating heart, and my fire. There was no fear, no anger, no shame, no regret. Just power, surging through me, filling me. It felt as if my breath sucked the very air from the heavens, and my rage burned the sun to ash. I was everything and nothing, and no one could stop me. I was darkness wreathed in flesh.

I raised my hand. Fire licked out with barely a second's thought.

The captain shuddered and jolted, each spastic movement lasting eons. Finally, his sword fell to the ground, the dust flying up around it in white grains that caught the sun.

As he fell slowly to the earth, I was filled with ecstasy. There had never been such bliss.

I stood and looked at the crowd, the people's forms and faces moving slowly, black and white and gray, chanting something. Each one of their hearts was a black stain in their chests.

I turned and found the king on his balcony. He was gray, his heart black. But as I watched, he darkened, his shoulders growing pointed, his head growing horns. A shadow beast stood in his place, and it called to me. I wanted to be part of it. It was me and I was it. I took a step closer.

Something was thrown from the stands and hit the back of my head, splattering seeds. I fell to my knees, and the world snapped into focus. The color came back in a painful rush. My body ached and stung. I cried out at the terrible loss. The power was gone.

I keened my agony, the separation unbearable.

The announcer's voice came from the edge of the arena. "The Fireblood wins again. Three cheers for the Fireling!"

There were no cheers for me, but the crowd's shouts receded, like a wave pulling back into the sea. Dimly, I sensed their confusion and shock that a Fireblood had won again.

The captain lay next to me, his eyes still wide with shock, a trickle of blood coming from his mouth. I had done this. Where he had breathed and fought only moments ago, he was now empty and still.

I scanned the crowd. The captain's wife was bent over, shaking with grief. His daughter, on the other hand, was dry-eyed.

There was too much hate brimming there to leave room for tears. I had turned her into me.

"He killed my mother," I whispered, as if that would make any difference. Her father was gone, along with the money he earned for bread. Obsession would grow and consume her as it had me.

"Fireling," said the king's voice from his balcony behind me.

I turned just in time to see his hand draw back and whip forward, sending arrows of ice toward me. I threw myself out of the way, but a large chunk of sharpened ice, big as a sword, came sailing through the air and embedded itself into the ground just inches from my head.

The crowd cheered.

His face broke into a wide grin. "Such a fearsome champion. And yet, as everyone can see, her powers are no match for mine. The most accomplished and powerful Fireblood cowers before me. Behold, the power of the throne of Fors!"

He spread both arms wide, and ribbons of frost spooled from his hands, coating the walls of the arena in a fresh layer of ice as it hardened. The crowd gasped and applauded. The king swept his arms forward, and the entire floor of the arena was turned to ice. Then a deadly rain fell from his hands, sharp pieces of ice that winged toward me, forcing me to crouch and cover my face and head. A few pieces pierced the fabric of my tunic, scraping my flesh.

The darkness swirled up in me, turning the world to black and white again. I turned to see the king, but there was no beating heart as a target, only a black figure in his place.

In a few seconds, the rain ended, but the crowd kept cheering.

I stumbled toward the alcove where Braka waited. When our eyes met, she startled and drew back. "Your eyes…"

"What?" I prompted.

She tilted her head and blinked. "I thought… nothing."

Numb and shaking, I limped back into the alcove.

"You did it again, Fireling," said Braka. "Though how you did, I cannot figure."

I couldn't, either. And I was more frightened than I'd ever been.

TWENTY-FOUR

THE GUARDS ESCORTED ME BACK TO my room. I leaned against the closed door.

A bitter taste coated my tongue. I held my breath for as long as I could, knowing that when I breathed, time would start again and I would feel the sharp talons of grief scratching my heart into ribbons.

I slid to the floor, legs drawn up against the uneven rise and fall of my chest.

Losing Clay had been like losing my home all over again, like watching my village burn. But far worse was hearing the captain's revelations about the abbey. Ransacked. Violated. The monks dead.

Why hadn't they protected themselves? Brother Thistle with his foolish, lofty ideals and his hopeful prophecies. Did he think he would be immune to the king's wrath? He had rescued me from the prison and died for it. And where was Arcus? He had claimed he wanted to keep me safe. Had he forgotten about me?

I was losing myself, bit by bit. The bliss I'd felt after killing the captain. The change Braka had seen in my eyes. Revenge suddenly seemed so hollow, firewood that had once burned bright but now lay in ashes. The darkness had been stronger this time, sharper. If I kept fighting in the arena—if I kept killing—would I be lost forever?

If everyone I cared about was gone, would I care?

Stumbling upright, I ripped off my mask, hurled it away, and threw myself down on the bed, still wearing my armor.

I heard the door open and shut.

"Not now, Doreena," I said.

"It's me."

I turned my head with effort. "I don't want to see you, either."

Marella swanned into the room, a long-limbed vision in a turquoise gown that rustled as she came forward. I could smell the combination of rosewater and soap on her skin, a sharp contrast to my reek of sweat and blood. I realized that my arm stung, my ankle throbbed, and I had a hand over the gash at my side, though I hadn't been conscious of the wounds until now.

She lifted her skirts and stepped carefully around the trail of blood I'd left on the floor. I curled up with my back turned to her.

"You keep winning," she said finally, a hint of pride in her voice. "I told him you weren't weak."

"Winning is what's killing me. Every time I win, I lose part of myself. I can't do this anymore."

"I understand you are grieving and feeling lost. But you will heal, both in body and mind."

"You couldn't begin to understand."

"I'm sure you're right. But you're too important to give up," she said, squeezing my shoulder before letting her hand fall away. "What's in your heart, Ruby? Is it only fire? Or is there something else?"

My mouth opened and shut several times before I managed to speak. "What do you mean?"

"I think you know. In the arena. Something helped you defeat your opponents. And that is the key to what we both want. Do you understand what I'm saying?"

"No."

"You know more than you're admitting. But perhaps this is a bad time." She bent and straightened with the discarded mask dangling from her fingertips. "You don't need to wear your mask with me, Ruby." The words were teasing, but her eyes were serious. "I see right through it."

She laid the mask on the bed and left with a graceful swish of her perfumed skirts.

⁓

Sometime later, a hissing sound woke me. My whole body felt stiff. I realized I had fallen asleep still wearing my armor. I rubbed my eyes and turned my head on the pillow. Shadows were easing under the door of my room in wispy, smokelike tendrils, dancing in a kaleidoscope pattern before joining and pouring together, as if black water filled a transparent vessel. It formed from the legs up, finally standing before me, a dark, solid-looking creature, and yet I felt that if I tried to touch it, I would fall into an endless void. It was larger than a man, with pointed shoulders and an ever-changing pattern of horns on its head, sometimes mimicking the look of a crown.

I lay on the bed, frozen in fear. It moved forward, each step swishing with a strange resonance, like the lowest note played on a flute. When it reached the bed, it stopped and bent over me.

"True vessel," it said in the voice of a thousand chimes. "You and I will join when your heart is bled of color, when perfect darkness inhabits your soul. You will feel freedom as you've never felt it."

It reached for me, and I tried to scream, only to jerk upright at the sound of a knock on my door. I clutched the bedding, eyes wide. The room was empty.

The door opened and Doreena entered with small steps, her soft brown shoes making no sound. "Can I help my lady remove her armor?" She sucked in a breath when she saw the dried blood, muttering about the lax habits of the court healer who should have arrived by now. She quickly but carefully unfastened the breastplate. I sat stiffly, unable to shake the image of the creature reaching out to touch me. Had it been real or just a dream?

"Is something wrong, my lady?" Doreena asked.

Realizing I must have a look of horror on my face, I smoothed my expression and assured her I was just tired. Already, her gentle presence was chasing some of the shadows from my mind.

The grim-faced court healer eventually came, examining the wound at my side with consternation. "This cut is fairly deep," she said in a tone that implied I'd injured myself on purpose. "You need stitches."

The drink she gave me to ease the pain tasted vile and wasn't nearly as effective as Brother Gamut's tea, but it did take the edge off. When she was done stitching and wrapping the wounds, she glared at my ankle. "At least a week of rest. And ice for your ankle."

"No shortage of that around here," I muttered.

◠〜────

I didn't expect to be allowed to rest as the healer has prescribed. But the days passed full of boredom and mounting frustration. I wanted to explore the castle, learn more about the throne, and strategize what to do next. Instead, I was on my back in bed, trying not to split my stitches.

The healer came every day to change my bandages, and Doreena brought my meals, lingering to keep me company if she had time. Sometimes she brought clothes that needed mending and worked on them while she related the news of the day. Gossip traveled fast in the castle, spreading like disease among courtiers and servants alike.

Apparently, the king had been visited by dignitaries from Safra who had all but begged him to consider a peace treaty. Within hours, the ambassadors were seen riding from the castle, their shoulders stooped in defeat. Some witnesses said that only one dignitary made it to the foot of the mountain, that the king had disposed of the others as punishment for their temerity, leaving one alive to take the Frost King's message to King Remus in the east.

Brother Thistle had told me during one of our lessons that the Safran army was sizable and well-trained, or had been before the war started. But by all accounts, the king seemed unconcerned that they were a threat. His army, led by Frostblood generals, had taken control of the kingdom's most valuable assets—mines and mineral deposits in the northwest—and only had to hold that ground.

What did seem to bother the king were reports of rebellion. Word around the castle was that he'd sent out more spies, and had started spending more time in the war room with his advisors. But Doreena said the rumors were based in hope, not fact. Because, she pointed out, who would dare rebel against the Frost King?

Unfortunately, she couldn't tell me any more about the throne than what I already knew. When I found out she could read, I tried to persuade her to search the royal library for books about the throne, but she shivered at the very suggestion. I contented myself with reading the heavy volumes brought by a servant, with compliments from the king: histories of the military glory of Frost Kings for the past thousand years. If nothing else, they helped me to fall asleep.

Marella didn't visit. I wondered if she still had plans for me, or whether she'd lost interest, perhaps deciding my injuries meant that I wasn't as strong as she'd hoped.

Finally, after the prescribed week, the healer was satisfied with my progress and declared me fit for regular activity. Within minutes of her departure, a guard clumped into the room.

"Do you never knock?" I asked stiffly, putting down one of the thick history books.

He gave me a sour look. "You are to join the king for dinner."

I was taken again to bathe and dress, with help from Doreena. This time, my dress was robin's egg blue with white ribbons that crisscrossed under my breasts and at my waist. Elaborate filigree earrings with blue stones hung from my ears. My hair curled in ringlets at the ends, left loose down my back. Doreena spread something waxy on my lips to make them shine.

"You look lovely," Doreena said. "The king is in danger tonight."

"What do you mean?" I asked sharply.

"Of falling in love with you when you look like that."

I shuddered. "Bite your tongue."

Her head tilted slightly. "It wouldn't be the first time a Frostblood king fell in love with a Fireblood, you know."

Her words reminded me of a conversation with Arcus the night we'd sat side by side under a crescent moon, his profile barely visible in the fading light, his cloak billowing in the wind, his eye glinting in the starlight whenever he looked at me. It had been the first time he'd trusted me enough to tell me about his past. He'd also told me about the Frost King who had loved a Fireblood lady. The memory brought a little flutter in my stomach.

"I've heard the story of the Fireblood who became queen. Did the people accept her?"

"Well…" Her eyes flicked to mine, then away. "Actually, it ended tragically. The queen was murdered. It's said that a noblewoman who loved the king was jealous and plotted the queen's death. She died on their first anniversary."

A shiver traced my spine. "What a terrible story."

She nodded thoughtfully, a crease between her brows. "Affairs between fire and frost rarely end well."

I stood still while she finished with my hair, but couldn't help dwelling on the fate of the poor Fireblood queen.

A few minutes later, the guards deposited me in the dining room. Candlelight bounced off the icy chandelier and fluttered against the frost-tricked walls. The smell of roasted meat and spices filled the air.

This time, there were no richly gowned women, no courtiers, only the king at the head of the table, his hair gilded by candlelight. My gaze went to the chair where the captain had sat the last time I'd been in this room. I'd sat just two seats over, wishing he were dead. Now he was, and he'd died by my hand.

The king was dressed in black, the color so stark against his pale skin and hair that I was reminded of the moments in the arena when the world had turned black and white. But the candles were still gold, the walls tinged with blue. I took a deep breath and blotted out the memory.

Once again, the king motioned to the chair next to him. I walked toward him slowly, heart pounding in my ears, and sat on the white fur.

He looked handsome and austere. My hands trembled in my lap. The last time I had sat here, he had lied to me about the monks. I had an impulse to leap forward and take him by the throat. Or to burn him where he sat. But even away from the throne he radiated power, and he'd demonstrated that in the arena. My fire had no chance against him.

He regarded me steadily, his lips showing slight amusement but his eyes narrowed. I was struck by the strangeness of his eyes, mostly black with just a rim of deep blue around the edges.

"You look even lovelier tonight, Ruby."

I stiffened at his familiar use of my name.

He eased back in his chair. "I fulfilled my end of our bargain," he said evenly. "I gave you the captain. Aren't you grateful?"

"I didn't want to kill him. Not like that."

"'Not like that,'" he imitated with a dismissive wave of his hand, his eyes sweeping my straight-backed figure. "You're very finicky, Fireling. You wanted to kill him and now you have. That's all that matters."

"His wife was watching," I said through numb lips. "His young daughter. And he told me the monks are dead. By your orders."

His brows creased, his expression turning to intent speculation before it smoothed into his usual blank carelessness. "Ah. Well, perhaps I have forgotten."

I wasn't surprised that he had lost track of all the deaths—how could anyone remember so many?—but the casual way he had said the words stunned me.

Rasmus made a motion with his hand and a steward came forward, piling his plate with food. When the servant went to do the same for me, I put my hand over my plate and glared until he stepped away. The king regarded me for long moments with a heavy-lidded gaze, both of us silent and still.

He stood and grabbed my wrist in a biting grip. His cold skin burned into me more than fire ever could.

"You're hurting me," I said, trying to twist away.

"Your touch hurts me, too," he replied, his voice as rough as his hand as he pulled me closer. "But it's a pain I enjoy."

Arcus had once told me that my touch unsettled him, made him uncomfortable because it penetrated his defenses and made him feel things he didn't want to feel. But this was different. The king's touch hurt me and mine hurt him. If it gave him pleasure, it was a twisted one.

He drew me along to the wall opposite the head of the table, then pressed a barely visible recess on the stone wall that must have been a kind of mechanism. A hidden door swung open. We entered a narrow tunnel lit with torches. The ceiling was so low he had to bend his head.

"This tunnel is for me alone," he said, his hold on my wrist easing as we walked, his voice muffled in the tight space. "You enjoy an incredible privilege by seeing it. I do so only as an act of great trust."

My senses quickened. I hadn't done anything to earn his trust. And yet, if it was there, I had to use it to my advantage.

After a minute, we came to another door. The king pushed it open to reveal the throne room, draped in torchlight and shadows, the sky black against a moonless night. The throne was a large, menacing presence. Ice flowed down it and into the hallway and, I knew, all through the castle, even out into the arena. When I'd first seen it, I'd thought it looked like veins connected to a heart. Now, as shadows darted about in the walls, I realized the Minax lived in the throne but moved about in the ice connected to it.

I stifled a gasp as the familiar invisible force stole my fire.

"What are we doing here?" I asked, my voice subdued by the pressing shadows. "I thought we were to dine."

"You refuse to eat. I'm tired of games. This is where you really want to be. I give this to you as a gift."

He pulled me forward until we stood within arm's reach of the throne. Its dark power beat against me in waves. I wanted to cringe away, to run, but at the same time, I felt an insistent pull, moth to flame.

"Do you feel that?" he asked, pressing my hand to the throne. "Pure power. The throne was created by Fors himself as a gift to his Frostblood people. Did you know that?"

"Yes," I whispered, cold spreading up my arm. "But Fors is your god, not mine. It burns me."

"A further gift was bestowed by his brother, Eurus. Some call it a curse from a jealous god who sought to destroy his brother's creation. But it's really a gift of power that only the chosen can feel. To unlock it completely, you must have the right person. Someone who was created to bear a power so great."

"The child of darkness," I murmured, pulling against his grasp.

"Yes. When I took the throne, it told me to find the child. Together, she and I will bring darkness to the land. And with her, I'll be complete."

His eyes burned with intensity, an excitement I'd never seen before. I shook my head, my mind writhing with denial as his meaning sank in. "I'm not. I'm not the child of darkness."

His icy fingers touched my chin, tilting my face so my eyes met his in the flickering light.

"The prophecy says the child of darkness will have a powerful gift. I've tested all the strongest Frostbloods and Firebloods in my arena. You are the first to show a connection with the throne. Stop resisting, Ruby, and you'll never know pain again."

I shook my head. "But others will. People are suffering and you don't see it. The throne has taken away your mercy. You've become a monster."

"Not a monster," he said, stroking the curve of my cheek with his thumb. "Together, you and I will be like gods."

"I don't want to be a god!" I twitched my chin from his fingers. "I want to be a healer like my mother."

It was a truth I hadn't known until the words were spoken. I wished I had been given a healer's touch, a healer's gentle patience, instead of the rage of emotions that went with a power that killed and maimed.

"You deny it, but killing gives you pleasure. It allows the darkness to seep in further, merging with you more with each death."

He pulled me to his chest and found my lips with his. Cold and hot merged with darkness to create a new flame. His lips were hard, but they warmed under mine and filled me with a twisting excitement. His hand came to my face and tangled in my hair, the sharp stone of his ring cutting into my cheek.

His lips found the hollow under my chin, moving down my throat in a cool caress. A rush of sensation blurred my thoughts, pleasure mixed with distaste in equal measure. My hands found his shoulders to push him away but held on instead. The king lifted his head and smiled.

"My bloodthirsty Fireling," he whispered, smoothing the pads of his fingers across my lips. "Just one more fight, I think, and you will be ready. Once you let the Minax merge with you, its power will increase tenfold, and together we'll share it."

"I won't merge with it."

"You've already been doing so in my arena. Surely you've sensed it helping you? It lends you power to kill, and your killing makes it stronger. With it comes perfect bliss."

His words reminded me of the dream, the dark thing telling me that we would merge when my heart was black.

"But the Minax is already part of *you*," I said.

He shook his head slightly. "It advises me, lends me the power of the throne, eases my worry. Yes, by virtue of my crown, I share some of its power. But I can't merge with it completely, not the way you can. Once you and the Minax are one, we'll create a perfect rule over a perfect kingdom. No rebellion could withstand our combined power. No country will be able to defy my rule. And with it inside you, we won't be restricted to the castle. We can go anywhere, and its power will come with us."

Now I understood why the king had forced me into the arena. He could manipulate me so easily, forcing me to kill or be killed, every time opening cracks in my soul to let in more darkness. What would I become if I let him shape me into the creature he seemed so intent, even excited, to create? Like Eurus creating his shadows, there was no thought of right or wrong, only pleasure in the act of creation, of having control over another being.

I tried to pull away, but it felt as though I were caught in amber. His hand came up and caressed my throat. Revolted pleasure surged through me.

A great shadow rose from the throne, its shoulders pointed and two great horns growing from its head. The Minax looked more solid than it had in the arena, the same shape, only gaining bulk and dimension, as if it were becoming more corporeal as I watched.

A tendril morphed into a black hand that reached out and stroked the tip of my finger, sending tingling darkness up my arm and over my chest. Grief was sucked away and replaced with heady power. It was draining all the painful feelings from me, replacing them with a blank, empty kind of joy. I wanted to throw myself into that embrace. I wanted to forget everything and welcome oblivion.

It took a few seconds to realize that my heat had come back to me. The Minax had given me my fire.

The chiming voice of my dream whispered in my mind. "Let us be one. Together we will be free."

I suddenly had an overpowering urge to use my heat on the throne, to melt every last bit of ice until only a puddle remained in its place.

To set the Minax free.

Before I could react, Rasmus's lips came back to mine, harder, more insistent. My mind scrabbled to take hold of something stable, something that would ground me in this storm of confusion. A jolt of memory tore through me, another set of lips, cold but ardent, moving against mine. For a second, it was Arcus kissing me. I felt his cheeks under my palms, the silky strands of his hair at my fingertips. I saw his lips descending to mine. Other images came thick and fast: his profile in the dark, the waver in his voice when he'd told me he didn't want to let me go, his conviction that I was strong.

As hope and longing swelled inside me, the dark thing quivered and retreated. It was poised, though, ready to come back to me. I took advantage of its retreat, shoving the king with all my strength and running to the main doors, pounding on them with both fists.

I heard a laugh. I didn't know whether it was the king or the shadow hovering over the throne.

At the king's command, the guards opened the doors, took my arms, and led me back to my room.

I sat on my bed, my arms wrapped around myself. The king had seen the darkness inside me, and I couldn't deny it was there. I had welcomed it, and him, not just letting him kiss me, but returning his kisses. I closed my eyes against a surge of shame. Much as I wanted to deny it, I had enjoyed it, almost as much as I'd enjoyed killing in his arena. And now the Minax was speaking to me, telling me we would merge, that we would be one. I could no longer dismiss my earlier vision as a dream. The thing was becoming more powerful, more solid, the longer I stayed here, the more I killed.

Hands over my face, I rocked back and forth. What had I become?

Even now, I longed for that darkness, for its sinuous caress, like Brother Gamut's tea that eased all pain, only a thousand times stronger. I ached for the obliteration of worry and pain, even as the implications of what I would become repulsed me.

I hated the king. Hated him to the depths of my spirit. And yet he'd woken something in me: a thirst for mindless power I couldn't control.

I hopped off the bed and paced back and forth from stone wall to wooden door. When Brother Thistle had explained the plan to me, the evening sun streaming through the windows of the chapter house, he had seemed so confident. I would come to the castle and destroy the throne.

Now that I was in the castle, nothing was simple. I couldn't kill the king because the throne protected him. I couldn't destroy the throne because I had no power in its presence, except when I was in contact with the king.

Part of me just wanted to surrender. To let my next opponent strike me down. I could finally join my mother in the afterworld in the sky.

If I truly were the child of darkness, it would be better for the world if I was dead, rather than becoming some unstoppable power at the right hand of the king.

The thought hovered there, dark and heavy and undeniable.

Unfortunately, I didn't think the darkness would let me die. In the past two fights, it had snaked up and taken me over when I was under threat. Every time, it was stronger. Even if I fought against that shadow power, I didn't know if I could win.

Let the darkness take me, then. The king has won.

With the suddenness of a shutter being thrown open to let in the light of day, an image came to mind of my grandmother telling stories in front of the fire. I saw her lips moving, felt her hand on my hair. When the story was done, she would often give me a piece of wisdom to take from it.

"There is always light in darkness. It may only be a pinpoint, but it is there. Follow it and you will find your way free."

Letting myself be taken by the dark was forfeiting my choice.

Surely I was stronger than that. I could fight the Minax and its plans for me. I wouldn't kill again, no matter how strong the urge.

I would lose in the arena, but I would win the battle against the king. With my death, his hopes of finding a vessel for the Minax would be crushed. And perhaps another Fireblood, someone more powerful, more cunning and strong, would come along and destroy the throne.

It just wouldn't be me.

"I will find the light, Grandmother," I whispered.

TWENTY-FIVE

"RUBY!" BRAKA CALLED.

I blinked, and the familiar sounds and sights of the arena came into focus. I was half sick, half numb at the prospect of what I had to do. "What is it?"

"Your opponent," she said, her gray eyes serious. "He calls himself Kane. He is rumored to be a seasoned warrior come back from the wars. Like Gravnach, he uses no weapon but frost. Keep your distance and look for points he leaves unguarded, then focus on his weak spots."

My brows rose, her earnest words pulling me out of the fog of resignation. "Braka, are you actually giving me pointers? Be careful or the others will think you like me."

She smiled, displaying her missing tooth. "I do like you,

Fireling. You are brave and strong, and you have powers that, well, frankly confound me. I believe you can win any fight. You will even win the crowd eventually."

My lips twisted. "Unlikely. I see them preparing to launch their vegetables as we speak."

She chuckled. "There is something about you," she said thoughtfully, "that grows on a person. Like icicles."

I smiled up at her. "I'm nothing whatsoever like icicles."

She paused in thought. "Like fungus, then."

I chuckled. "Much better."

She clapped me on the back, the jovial pat reverberating through me. "No fear, Fireling. You haven't lost yet."

The current match was longer than usual, with one of the few female Frostblood challengers I'd seen. The two opponents were similar in size, but the woman had a clear advantage because of her stronger frost, though her male opponent often made gains with brute strength. Every match still made me sick to watch. That sickness reassured me. It meant I wasn't numb to the waste of life, at least not yet.

I caught a familiar floral scent and turned to see Marella standing behind me, goddess-like in a silver dress with silk flowers sewn onto the full skirt. Some of the same silk flowers were woven into her elaborately coiled hair. Icy gems set in silver winked from her earlobes and fingers, catching shafts of light from the arena.

"I came to wish you luck," she said with a dazzling smile.

"I appreciate the thought," I replied, adjusting my mask, "but I don't need luck. I don't want it."

Her lips quirked. "You're right. Luck is for fools. You're quite capable of destroying this challenger the way you've obliterated all the others."

The words sent a chill across the back of my neck. "I'm not going to destroy anyone. I can't do this anymore."

Her brow puckered. "You have no choice, Ruby. It's not your fault you're forced to do this. It's kill or be killed."

"Exactly. And every time I kill, something takes hold of me. A darkness I can't control." I paused. "I've decided not to kill again."

"Perhaps your guilt—"

"It's not guilt. I believe it's the Minax from the throne." I waited to see her reaction, but her face remained perfectly blank. "I'm sure it sounds like I've gone mad, but—"

"I know about the throne," she said simply. "I told you. Don't wear your mask with me. I was inviting you to confide in me and allow me to help you."

"How can you possibly help me?"

"I've been preparing for this day for half my life, reading the dustiest tomes in my father's library, researching the throne, sneaking out at night to consult with scholars." She smiled at my consternation. "My father may be a fusty, old sermonizer, but his saving grace is his collection of books. I know the old stories, and I've seen for myself that there's more truth to them than most people believe."

A cheer went up from the crowd, but I didn't bother to turn and look at what had caused it. I was too ensnared by Marella's revelations.

"King Akur went through a marked change during his reign," she said. "His wife and children saw it. My father and the closest court members saw it. And so did the royal scholar, who believed the throne was the real cause of our war on Firebloods. He believed the curse in the throne woke and was growing in influence. He told the king that as long as we treated Sud's people unfairly, the repercussions and fighting would be endless. And then King Akur's wife was murdered, proving Brother Thistle's theories right. The only reason he wasn't executed for his treasonous opinions was that he shares the same blood as the largest landowner in the eastern provinces. If Thistle's cousin, Lord Tryllan, had pulled his support for the king, it would have meant disaster for the border wars. So Thistle was banished to a crumbling old abbey on Mount Una, and he and his predictions were forgotten."

"Why didn't you tell me sooner?" I asked, half accusingly. "I would have told you everything."

"I didn't know if I could trust you. You have a bond with Raz. He looks at you in a way I've never seen him look at anyone." There was a brief flash of emotion in her eyes. "There are a great many reasons you could choose to reveal me, and I didn't want to take the chance. But now you're talking of dying in the arena today, and that risk is much greater. To all of us."

I paused. "You think I can destroy the throne, then?"

She took my hands in hers, her fingers cool but not frigid. "I know you can, Ruby. Today is the summer solstice, when your powers are greatest. If it's any day, it must be today."

Solstice. I remembered Brother Thistle saying that it was just over three weeks away, but the days had passed and I'd lost track.

"But, Marella, I'm afraid I'll be lost and I won't even want to destroy it. It'll merge with me and then—what would I become?"

Her fingers tightened on mine, her voice becoming urgent. "Merging with it is the only way to destroy it. Don't you see? If you do that, you can turn its power on itself. It's not only your fire you need. It's your darkness. That's what makes you special."

"How do you know?"

"I've watched countless Firebloods fight and die in this arena, and I've never seen any of them do what you can. The Minax has chosen you."

"Oh Sud, help me," I whispered, pulling my hands from hers and covering my face.

"You already know it's true. That's why you decided not to fight today. You're scared of what you'll become. But I promise you're stronger. You can merge with the Minax and still control it. You can do this, Ruby."

"You're *wrong*. I won't risk it."

I turned away.

"Then let me tell you something that might change your

mind. Your opponent today, Kane. He was one of the soldiers who raided the abbey."

I spun back to her. "What?"

She nodded. "I inquired about him for you, hoping I could discover his weaknesses, and I found out that he was assigned to Captain Drake when they went to Mount Una. I heard he was merciless. It was carnage, Ruby. And . . . the young man with scars was killed, too."

"Arcus?" I breathed.

She nodded, her eyes full of sorrow. "A fierce Frostblood warrior that fought madly to protect the abbey, despite the impossible odds. He killed a dozen soldiers before archers brought him down with flaming arrows."

A haze blurred my vision. The burning arrows wouldn't have been enough to subdue his frost, but he would have been terrified of those flames. It would have knocked him off guard, weakened his focus. I could see it clearly in my mind, the moment when he had been overcome.

I didn't realize I had doubled over until I felt Marella pull me up into a tight hug. "I'm so sorry, Ruby," she whispered into my hair. "I wasn't going to tell you. But now you know why Kane must not leave that arena alive. He deserves this death."

I gasped and shuddered, feeling myself falling into a million pieces but helpless to stop it.

"You can do this. Destroy Kane. Destroy the throne. Otherwise, there is no end to the darkness."

With a final squeeze, she pushed me from her, watching the

fight with a regretful expression. I followed her gaze and saw that both opponents were on the ground, the announcer raising the Frostblood woman's lifeless hand into the air. The crowd cheered, and servants came and pulled the bodies from the ring, leaving a trail of glistening blue blood behind. The Frostblood woman had apparently won, but she had paid with her life.

The announcer gave a signal. I stepped into the sunlit arena.

There were the usual jeers and curses, the drizzle of rotten food or rocks landing on the edges of the field. But shockingly, a couple of voices could be heard calling "Fireling!" I was numb to it all as if I floated above myself, a bystander with no stake in the proceedings. I hoped I would never have to feel again.

I turned and found the king on his balcony, Marella now seated like a painted doll to his left, her silver dress billowing out over the arms of her ice-carved seat. His robes were deep black with silver piping. I wondered if she had deliberately dressed to match him. It seemed that in subtle ways, she was always trying to catch his attention. I remembered what she'd said about the way he looked at me, and I saw it now. Rasmus inclined his head, the intensity of his gaze shivering over my skin. I stared, drawn despite myself to the shadows that shifted in the ice behind him, just out of sight.

As I gained center stage, the doors on the opposite side of the arena opened, and a figure strode out. He wore black leather armor with metal buckles and a steel helm with rectangular nose

and cheek guards that reached down to his chin, the only openings over his eyes and mouth. A black cloak flowed down his
back. He was larger and broader than the captain but not as big
as Gravnach had been. He held no sword.

He uses no weapon but frost, Braka had said. I shivered, remembering Marella's assertion that I had to merge with the Minax to
destroy it. I had vowed to find the light, even if it meant death,
but that was before I knew that this man was guilty of murder.
Arcus's murder. There was nothing in this world that would save
him from death by my hand.

He stopped some ten feet away and bowed to me. I took my
fighting stance, fists raised in readiness. He raised his. We circled
each other.

After a few seconds, the crowd began their chant: "Die, Fireblood, die!"

But the Frostblood warrior made no move, perhaps assessing,
waiting for some indication of my strength. I wasn't so patient. I
sent a sizzling jolt of flame at his feet.

He jumped nimbly out of the way and countered with a blast
of frost that hit the ground in front of me, sending up a cloud
of dust.

I spun a tornado of hot air at him. He put out his hands and
the air dispersed in a hiss.

Pinwheels of fire roared from my hands. He slammed each one
down with his steel wrist guards and blasted cold air back at me.

"You think this is a nice game, don't you?" I called, twisting my hands to send twin vortices of air so hot that the water in the air turned to vapor. He let it pass over him without a flicker of reaction, as if it were a spring breeze. "But what you don't know," I said, throwing out a cloud of bristling heat, "is that you won't leave this arena alive."

My chest heated and I punched out a series of attacks, fire bolts and fire arrows and a ferocious tail of the dragon in rapid succession, the whipcrack echoing off the ice. He dealt with each lazily. The crowd laughed and started to cheer.

"Kane! Kane! Kane!"

Annoyance tightened my shoulders. His frost was even stronger than Gravnach's.

I threw a bolt of fire at his helm. That got to him. He stumbled back before sending a gust of frigid air that made my legs shake with the effort of holding my ground.

Our attacks grew more rapid. I kicked up a sheet of flame. He coated himself with protective ice. I melted the ice with heated air, then sent another tail of the dragon. He frosted the ground under my feet, catching me in the middle of a movement. My foot twisted as I slipped and fell. I tried to push myself up but fell back to the ground.

Kane stalked over to me, his silhouette blotting out the sun. I turned my head to see the king leaning forward in his balcony, Marella rigid beside him. And between them, a dark shape hovering, its pointed head and shoulders growing and sharpening. There was no indication that anyone else could see it, but I could feel its presence, even with my eyes closed.

As I felt the darkness rise, I sent another stream of fire at Kane. Whether it was because of the solstice, or the darkness filling me, or just the fact that my hatred had finally freed me of all restraint, my fire seemed to burn hotter than it ever had. His tunic caught and he threw out frost to quench it.

He struck at me with frost that hissed into harmless steam, then sent icicles screaming toward me. They melted in the cloud of heated air that surrounded me like a shield.

I was too powerful already, bright as a piece of the sun. I was sure I could kill him with my fire alone. But I wanted the oblivion only the Minax could give me.

"Come, darkness," I whispered. "Use me to kill this murderer."

The Frostblood warrior halted a few feet away and spoke.

"So it's true. You're lost to me."

But his words had no meaning, lost in a glorious hum of power. And whether I had the power to control the Minax afterward didn't matter. All that mattered was losing myself in vengeance.

My vision changed, the world turning to the now familiar black and white. Sound faded to the beat of my heart and the breathing of my opponent. Onyx tendrils arced out from my mind seeking the convulsing black lump in his chest.

"Don't make me hurt you," the warrior said, the words distant, like raindrops against glass.

I sent out a steady stream of fire and he met it with a column of frost. Meanwhile, the sinuous threads of shadow circled, spiraling tighter and tighter toward his heart.

"Please, Ruby," he said, his frost building, pushing me back, forcing me to end things now.

But some part of me had registered that I knew the voice of this warrior.

I *knew* that voice.

But it was impossible. He was dead. Had I lost my mind?

"Arcus?" I breathed, trembling with the effort of holding back.

"So pleased you remember me," he answered, the attempt at humor ruined by the way his voice cracked with emotion.

Shock trembled through me. I pulled back my hand, stopping the stream of flame, while he did the same, both of us reeling backward with the effort. The fire was easy to control, but the darkness wasn't. It still twined around his heart. He grunted in pain and clapped a hand to his chest. I groaned with the effort of controlling the killing frenzy inside me. *I will find the light.* With a massive effort, focusing all my energy on those sinuous tendrils, I drew them back and pushed them away. The world exploded back into color with a loud pop.

"Is it really you?" I whispered, trying desperately to see beneath his helm. My eyes roved over him. Broad shoulders, broader than I remembered, but that could be the armor. And the helm, damn the helm that hid his face! Hope and fear that I was mistaken warred with each other.

His hand dropped to his side. "I told you that you'd be a threat once you gained some control. Though I hear they still don't like you much in these parts."

Heady joy surged through my body, then burned into fury as I thought of what had almost happened.

"I could have killed you!" I shouted, but it came out high and thready as I stumbled toward him and threw myself into his arms. He grasped me so tightly I couldn't breathe, but I didn't care.

A voice resonated from a balcony. It was the announcer, his magenta robes a bright slash of color against the colorless ice.

"Champions! The arena is not a matchmaker's ball." The crowd erupted in laughter and shouts of agreement. "These people came to see blood! Do we need to send some challengers in there to pry you apart?"

"Arcus," I whispered, my eyes finding his. "The doors don't open until one of us is dead. I won't kill you. You have to kill me."

His eyes widened and then hooded. "Have you gone quite mad, Ruby?"

"No, listen," I pleaded. "Brother Thistle was right about the throne, but he was wrong about me. I'm not the child of light. I'm—"

"Just another foul-tempered Fireblood." He grinned to take the edge off the words and offered his hand again. "Calm yourself, Ruby. I know you didn't manage to destroy the throne. But I have forces all around us. I needed to buy time for them to get into place without drawing suspicion. And, to be honest, I wasn't sure where your loyalty lies. I'd heard rumors about you and the king…." His eyes searched mine before he continued. "Anyway, I didn't mean to hurt you. I'm sorry it took me so long to—"

"I don't care about that!" I couldn't believe he was speaking so calmly, as if everything were fine. "Listen. The curse in the throne—"

As I spoke, doors rumbled open and fighters poured out. They came from all sides with spears, swords, maces, and gales of frost and ice.

Arcus pushed me back and stepped in front of me, as if to shield me from the approaching chaos. He took a deep breath, put both hands to his helm, lifted it from his head, and threw it on the ground, the movements deliberate, unhurried, but filled with purpose. He raised his hands, palms out. Power emanated from him, a regal manner that brooked no opposition. The fighters slowed and came to a halt around us.

Bits of dust and cold mist swirled in the air. The crowd grew quiet.

"Good people, hear me!" he shouted above the din. "I come to you not as a peasant fighter, or a warrior, or a champion, as you have been told."

No, not a mere champion, I thought. Despite his stature, which could pass for one of the king's champions, he had a proud bearing that hinted at his noble birth, now more than ever before.

"I come to you as the man who would sit rightfully on the throne of Fors!"

I heard the words, but my torpid mind couldn't take in the meaning. He was pretending to be someone else, saying things that weren't true. And he didn't stop.

"I come to you as Arelius Arkanus, son of Akur, elder brother to Rasmus. I was burned by an assassin and left for dead. But I did not die."

I fell back, my heart racing, but my mind still stuffed with feathers.

"I lived to fight," said Arcus, more power in his voice than I'd ever heard, "to return to the people I love. I come to you now and present myself as your faithful servant. I come to you now as the rightful Frost King!"

TWENTY-SIX

*T*IME LOST MEANING. *T*HE SOUNDS
of the arena faded to a distant roar.

Arcus towered over me, his face bared for all to see, scars standing out in the bright afternoon sunlight. It was like looking at a stranger. He addressed the crowd, saying things I only half heard, about it being up to them, his people, to choose which ruler belonged on the throne, that they should fight by his side because his rule would be fair, his memory of their loyalty long.

He exhorted them with the skill of a seasoned orator, convincing and confident, his shoulders thrown back, his chin held high. Gone was the mysterious figure skulking in a hood. Gone was the young man who had feared my fire. Gone was the person whom I'd come to trust, whose scars I had gently touched, whose lips had moved over mine with sweet, ardent pressure.

A king stood before me. The Frost King. Towering and merciless, ready to take his seat on the corrupted throne and gorge himself on its power.

My skin roughened with gooseflesh. This time there would be no hope. Arcus radiated banked power, a hum of energy kept leashed and dormant but waiting for a chance to break free. It was in the very air around him, and always had been, though I hadn't recognized it before now. Where Rasmus drew his power from the throne, Arcus had inner strength. He would harness the throne's power and amplify it tenfold.

Then he turned to look down at me. His cold blue gaze softened, his eyes meeting mine with a hint of deep warmth.

I shook my head, the fearful image of an invincible king on the throne clearing like morning mist. This was Arcus. He might be Rasmus's brother, but he was still the same person I knew. I offered my hand and he took it, pulling me to my feet and against his chest. A smile curved his lips.

"My bundle of firewood," he said softly. "It's good to have you in my arms again."

A blast of ice exploded at Arcus's feet, bringing him to his knees.

I turned to the source and found myself facing the king's balcony. Rasmus's hands were out, his eyes fixed on us, fury blazing in their depths.

"Kill this imposter!" Rasmus shouted, the words echoing

around the arena. "My brother is dead. You see a usurper before you. Kill him or be named traitor!"

Many of the spectators drew swords or clubs from underneath their ragged clothes and poured from the stands into the arena.

As Arcus stood and pulled me back to him, I struggled out of his arms. "Go!"

"Ruby, stop," he said. "These are my rebels, people who have chosen to fight for me. And others may choose to follow us."

He was right. As the people rushed forward at the king's soldiers, swords clashed in a deafening cacophony of steel on steel. Those with the gift threw frost and ice in a dizzying display of shining white.

Full-scale revolt had landed on the king's doorstep. I turned to find his balcony, but I couldn't see past the forest of bodies.

"We need to get you out of here," said Arcus. "I can't be sure you're safe, even among my allies."

He sprang to his feet and pulled me by the hand toward the side of the arena, an alcove opposite to the entrance where I usually stood waiting to fight. A blast of frost at my heels made me stumble. Arcus pulled me into a shady recess.

I twisted to look at him. "The king will put down your little revolt in minutes, starting with you. Why would you be so foolish? This was never the plan."

"This was always part of the plan, just not the part that involved you. I've been meeting with my supporters in secret for the past year. But we hadn't planned to move on the castle until the throne was destroyed."

"And you know it hasn't been. You shouldn't have come!"

He shook his head. "That plan changed the moment you left the abbey without me. I couldn't let you face this alone. We came as quickly as we could…though I didn't know for sure whose side you were on anymore. I heard how you became a champion. There were reports that you were getting quite close to the king."

Our eyes met, his asking a question that he wasn't sure he wanted me to answer.

I slid my hand to the side of his neck and his hands came to my lower back. "My allegiance hasn't changed, if that's what you're asking. I'm with you."

As I spoke, the hair on the back of my neck rose. An invisible fingertip traced my collarbone, making my skin tingle. An amorphous shadow blotted out the sun like a moving stain. My throat convulsed. The tendrils flowed into me and erased all worry and care, replacing it with a heady sense of limitless energy. The world lost color. Arcus turned light gray outlined in black, his heart dark and clear in my sight.

"Kill him." It was the familiar ringing voice, excruciating and undeniable. I would do anything to please that voice.

No. I ripped my mind free with a sharp cry. The world regained its color, but somehow off, painted in faded hues, leaving me half in, half out of reality. The dark wisps licked at the edges of my awareness.

"Ruby?" said Arcus, his brow tightly creased.

The feeling was rising, the bloodlust sharpening. I had invited the Minax in, and now I didn't know how to get it to leave. And it thirsted for Arcus's death. I could feel my fingers itching to reach out and send dark tendrils into his heart. My control was slipping away by the second.

"Let me go!" I snarled, pushing against his chest. "The Minax is becoming a part of me. I can't explain now. I have to destroy the throne before I hurt you!"

As he loosened his hold in surprise, I turned and bolted into the arena. The alcove that led to the castle was on the opposite side. Somehow, I had to make my way through the crush.

"Ruby!" Arcus shouted, fury tinged with fear.

But there was only one thought in my head: *Destroy the throne.* Marella had told me I was more powerful today than any other day. And now, while the king was distracted, might be my only chance. Even if the chance was small, I had to try.

I scrambled into the throng, a screaming whirl of swords and frost. I dodged and ducked, sometimes narrowly avoiding the clash of soldiers and Arcus's supporters, impeccable blue tunics over armor pitted against people dressed as ragged peasants. I wove my way between them, sometimes using blasts of heat or flame to shield me from shards of ice thrown into an opponent's face. It took several minutes just to get near the alcove where Braka and her champions fought with fierce, muscular efficiency.

"Fight for Arcus!" I shouted to Braka.

Her icy braids danced as she blocked and kicked and swept her sword in lusty arcs. At her blank look, I realized she knew Arcus by a different name.

"Fight for Arelius Arkanus!"

"I can't, Fireling," she said, parrying blows from three men at once. "We're the king's champions!"

"And who is the true king?" The question hung in the air as I darted into the alcove. I didn't have time to convince her.

I streaked down the tunnel and into the courtyard, where fighting had spilled to and taken over. The arena was nothing compared with the battle that raged outside the castle. Steel rang against steel over cries and shouts. Archers loosed arrows from their position in the battlements. Frost wolves twisted and leaped, their teeth bared, eyes wild as they protected their masters. Blood darkened the cobbles underfoot, the metallic scent mixing with the reek of sweat and fear.

As I gained the castle wall, the guards were closing the massive doors. With a frantic rush, I focused on armor and swords, sending heat into the metal. Two of the guards dropped their weapons and cried out. One of them held on, coming at me with a shout. I darted to the side and threw heat into the air to cover him in a cloud of fog, then slipped past. Momentum made the doors continue to slide shut. When they closed, I pulled a heavy bar into place, sealing everyone out.

The corridors were empty. Most of the castle guards were outside in the fray. I was sure the throne room doors would still be guarded, though, so I headed for the dining hall's secret passage.

I ran to the wall where the door was hidden and slid my hand along the wall, searching for the mechanism. I couldn't find it.

"Ruby!" The voice was muffled but familiar.

There was a click, and then the door opened a crack to reveal someone inside the passage. It was Marella, one of her violet eyes and the elegant curve of her cheek visible in the finger-wide opening.

"What are you doing here?" I whispered.

"As I said, my father has served as advisor to three kings. I know every hidden room, every forgotten staircase, and every tunnel in this castle. I didn't know if the king had shown it to you, but I hoped.

"Come." She opened the door wider and started to move away.

Remembering what she'd told me—that Kane was one of the soldiers who raided the abbey, that Arcus was dead—I grabbed her shoulder, spinning her around. "Why did you lie to me?"

"Shh," she hissed. "Do you want to bring the guards in here? We can talk in the tunnel."

"I'm not going anywhere with you. I don't trust you, Marella. Why did you tell me Arcus was dead?"

She sighed. "You were talking about giving up, letting yourself lose the match. I couldn't let that happen, Ruby. I needed you to fight."

"It would have been enough to say that Kane was at the abbey with the captain. You didn't need to tell me my closest friend was dead. I could have killed him! When I think what almost happened because of you—"

She smiled knowingly. "Is he really just a friend, Ruby? I saw the way you looked when you thought he was dead."

I stepped toward her and she stepped back, palms out. "And yes, I suppose I did go further than I needed to, but I wanted you angry. I wanted you thinking your darkest thoughts, feeling your darkest feelings. That's the only way the Minax will be able to merge with you, and that's the only way to destroy the throne. You still want to destroy it, don't you?"

"Of course I do," I said, struggling not to shake her for what she could have caused. "But that doesn't mean I forgive you."

"I'm sorry, Ruby," she said, finally looking contrite. "I didn't know it was...Arcus, you call him? I had no idea what had happened to him when you were taken from the abbey. Frankly, I didn't even know for sure that he was the king. I had only suspicions. Now, come. We're wasting time."

She turned her back and moved away, and I followed this time. Destroying the throne took precedence over my anger at her betrayal. Whether I liked it or not, I needed her knowledge.

"Do you really think I can do this?" I asked as we half walked, half ran through the narrow space. "Whenever I've been in the throne room, I can barely connect to my power. My only hope is that the throne is weaker without the king's presence."

She stopped and turned, taking my wrist in her hand and squeezing in a comforting gesture.

"You can do this, Ruby," she said, her conviction flowing into me. "Let the Minax inhabit you. Once you become one with it, you share its power. It's the only way to destroy the throne and give us some hope of winning. Some hope for..." She trailed off.

"Rasmus?" I asked softly. Her eyes snapped to mine. "It's clear you care for him."

Her nostrils flared. "Perhaps I shouldn't. Even before he

took the throne, he was moody, unpredictable, and, well, troubled. But I cared for him anyway, for as long as I can remember." She pressed her lips together. "When he became king, he turned into someone I didn't recognize. His petty cruelty became monstrous, his unpredictability became wild changes in temper, and his black moods became..." She shook her head. "I lost him. If you destroy the throne, there is a chance I'll have him back, the real him, and maybe I can help him return to something worth loving."

Her confession stunned me, both the idea of loving Rasmus and the fact that she had confided in me.

We arrived at the tunnel exit, a stone's throw from the looming outline of the throne.

"You have to do this, Ruby," she whispered. "There are things I haven't had a chance to tell you, but I know more about the throne than you can imagine. It has waited for you all these years. If you fail, every hope is lost. And I will be executed for helping you."

"Yes," a silky voice agreed. "But it wouldn't be much of a loss."

TWENTY-SEVEN

$\mathcal{A}$ FIGURE ROSE FROM THE THRONE, his bright hair haloed by light that burst through the window and ricocheted off facets of ice.

"Marella, my dear traitor." He beckoned her forward.

"I didn't betray you," she said, her face ashen. "I'm trying to save you."

He gave a short, disbelieving laugh. "The only person you care about saving is yourself. You may have fooled Ruby, but I know you too well. Come closer. I want to see those lovely little tears you manufacture so easily as you beg for your life."

She turned and raced for the tunnel. When her hand touched the stone door, she cried out. Ice covered her fingers, fusing them to the handle. I put a hand out to melt the ice, but the familiar weight pressed on my chest, hiding my fire.

"You seem surprised to see me," Rasmus said to me, his lips curving.

I willed my heart to slow and stepped forward. "You aren't leading your men in battle?"

His eyes hooded. "I'll reward the loyal ones and string up the traitors. The throne is only strengthened by battle."

He spoke with lazy satisfaction, as if he'd shared some bit of arcane knowledge as a matter of idle curiosity.

"When people die by violence, the throne grows stronger and feeds its power to me." He closed his eyes, leaning his head back against the ice. "What were you planning to do here, my lovely Fireling?"

"I wanted the throne's power, as you offered."

His eyes opened, flaring. "Is that so? Well then, come."

He strode forward, his hand circled my wrist, and he pulled me to the throne. As he pressed my hand against the ice, dark power surged into my fingers and up my arm, making my body hum with cold delight.

"You belong to the throne," he said, sliding an arm around my back and holding me close, "and it belongs to me. That makes you mine, Ruby."

He took my chin in his hand and turned my face to his. Overpowered by sensation, every sinew alive with the feel of the throne under my hand, I could only shake my head.

His lips found the pulse that beat in my temple, sending liquid sparks into my veins. "Take it into your heart," he whispered, the words piercing my skin.

"Let Marella go," I managed to say. "You have no quarrel with her."

His narrowed gaze moved to Marella where she was trying to free herself. Icicles had formed in her hair.

"She didn't tell you?" he asked. "Lady Marella conspired against me with my own captain. In exchange for a pile of coin to pay off his gambling debts, he took you to Blackcreek Prison instead of bringing you here. She hid you from me."

My shocked gaze locked with his. "That's why you gave him to me in the arena. Because he betrayed you."

"I don't regret his death."

"Have you ever regretted anyone's?"

A pale brow rose and his lip twitched.

"She betrayed me. Spies in my inner circle." He ran a finger along my chin. As a bit of my heat returned, I realized that when he touched me and the throne at the same time, it returned my gift to me, at least a part of it. "They'll have to be purged. I'll let you kill her when I finish questioning her. It will increase your power."

The shadows in the throne thickened. I was able to summon enough of my gift to send warm air at Marella's hands. She pulled free of the ice and darted back into the tunnel, the slap of her shoes echoing into silence.

Rasmus took my shoulders and shook me. "Your mercy is wasted."

His lips covered mine. The pressure sent a surge through my body, glorious delight that obliterated all worry and fear, all concern for what I should and must do. There was only bliss and darkness. A shadow rose and towered over us.

"Do you want me?" asked Rasmus against my lips, his hand sliding to my lower back, his hips pressing against mine.

As I was lost in ecstasy, part of me wanted to say yes. I wanted the darkness. I wanted the power. I wanted the bliss. *You give me all these things, and therefore I want you.*

But something flickered at the corner of my mind, memories of warmth. Most of the people I loved were gone, but there was someone who needed me, someone I cared about more than darkness and power. I saw eyes a dozen shades of blue that went from cold to hot in a heartbeat. I had told myself to forget him, but he had come back and he depended on me. I couldn't turn away from Arcus now.

As Rasmus's lips moved over mine, connecting me to his darkness and the darkness of the throne, heat came rushing back into my chest. I sent it into the hand that rested on the throne, fire flowing from my heart through my arms and into the jagged ice. The surface began to melt, a hand-shaped indentation forming in the ice. Drops of water hit my feet. Rasmus sucked in a breath and shoved me away, something stark and vulnerable flashing through his eyes before his expression hardened.

"Why did you really come here?"

He swept his hand around the room, sealing the door with a sparkling layer of frost before offering that same hand to me. Instinctively, I moved backward, toward the door.

"Have you ever loved anyone, Ruby?"

The question took me aback, but I needed to keep him talking, stalling while I tried to think of a way out. "I loved my mother. M-my grandmother."

"How about now? Whom do you love now?"

I hesitated. "I love... my people."

"You don't even know your people. Why would you want to?"

"A million reasons you'd never understand."

"So you can feel like you belong?" he suggested. "Well, I was raised with my people and I never belonged. My frost was weak compared with my brother's, and my father hated me for it. He used to fill me with bits of ice, enough to cause excruciating pain but not enough to kill. He hoped to make me more powerful, to strengthen my gift."

I swallowed hard. "That's terrible."

"It cut me off from everyone, never understood, never accepted. When I took the throne, the advisors thought they could make sport of me, stealing from the royal coffers, belittling me just out of hearing, making a farce of my reign. But the throne understood my fears and helped me kill one of them in front of the rest. Suddenly, they respected my power, and the darkness brought me joy and took my pain, much as it takes your heat. It feeds off things that are hot: passion, hatred, violence."

I pressed a hand to my stomach, battling nausea. My own hatred and violence had fed the very throne I had come to destroy.

"But I was still frozen," he continued. "The throne has no cure for that. When I saw you in my arena, when I watched you burn the hearts of your enemies without a second of hesitation, I thought, *There she is. She is fire. She is heat. She was meant for me. I found out about your pain, your sorrow, so I would know how to blacken your heart, to make you strong.*"

The throne still pulled at me, and, despite myself, so did his soft words.

"I'm already strong," I said, "just in a different way." I took a breath, remembering that I was a healer's daughter. "Perhaps there is a chance for you. He always wanted me to heal you."

His eyes narrowed. "Who?"

I made a helpless gesture. "Arcus. He wanted me to break the curse and heal you. I don't know how we can do it, but maybe we can find out."

He moved closer, slowly, like one would approach a wild dog. His voice shook, his eyes shining like polished onyx. "The way you say his name, Ruby...I felt you rip yourself from the darkness, from me, to protect my brother when you should have killed him." Hurt flashed in his eyes, swift as lightning, leaving them darker than before. "Why didn't you kill him?"

I spread my palms. "I never wanted to kill anyone."

"You killed before. Why not *him*, Ruby?"

I felt as if I was being backed into a trap. "He's my friend."

Rasmus took my chin between his finger and thumb in a bruising grip. "Why wouldn't you kill him?"

"I would never hurt Arcus," I said, shoving him away with all my strength, any thought of healing gone. "I would die first!"

There was a thick, pulsing silence before he spoke, his voice tempered steel. "If you refuse the throne, you refuse me. You're not strong in the way I need you to be. And I detest weakness."

He flicked his hand at me, and I was covered in ice up to my waist. I willed my skin to grow hot, but the ice thickened and crept up my body.

"Good-bye, Ruby," he said. "Know that your death will increase the throne's power. So it wasn't a complete waste."

TWENTY-EIGHT

THE DOORS TREMBLED AS SOME-thing crashed against them, cracking the ice that sealed them with each blow. They split open and Arcus pushed through, breathing heavily, his head bare, a blood-smeared sword held in his hand.

Rasmus, poised and ready, hit Arcus in the chest with a bolt of frost, slamming him into the stone wall. Another bolt caught Arcus's wrist, opening his hand. The sword clanged as it fell to the tiled floor, then froze with a thick block of ice covering it.

"Let her go," said Arcus in a calm tone at odds with the fury in his eyes. He levered himself away from the wall and came forward. "And we can talk like brothers."

"Isn't she pretty there, all trussed up in ice?" Rasmus said with amusement. "Perhaps I'll keep her as a statue in my court-yard. Fire trapped in ice. An elegant metaphor, don't you think?"

".The throne controls you," said Arcus, his voice low and even, moving forward slowly.

Rasmus breathed a laugh. "The throne is my ally."

Arcus stopped a few feet away, his eyes moving over me, per-haps looking for blood or signs that I was hurt. A look of relief passed over his face when he didn't find any.

"I'm not your enemy, Raz. We can find a way to free you from the curse."

Rasmus bared his teeth in a feral grin. "Fors and Eurus are brothers, too. Eurus made the throne stronger as a gift."

"He poisoned it out of jealousy," said Arcus.

"You were scared of your own throne. Is that why you didn't come back until now?"

"You hired someone to kill me! Forgive me for not being eager to return."

Rasmus shook his head. "Not me. I was barely more than a child."

Arcus blinked several times. "You're saying you didn't send the assassin. I don't know if I believe you."

"Believe what you wish. I don't need you." Rasmus turned to me and spoke with feverish emphasis. "And I don't need her."

Ice crept up my chin and coated my lips, cutting off my air. I struggled in blind panic. After a few seconds, my heated breath melted the ice around my mouth. I took in gulps of air and watched the brothers face each other.

"Let her go, Raz," Arcus said, his voice stern. He had an air of command, of an older brother and a king. "We can make peace now, but if you kill her, you're as good as dead."

"All I have to do is raise a finger and I can stop her heart," said Rasmus softly. "Just one breath. A thought, even. You won't even know I've done it until it's too late. Another lying Fireblood whom no one will miss."

I focused on my heart, willing the heat to come forward, to melt the ice around me. Barely a flicker answered, not even a tendril of flame.

"*I* will miss her." Arcus's voice was harsh, threatening, but it held a desperate undercurrent.

"I missed you," said Rasmus. "For a while."

"You said you never wanted the throne. Together we can destroy it. You can rule at my side, at my right hand."

"I rule *now*," Rasmus said, raising his voice.

Arcus took a breath. "I admit I was proud. And in my pride, I refused to believe in the curse. I watched Father grow paranoid and cruel, but I blamed the wars, the pressures of ruling. When I took the throne, I fought the knowledge that I was being changed, corrupted—"

"Perfected," Rasmus bit out. "Strengthened. If you had only accepted it, the limits would have fallen away and you would have become so much more than you imagined."

Arcus shook his head. "You've lost yourself. The thing in there"—he gestured to the throne—"has eaten you up from the inside."

"The only thing my throne feeds on are the spirits of traitors and Firebloods." He waved a hand, and the ice pressed tighter until I cried out. Arcus's eyes widened, his face paling.

"Keep the throne," Arcus breathed. "I'll take her far away, across the ocean. I'll forfeit my title, denounce my claim. Whatever you ask. As long as you let me take her."

No. I tried to shake my head, but ice held my neck fast. I wanted to shout at Arcus, to scream that he couldn't make such an offer. If there was one thing I knew about him, it was that he was steadfast in his loyalties. It would kill him to abandon his people.

"You might come back," said Rasmus. "You have too many supporters who could rise against me. Assassinate me."

"I never wanted you dead. I only wanted our kingdom to be what it once was. For you to stop the wars, start helping people again. But I will let that all go."

Rasmus shook his head. "I don't trust you."

A silence. "Then kill me if you must. But let her go first. I will let you kill me when I see her safely leave your city."

No, no, no.

I went wild inside. I opened my mouth, but only a squeak emerged from my frozen throat. My lungs bursting, my mind flailed with the effort of making my limbs move, to smash out of the bonds of ice. It was like being buried under a mountain, every muscle straining in vain.

"You would die..." He looked down at me, then back at his brother. "For *her*?"

"Yes. I would," said Arcus firmly. "That is the bargain."

No, I couldn't let him do that.

Indecision hung in the air, as palpable as a dense fog. Shadows played against the walls. Something whispered from the throne, a sibilant, barely detectable hiss.

Rasmus smiled, the expression so cold it was like seeing a corpse grin. "You have only made me want to kill her more." He turned back to me, meeting my eyes. "You are nothing."

The ice slipped from outside my body to the inside. A scream froze in my throat as pain bit into my chest, worse than a sword thrust, icy where I was hot, but unmelting. Slicing into me, driving, relentless, inescapable.

I caught a glimpse of Arcus launching himself at Rasmus as my eyes closed against the pain, a dim thought of grief that Arcus couldn't win flitting through my mind. With the throne behind him, Rasmus was far too powerful. *Sud, let it be over. Please, just let it be done.* I would go to the afterworld in the sky and be with my mother. I would be warm. I would be free.

But one thought, Marella's words, suddenly came back to me. The only way to destroy the throne was to become one with it, to let the Minax merge with me. The throne of Fors was made to repel and weaken Firebloods. Right now I was all fire. But if I let in the darkness, which already moved freely from the throne to the ice connected to it, I could slip past the throne's defenses and destroy it from within.

Come, darkness, I thought.

Hissing filled my ears and dark tendrils snaked into my

fingertips, up my arms, and over my face. There was a sensation of pressure. My ears popped and I gasped a mouthful of air, unable even to writhe against the strange feeling because of the ice holding me. Then the feelings settled and eased, my body growing accustomed to its new occupant. With a sense of triumph, I realized my heat was my own again, roaring into my chest and through my limbs in a glorious, hot surge. My mind was lifted free of all worry, my thoughts growing simpler, more elemental, with a sharp, soaring joy.

"You and I are one," a ringing voice said, only now it came from within. "Free me, and then we will search for my brother in the fire throne, so that we may achieve the destiny our father laid before us. Daughter of Darkness, be ready for that day. It comes soon."

The room had been leached of color, the icy blues now gray, the shafts of sunlight from the window pure white. I looked at my fingertips and saw a haze of onyx smoke curling from them.

Arcus and Rasmus struggled a few feet away, and though Arcus's arms bunched with the effort of holding his brother off, his knees buckled as Rasmus's hands squeezed his throat. I watched them with detached interest, trying to remember what I had wanted so badly only moments before. I tried to move and found that I was still encased in ice.

Break this ice, I thought, and the ice exploded into half-melted shards, glistening like white gems as they filled the air and skidded across the floor.

Hadn't I been part of the king only moments ago, my darkness inside him? He was my ally.

"My king," I said, and my voice was tinged with the sound of chiming bells, haunting and resonant. I sent a whirlwind of heated air at Arcus, and he was thrown several feet away, sliding across the floor in a screech of armor on stone.

I walked slowly to Rasmus, and he watched me intently with eyes that were no longer as black, but showing a wider rim of dark blue. He took a shuddering breath. "You merged with the Minax."

"We are one," I answered with my strange new voice.

He reached out slowly, put his hand to the back of my neck, and pulled me forward, his lips meeting mine. He gasped when they met.

"Your skin burns," he said. But his lips returned to mine and I pressed myself against him, returning his kiss.

"Ruby!" said Arcus, my name the very sound of shock and betrayal.

"She chose, brother," Rasmus replied, smoothing a lock of hair from my cheek. "She chose power."

"I *am* power," I corrected, pointing to the throne.

Not a scrap of shadow marred it now. The Minax had left the throne and was in me, and *was* me, and I was it, and I would never give up this incredible power. But some part of the Minax was still linked with Rasmus. He still held some of my shadow energy, and I wouldn't share this. I wanted it all.

"Leave the king," I told the Minax, and a ropelike cord of shadow swirled from him and into me. Rasmus doubled over, putting his hands to his knees for support.

"Don't take it all, my sweet," said Rasmus shakily. "We need to share it."

I hesitated. I didn't want to give up even a shred of this feeling. The Minax spoke in my head. "You have freed me. You needn't share our power long. Give him only enough to kill the brother, and we will feed on their grief and hatred and leave this place strong."

I nodded, then touched Rasmus's cheek and poured darkness back into him.

"Thank you," he said with a smile.

"Kill him," I commanded.

Rasmus drew his hands back and snapped them forward, hitting Arcus with a massive blast of frost. Arcus turned to take the blow on his shoulder, raising one hand to punch out his own onslaught.

"Need more," Rasmus whispered, and I touched him again, giving him my dark energy.

As some of the darkness left me, the world gained color and I looked at Arcus with new eyes.

"You're hurting him," I said, expressionless. The Minax had said this would make me stronger, but I felt a vague sense of discomfort that even the oblivion couldn't touch.

"Yes," Rasmus gritted, "if only he would die faster." His muscles coiled as he slammed out blow after blow of sharpened ice. The room filled with an echoing howl as it cut into the tender skin of Arcus's neck, who used one hand to staunch the blood as he fought with the other.

I continued to watch until a gash formed on Arcus's hand, making him cry out and curl up to take the blows against his back.

"Something is wrong," I said, putting my hand around Rasmus's wrist and pulling his arm down. His frost swirled against the floor and ceased. "I don't want him to die."

Rasmus met my eyes, his own nearly black again. "Don't let your resolve weaken. We're so close."

"Ruby," said Arcus, sitting up, bloody and panting with exhaustion. "Help me."

"No," said Rasmus. "He must die so we can take his power, and together we'll be unstoppable. Do it, Ruby. Show me your strength."

A rush of anticipation filled me. Hesitating for only a second, I raised my hand and let my fire explode at Arcus. He met it with frost. As the two columns merged, they sparked into white-and-blue fire that flowed toward the ceiling like a geyser.

"Frostfire," Rasmus breathed, laughing delightedly. "The fire that can burn through anything. It was said only a divine being could create it, but here you are, making the stuff of gods. I knew you were special." He turned to gloat. "Even you're no match for it, brother!"

He added his frost to the columns, all three jets joining and creating a blinding-white pinwheel with a blue center. He used the force of his frost to bend the sparking flame, the blue center moving inexorably toward Arcus.

"When it reaches him," Rasmus said, grinning, "he'll be nothing more than a stain on the floor."

Suddenly, a frantic inner warning clawed at me, a bubble that formed in my heart and made my chest ache. This was Arcus. *Arcus.*

A hundred images danced through my mind. Arcus carrying me from the prison, Arcus saving me from my own fire by putting me in the stream, Arcus helping me train. I remembered the first time I'd looked into his eyes, the first time he'd smiled at me, how dazzled I'd been to realize there was far more to him than even he seemed to know. And he'd changed for me, or at least he'd tried. He'd reined in his impatience after the first dueling lesson. He'd shown me in the forge how steel needs flame. He'd unwittingly shared pieces of himself with me, his love of stories, his concern for people who were suffering. He had pushed me away so many times, but now I knew that he had only been trying to protect himself from feelings that were too big to deny or control. I had felt the same way, spun off my axis by my longing for his attention, his trust, and even his touch.

I remembered how he'd kissed me and the things he'd said about wanting to protect me, not wanting to let me go. He'd shown time and again how much he cared, whether he'd meant to or not, and I had grown to see the depths of him, so different from my initial judgments. He felt things deeply and so did I. He had become vital to my existence.

He had offered to die for me. And I would do the same for him. I knew deep in a place that was still purely *me* that I wouldn't hurt him for anything in this world.

The rush of feelings helped me gain control, to find a little of myself again. I found a sense of hope, something warm and bright that I'd held on to when things looked bleak. I wrapped that feeling around me and I shifted position, inching toward Arcus so I could bend the frostfire toward Rasmus. The blue center moved in his direction.

"What are you doing?" Rasmus asked, his eyes wide.

"Melting your throne." With every second, I felt my mind gaining control, shaking off the influence of the Minax. This was what I had come to do. Destroy the curse.

"No!" Rasmus used his frost to knock me back. I hurled a blast of heat at him that sent him careening across the room, his head hitting the wall before he slumped to the floor.

I turned back to the throne, letting my heat build. But the throne clawed at my heat, trying to pull it away from me, its very nature designed by Fors to weaken and destroy Firebloods.

"You can do this, Ruby," Arcus said. "Don't hold anything back. Let go!"

There was a moment of terrible doubt, when every past failure came back to me: my village, my mother, my early attempts at harnessing my fire, how I'd let the Minax control me, the fact that it had persuaded me to kill Arcus just moments ago.

But I was stronger than that. I hadn't let it rule me. Even as I felt the shadow presence in my mind, I was in control. My gifts, whether fire or darkness, were no longer wild. They were mine to command.

"Arcus," I breathed. "Cover yourself with ice."

I heard the crackle of ice forming and saw out of the corner of my eye that Arcus had first sent a thick sheet of ice to cover his brother, who lay slumped on the floor, then surrounded himself with ice.

And finally I let go.

My heart beat once, twice, and I was filled with a terrible pressure of countless sunsets. Orange seared my eyelids, white fire engulfing me in torturous waves. It was a hundred times hotter than the flames Arcus had rescued me from when I had burned my clothes by the abbey stream. It was like being dropped into bubbling lava.

I focused on the black outline of the throne. It still tried to siphon away my heat, a churning, insistent pull that felt as if it were tugging my heart right out of my chest. But I was no ordinary Fireblood. Whether I was born for this destiny or not, I alone had managed to control the Minax inside me. I could do this.

Pulling up every thought of heat and fire in my mind and heart, I let the excruciating pressure build inside me until it was unbearable. Then I let it all explode into the throne. The blast sent me flying backward to slam against an icy pillar. Dazed, I saw that the throne was only half melted, and I repeated the same process. Let the heat build, the way Grandmother had taught me. Harness it, the way Brother Thistle had taught me. Let go, the way Arcus had taught me. Again and again I poured heat, pushed against its resistance, let my power build, and released it with a heady confidence I'd never felt before.

As sweat poured down my face and my hands shook, I

shouted with the effort of forcing out so much heat. Finally, the remaining ice of the throne swelled like an overfilled cask and then burst into a cloud of tiny droplets that hissed and steamed and filled the air with rivulets of light.

The Minax swirled inside me, reeling at the sight of the bare space where the throne had stood, its home for a thousand years. I felt its confusion, its brief sense of loss, but its feelings shifted to elation as it realized the freedom of living inside me instead. It settled into me, pushing at the edges of my consciousness.

There was a sound like shattering glass. Arcus was smashing through the protective ice that had kept him safe from my fire. He came to my side, and I dimly heard him calling my name, felt his hands on my shoulders. But my consciousness was disappearing like grains of sand being sucked into the sea.

The voice of a thousand bells spoke, each word resonating with excruciating triumph.

"My true vessel, you have freed me. We will always be one now."

As the darkness expanded in my chest, I realized it hadn't been using its full power on me before. It had let me destroy the throne because it wanted me to. I had been part of its plan. And now it was growing, consuming my identity, my very self.

I needed help, someone who had power greater than my understanding, someone with golden hair and eyes who had helped Arcus before, someone I had seen when I was lost in the blizzard-white woods. If that had really been the seer, the prophetess who had healed Cirrus, I needed her help now.

"Sage," I said, some part of my spirit, some part that knew more than my mind, reaching out. "Help me."

The voice from my visions spoke in my ear. "To be filled with light, you need only to make a choice. Choose to forgive yourself. Choose to love."

Her words lent me strength to struggle harder against the shadows. I willed myself to focus on things that were from the light: love and hope and healing, new beginnings and forgiveness. The life I wanted to live, rather than the pain and guilt of my past. I pictured Mother, smiling and proud, Grandmother at her side as they beckoned and welcomed me into an embrace. Love was a purifying force, like fire. I embraced it.

Blinding golden light filled me. A scream pounded in my ears, an inhuman cry of agony, and then the darkness that had been inside me snapped free, like a clothesline that had been cut, sending all the sheets whipping into the wind. I would have fallen, but Arcus held me upright, pulling me against his chest.

The Minax hovered above us. It tried to seep back into me, but I filled myself with every loving thought, keeping the light steady and bright.

The shadow beast flickered from opaque to transparent, clearly struggling to keep its solid form. It shivered forward and retreated, as if wanting to come back to me but knowing it couldn't.

Movement caught my eye. Rasmus had smashed through the ice and was crawling across the floor toward us. He was trembling, his face a sickly gray, his eyes pure blue and filled with pain. "Come back to me, Minax," he said hoarsely.

He looked so weak I had no sense of fear of the once powerful king. "You can't let it merge with you," I said. "I've felt its full power. If you invite it in, it will erase who you are completely. You can't survive."

He shook his head. "I'm dying anyway." He raised his arms. "Come, Minax, my only friend. Return to me."

The shadow beast only hesitated for a moment before moving toward Rasmus. Arcus leaped toward him. "Raz, no!"

Even as Arcus reached for his brother, the darkness had filled Rasmus, turning his eyes black once again as he breathed a sigh of relief, his lips curving in a shaky smile. "Nothing matters but power," he whispered.

Then his brows drew together, and he threw his head back in agony. Veins stood out against his light skin, the blue turning black, like oil. The veins spread out like tiny tributaries and streams, connecting and swelling. Rasmus screamed and clawed at himself, staring at the ceiling as if searching for some hope of rescue. He convulsed violently, then fell limp against the floor as the Minax flowed back into the air, hovering above us again. It looked stronger, more opaque and solid. It moved toward Arcus, and I threw myself in front of him, my hands out.

"Sage, protect us," I said under my breath.

The Minax shook in a way that mimicked laughter. "I don't need this one, the king who fought my influence when he took the throne. I have fed on another king. That will sustain me until I can find my next host. Though you are my true vessel, Daughter of Darkness. When despair fills you, when everyone you love is gone, we will be one again. Remember me with this."

Something seared the skin near my left ear and then I felt the presence of the Minax leave.

The world spun and righted itself. I sucked in a painful breath. I was on all fours on the stone floor. I tried to speak, but my throat felt dry and shredded.

I opened my eyes and found myself staring into twin chips of ice, a myriad of colors from a warm summer lake to a cold winter morning.

"Is it you, Ruby?" Arcus said my name quietly, a caress of breath.

"Yes, the Minax is gone," I said. "For now."

"Thank Tempus you're all right!" He gathered me into his arms. I tucked my head into the space between his neck and shoulder. After a few minutes, his head turned toward his brother's still form. His breath shuddered against my neck. "He was my brother."

"I know. I'm so sorry."

For months I had dreamed of killing Rasmus. But Arcus had wanted me to cure him, and I hadn't been able to. I held Arcus as tightly as I could while he trembled, his tears cold against my collarbone. For long minutes, I just stroked his hair. I was amazed at Arcus's capacity for love, even after such betrayal. When he grew quiet, I pressed my lips to his cheek.

The sun had slipped behind the mountain. Weak light filtered into the throne room, making the dust motes dance. The shadows were growing longer, but they were just shadows now. The room felt different. The evil presence in the throne was gone.

"There are things that must be dealt with," said Arcus, blowing out a long breath. "My forces won the battle, but there are those who will look... unfavorably on what happened here. They could accuse me of killing my brother to take power."

I didn't mention that there was a moment in the arena when I had thought the same, that Arcus had been after the power of the throne.

"But you didn't kill him."

"They won't necessarily believe that," he said. "And I need to convince those loyal to my brother that they owe me allegiance. It'll be no easy task."

"I wish I could help, but as you said before, I'm not loved in these parts."

He smiled crookedly and touched my cheek. "You are, by some."

Something painfully joyful and light flared through me. I closed my eyes on an overflow of feeling and pushed my cheek into his palm, pressing his hand there with mine.

TWENTY-NINE

A TORCH BOBBED INTO VIEW. MARELLA stood in the doorway.

"Where is Raz?" she asked, but it was clear from her pained expression that she suspected the answer.

Arcus gestured to his brother's limp form. Marella put a hand to her heart as she stared at him. Her eyelids flickered and closed.

No matter what Rasmus had threatened, I had to remember that she had known him all her life.

"I'm sorry," I said softly to her.

"You destroyed the throne, as you were meant to do," said Marella, her voice strained. She took a few shuddering breaths, making a visible effort to compose herself. Then she made a frustrated gesture to the doorway. "Stop hovering, Father. You don't want the new king to think you a coward."

Lord Ustathius moved into the room, bowing to Arcus and looking slightly lost.

Marella moved to light more of the torches on the wall, illuminating the spot where the throne had sat for untold generations. There was nothing left but a blackened outline of where it had been. The room seemed cavernous without that menacing presence. I tried not to look at Rasmus's body, focusing on Marella instead.

"Marella, Rasmus said you paid the captain to take me to Blackcreek Prison. Is that true?"

She hesitated before spreading her hands in an open gesture. "Forgive me, Ruby. It was all I could do for you at the time. I couldn't stop the raids, but at least I could make sure Captain Drake kept any Firebloods he found away from the king."

"Why would you say such a thing?" her father demanded, his cheeks looking more sunken than I remembered, his hands unsteady at his sides. "You have just admitted to treason."

Marella wore a wry look. "I don't think this king will mind that I tried to save Ruby from the king's hatred. Do you, King Arelius Arkanus? Or am I to call you Arcus now?"

Arcus shifted, one hand coming to rest on my shoulder in a possessive gesture. "You've always called me by the name Arkanus, and I don't expect you to stop now. And I will not fault you for trying to protect Firebloods. But why would you do that?"

"I've always had a particular interest in the prophecies of Dru, as well as the history of our people and the history of Firebloods. One of the texts said that a powerful Fireblood would destroy the cursed throne, though I can assure you, no one here believed this throne cursed besides Brother Thistle. And me. I sensed it was evil from the time I was a child."

"Then where are all the others?" I asked, my voice catching. "The Firebloods you saved?"

Her eyes grew shadowed. "I'm afraid most were already gone, fled or killed, by the time the captain agreed to work on my behalf. You were the only one he found. I thanked Fors for that miracle."

"He killed my mother, Marella."

She turned her face away. "I hadn't thought he would be so brutal. I am sorry, Ruby." She looked at me again, her gaze contrite, almost pleading. "But at least I saved you. And when you were brought here, I made sure Rasmus gave you a chance to fight. You defeated every opponent, and I knew you were the one the books talked about, the one who could control the darkness instead of succumbing to it." A smile lit her face, making her even prettier. "And now we are like sisters, aren't we? I'll never forget how you destroyed the throne, and you must never forget how I helped you."

The shock and exhaustion were finally hitting me. I could barely process what Marella was saying, much less how I felt about it. My stomach flipped, and I groaned and pressed a hand to it as my head went light. I heard Arcus ask Marella to fetch a healer, and her footsteps fade from the room, followed by her father's, his chastising voice echoing down the corridor.

My eyes fell on the empty space where the throne had sat. The Minax had hovered there, triumphant, and said it would come back for me when I was weakest. When everyone I loved was gone.

Hadn't enough been taken? My mother, my home, months of my life. All that was left was Arcus. No matter how I had tried to close myself against him, he'd become a necessity to me. Losing him was too horrible to contemplate.

"What's that?" said Arcus, his fingers feathering over the tender skin near my ear. "It looks like . . . a heart. A small black heart."

"It must be a burn." But I knew that the Minax had marked me. Sickness twisted my stomach. I couldn't think about that right now. All I wanted was to bask in comforting arms.

Arcus sucked in a breath as he touched my cheek, drawing his fingers away quickly. "Ruby, you're burning up. Even for a Fireblood, you're wickedly hot. We need to get you into water."

I nodded and pushed up to stand. But the world tilted like a spinning top, and I was pitched from its surface and sent into the black sky.

I moaned and pushed at the hand that mopped my forehead with a cold cloth. I hated cold. I wanted to burn. I was fire.

A sigh. "You have always been stubborn. Now I fear it will be the death of you."

I fought through the heaviness that fogged my mind and opened my eyes. A lined face and hooked nose swam into view. He smiled, displaying a few missing teeth. The tufts of white hair on his mostly bald head shone like filaments in the sunlight. With his beatific expression, he looked like a messenger of the gods. And since I knew Brother Gamut was dead...

"This is the afterworld?" I asked, my voice as rough as quarry rock.

"If you were dead, would you be sponged with cold water, which you hate so much?"

My senses returned in a rush. My throat hurt. My skin hurt. My eyes felt as if they were full of sand.

"It depends," I croaked. "The gods might be punishing me."

He chuckled. "That is all too likely."

Tears filled my eyes. I was alive. Brother Gamut was alive. If the captain had lied about Brother Gamut, maybe he had lied about the others, too. With a grunt, I pushed up and threw my arms around his fine-boned frame. "You don't know how glad I am to see you safe."

He laughed and sucked in a breath. "Your skin is burning hot, Ruby."

I released him and fell back onto the soft mattress, putting my hands to my spinning head. I finally registered where I was: in a room I had never seen before, with gauzy curtains around the bed and heavy drapes at an open window.

"Where am I?"

"In the queen's old room." He gave his gap-toothed grin and

waved to a door in the wall. "With a door to Arcus's room. It is lucky for you that I am so happy to see both of you or I might question the prudence of his choices."

Before I could reply to his teasing, a wave of nausea hit. "I'm going to be sick."

"There is nothing left in your stomach but water. That is all you've been able to keep down. You have been through a trauma, and your body is just now starting to heal. I have been sitting with you since I arrived, talking to you in hopes that you would fully wake. I am glad you finally decided to do so."

"How many days?"

"Arcus sent for us before he entered the city. We arrived the day after you... became ill. I have been at your side for three days."

"And before that you were at the abbey? Safe?"

His wild white brows drew together. "Most of us are unhurt. After the soldiers came..." He met my eyes and sighed. "We had thought Brother Lack was unaware of the exit through the catacombs. We must have been wrong. Once the soldiers knew about you, they questioned us. But Arcus returned quickly, and he and Brother Thistle unleashed their frost on the soldiers. Those of us who are young and able helped fight."

"And you won?"

"We escaped. After that, Arcus left to bring his supporters to the castle. The rest of us hid in the caves in the mountainside until we received word from Arcus that it was safe to return to the abbey. But he wanted Brother Thistle here when it was all over, someone he could trust to advise him. And I offered to come provide healing to anyone injured in the battle."

"Brother Gamut, you won't look me in the eyes. What aren't you telling me?"

He shook his head, the words coming out slow and labored. "We lost a few of our brothers and sisters in the fight."

He told me the names of his lost friends, including the jovial Brother Peele. I held his hand tightly as he spoke, tears streaming down my cheeks.

"The rest of us are safe, though," he assured me. "Sister Clove's arm was broken, but it's healing. We all help her more now."

"And so will I," I said, sitting up and taking a deep breath. "As soon as I'm well, I'm going back with you. The abbey is my home now."

"I am glad you would call the abbey your home. I have had to drink many cups of my own tea to ease my worries about you."

"No need to worry anymore. But tell me more, please? I need to know what I've missed."

He patted my hand again, withdrawing it quickly with a grimace. "Only if you promise to let me sponge your face and neck. Even Firebloods are not meant to burn all the time."

He continued to dab my forehead, cheeks, and neck with the cool cloth as he spoke. I interrupted often, and he answered my questions, sometimes urging me to be quiet so he could finish a thought.

I tried, but patience is just not in my nature.

While I'd drowsed in my fevered state, Arcus had convinced

most of the nobility that he was the rightful king. It didn't take much convincing that a curse had been darkening the nation, as people had felt that truth in their hearts for a long time. But Arcus still had to deal with a nation that had long been spread too thin by war. He had ordered his armies to be withdrawn from neighboring countries and had sent ambassadors to begin the long process of mending ties with kings and queens. It would take time, Brother Gamut said, for people to forgive. The Minax's dark appetites had been embodied in the form of the Frost King. It would be a long road for the new king to regain trust.

"But is he all right?" I asked anxiously. "How is he dealing with his brother's death? Brother Gamut, you should have seen him. He looked... broken."

"I know, child. I see his sadness. He is not himself."

As we sat in silence, the door opened and Arcus came in, looking at Brother Gamut. He wore no hood, so his eyes were clearly visible. Today they were the color of a frozen lake dusted with snow. His expression was grim, shadowed, his cheeks hollow, as if he hadn't slept well in weeks. He looked as if he'd aged years in the past few days.

"I will watch her for a while, Brother," Arcus said heavily, closing the door behind him. "The coronation isn't for a few hours yet."

His eyes widened as they settled on me. "She's awake!"

"You can talk directly to me now," I pointed out.

"Ruby," he breathed, moving his broad-shouldered frame so carefully toward me that I wondered if he expected me to fly away like a startled bird. It both touched and amused me to think that after everything I'd survived and everything I'd done, he could still think of me as fragile.

He slid his cold hand under my palm. I shivered, but it was the sensation of his touch, not the cold, that ran up my arm and brought goose bumps to my skin.

"How do you feel?" he asked softly. I tried to pull my hand away, sure it must be uncomfortably hot in his. He tightened his grip.

"Like an overcooked rabbit," I answered.

His eyes crinkled with amusement, making him look closer to his own age again. "You're the fire. Muffle your flames."

"Ah, but that requires self-control. And we both know—"

"You have very little of that," he completed with a crooked smile that did nothing to lower my temperature.

Despite his light words, there were signs of tension in the line of his jaw, the set of his shoulders. "Are you all right?" I asked.

"Brother Thistle has been hovering over me like a mother hen. If he persists, I'm going to lock him in the keep."

"He loves you."

"And I love him, too." His face grew serious and I wondered if he wanted to say something more, but then his eyes flicked to Brother Gamut, who sat grinning happily from his perch on the brocade chair, and he seemed to think better of it.

"I'm so sorry, Arcus," I said, my fingers twisting together on the quilt. "I should never have gone into the throne room without you. If I had waited, maybe—"

He shook his head, his brows lowering. "Nothing was your fault." He paused. "There was a small service yesterday. We buried him in his ceremonial robes with some of his favorite items from when he was a child."

I nodded. And that was probably how Arcus preferred to remember him: as the boy he once was.

"We were all saved because of you."

"Then why do I feel like I failed?" I asked, looking away. "The Minax is loose now, unhampered by the throne. Who knows what chaos it's capable of now that I freed it?"

Brother Gamut, perhaps sensing that the air had grown thick, cleared his throat and stood. "I need to fetch some herbs to make your special tea. Would you like that?"

"Very much," I said sincerely. "You have no idea how much I've missed it."

The monk made a quick bow to Arcus and shuffled from the room. When the door had shut behind him, Arcus sat in the chair, his hand still holding mine.

"You did *not* fail," he said. "You rid the castle of a curse."

"But the throne brought the Frost King power." I met his eyes. "You'll be weaker now without it."

His eyes narrowed as he considered what I had said. "The throne did give the king power, but it was not always used justly. It had been growing dark for a long time, at least since my father's reign. My own father was . . . terribly cruel to my brother."

"Rasmus told me." I slid my fingers into his and squeezed.

He looked down at our hands. "So I intend to use not only

my frost, but my ability to speak to people, to persuade them to think as I do."

I grinned. "Because you're so loquacious."

One side of his mouth tilted up, puckering the scar. I suddenly longed to trace it with my finger.

"I used to be known for my persuasive arguments."

We sat in peaceful silence for a minute.

"Why didn't you tell me who you really were?" I asked.

His lips twisted. He met my eyes, his own intense. "It was a secret that, if exposed, could mean the death of the monks. I was using the abbey as a place to hide, a secluded and safe place to live while I built up my supporters. Rasmus might have taken his wrath out on the order. I couldn't risk that. Even if I knew I could trust you—and, Ruby, I did really come to trust you—it was more a question of what you might reveal if you were captured."

"I understand," I said. "I care about the monks, too."

He sat back and stroked my hair with his hand, then lifted my chin until my eyes met his. "Ruby, I want you to know I'd changed my mind. I was going to tell Brother Thistle we had to find another way. But then..." His hand convulsed. "I was in agony when I returned to the abbey and found that you'd been taken. I followed, but you were too far ahead. Once you reached the castle, I needed a strong force to fight Rasmus's soldiers."

"And you did it. You won."

"Things looked bleak until the champions declared they were for me."

My affection for Braka grew tenfold. "Good."

"They have been released from any servitude under my rule, Ruby. They are free men and women now."

I beamed up at him, bursting with pride for the new king. Arcus smiled back and my heart kicked up a fuss at the glorious sight.

"I thought you would like that," he said, his hands sliding around mine.

I screwed up my courage and told Arcus how the Minax had called me its "true vessel." His hand tightened on mine as I spoke.

"We will not let it take you," he said, his voice rough with feeling. "I won't let it, Ruby. I swear."

I squeezed his hand because he meant to comfort me. But how could we fight something as ephemeral as darkness?

"You look tired," he said more softly. "I should let you rest."

Reluctantly, I let his hand go. "You need to prepare for your coronation. I wish I could come."

He shook his head, his look stern. "You're too ill. When your fever comes down, you can do what you like. Until then, no visitors and no leaving this room."

I remembered telling him once that he could never control me, which he'd find out to his detriment if he tried. But he wasn't like his brother, exerting control over people for the pleasure of it. Arcus was imperious, but it came from the need to protect. And just then, tired and battered as I was, I didn't mind.

"You are very kingly when you give commands," I said, unable to keep my lips from twitching. "It makes me want to defy you, just for the sake of it."

He eyes danced. "And risk the charge of treason? Do you want to end up back in a cell, Lady Firebrand?"

I mocked his stern look with one of my own. "That is nothing to jest about."

He grinned and put a hand to his chest. "Your eyes scorch me. I wish I were half as frightening as you when I get angry, my little inferno."

"You're plenty frightening when you want to be."

His grin softened. "Not to you, I hope."

My pulse reacted to the tenderness in his eyes. "Only when I thought you were going to sacrifice yourself for me. How could you?" I looked down, then back up, fighting shyness. "It would kill me never to see your handsome face again."

Suddenly, he was crushing me to him, his chest rising and falling on a deep breath, before he put me gently back against the pillows. The once-cold blue eyes simmered as they met mine.

"Thank you, Lady Firebrand," he said, and his voice sounded as if it were coated with rust. "I will take those words to bed with me every night to comfort me."

Images of his bare chest covered by a sheet brought heat to my cheeks. He planted a kiss on my forehead and started to rise.

"Arcus," I said, still keeping one of his hands captive. "Someone told me that affairs between fire and frost never end well." I didn't say more, but he seemed to understand the question I wanted to ask. Would our end be as tragic as that of the Frost King who married a Fireblood queen?

He paused, and my heart stuttered. But then he sat back on the bed next to me, looking more thoughtful than concerned.

"I doubt our kind have been together often enough to answer that question. I'm convinced the throne had a hand in the death of the Fireblood queen. I don't fear your heat and you don't fear my frost. And besides…"

As he leaned in, I slid closer and lifted my chin. He dipped his head and pressed a kiss so blistering in intensity to my lips that his cold burned hotter than fire.

It didn't hurt, but it did burn, and not in a way I minded. My blood woke up and my fever spiked and my mouth went bone-dry. Little shivers ran from my lips down to every part of my body.

He was gentle but unrestrained at the same time, as if he were showing me something, giving me something of himself. It made me feel raw and new and precious. I gave myself back, showing him with my lips and my hands on his cheeks and in his hair and on his beautiful scars that I needed him in ways I was no longer afraid to share with him.

When we were both breathless, he broke away and smiled. I smiled back. And then he put his lips gently back to mine, his fingertips under my chin.

"When it comes to you," he whispered, "I like to be burned."

ACKNOWLEDGMENTS

If gratitude could be expressed in heat, these pages would all be burnt. There were a thousand different moments of good fortune that led to this book becoming a reality and a long list of people responsible for those moments. Here are a few:

First of all, thank you to everyone at New Leaf Literary, especially my intrepid agent, Suzie Townsend, who always knows the right thing to say to keep me sane and energized. I know how much you did to champion *Frostblood*, and I won't forget it. Squishy hugs to my original team members, Jackie Lindert and Jaida Temperly, who found my book and brought it to Suzie in the first place. I won the lottery that day. Gargantuan thanks to Kathleen Ortiz for being phenomenal at handling foreign rights, as well as to Sara Stricker, Danielle Barthel, Pouya Shahbazian, Joanna Volpe, and Hilary Pecheone for being awesome.

Endless gratitude to Deirdre Jones at Little, Brown for believing in *Frostblood* and for being the best editor I could have hoped for. Working with you is such a tremendously positive experience! Huge thanks to art director Sasha Illingworth, production editor Annie McDonnell, copyeditor Christine Ma, production manager Virginia Lawther, Emilie Polster and Allegra Green for marketing, publicist Kristina Pisciotta, editor-in-chief Alvina Ling, and publisher Megan Tingley. You all rock!

To the *Frostblood* team at Hodder & Stoughton, especially Emily Kitchin, Fleur Clarke, and Rebecca (Becca) Mundy, thank you for your unflagging enthusiasm, your stunningly cool marketing ideas, and your all-around magnificence. Cupcakes for all!

My journey toward publication didn't truly start until the day I joined RWA and TRW, and there are so many people to thank that I can't name them all. Just know I appreciate you! Behemoth thanks to Morgan Rhodes for rolling up the first five pages of *Frostblood*, hitting me over the head with them, and saying, "Finish it!" A million hugs to Eve Silver, who generously gave me notes on the opening chapters, gentle nudges, good advice, and mentoring. Thanks to Kelley Armstrong for providing a wonderful critique of the opening chapters. Thanks to Molly O'Keefe for being the first published author to tell me I could write and that I should keep going. Infinite hugs to my dear friend Nicki Pau Preto for critiques, commiseration, and a steady supply of laughter.

The Lady Seals, the original Table of Trust—how would I function without you? Guida, Crystal, Sarah, Brooke, and Anabel, meeting you must have been ordained in the stars. You are my always friends, my chosen sisters, and I love you more than I can say.

Speaking of people I can't live without, thank you to my other Table of Trust—the Pitch Wars 2014 group, especially Mara Rutherford, Nikki Roberti, Kristin B. Wright, Mary Ann Marlowe, Summer Spence, Ron Walters, and Kelly Siskind for providing awesome notes, endless compassion, and humor. Hugs and kisses to Kelly Calabrese, Jennifer Hawkins, Margarita Montimore, and Kellye Garrett for friendship and laughs. Brenda Drake, thank you for the time and love you put into Pitch Wars, a contest that has changed the lives of so many aspiring authors! Many thanks to Sarah Nicolas for choosing and mentoring me, and to Shannon Cooley for your excellent notes and support.

And thanks to the Agented Chamber of Secrets, especially Alexa Donne. If it weren't for your breadcrumbs, I'd still be lost in the revision forest. Chocolate and hugs to everyone in the Swanky 17's for your knowledge, encouragement, and support. Many thanks to early readers of *Frostblood*, including Ryan Iler, Rebecca Bartlett, Emily DiCarlo, and Isabelle Hanson. Big hugs to my coworkers at ECL, especially Mary, Laura, and Brittanie, for making the days fly. And special mention to Tony Nespolon, English teacher extraordinaire, who made reading and writing so endlessly fascinating, and to the members of the back-of-the-bus-reading-club, Robin, Skye, Renai, and Colleen, where my dreams of writing began.

All my love to my mom, Nancy. You are the sweetest mom in the world, which makes me the luckiest daughter. Your love of reading permeated our whole lives. Your unconditional love and support are everything to me. And thank you to Dan for being so supportive and proud!

All my love to my dad, Matt. I can still hear you reading *Ali Baba and the Forty Thieves* to me on the porch by the lake. I love how you told me that your Oma was a consummate storyteller so I knew it ran in the family.

All my love to my brothers, Erik and Mark, for being the best brothers on earth. And to the wonderful Takakis and Stevensons: Fred, Donna, Jill, Todd, Zoe, Quinton, and Heather.

Finally, thank you to Darren, Nicklas, Aleksander, and Lukas, for bringing me happiness every single day. I love you to the moon and back again!